THE MARKED DAUGHTER

BEAR & MANDY LOGAN

L.T. RYAN

with

K.M. ROUGHT

LIQUID MIND MEDIA

For information contact:
Contact@ltryan.com
https://LTRyan.com
https://www.facebook.com/JackNobleBooks

THE BEAR & MANDY LOGAN SERIES

1

THE SCORPION STRODE DOWN THE HALLWAY, HIS FOOTSTEPS echoing off the surrounding concrete. Only a few dim lightbulbs hung from the ceiling, silent and caged like the prisoners in the cells he passed. Shadows crept in from every corner, but he was familiar with their dark embrace. If it weren't for the stench of piss and mildew, the thick, sturdy walls surrounding him would be a comfort.

He paid no mind to the men and women behind the metal bars. He was here to see one person, and no one would distract him from his mission. Not that they tried. The Scorpion had a reputation, and he upheld it well. They knew it was smarter to remain silent than beg for their lives.

The hallway ended with one final cell. It was larger than the others, but it held no additional amenities. The iron bars were dark, the blood indistinguishable from the rust. The concrete floor bore a map of fissures, as did the walls. Light from the nearby bulb barely reached this area. Yet the stench of human waste grew stronger with every inhale.

The Scorpion reached inside the pocket of his suit jacket and retrieved a single bronze key. It was as old as the iron bars but it gleamed in the dim light. He had little interest in stepping inside the cell in his leather shoes and freshly pressed slacks, but it was all in a day's work. He didn't hate this part of the job—just wished he'd been better prepared for today's tasks.

He slotted the key inside its lock, turning it clockwise until the mechanism clanged open. Silence followed, heavy with promise, and the Scorpion imagined the other prisoners holding their breath in anticipation of what came next. Were any of them jealous they hadn't been paid a visit, or did they all know enough to be relieved?

One of the shadows inside the cell shifted as the Scorpion swung open the door and stepped over the threshold, careful to avoid a pool of viscous liquid to his left. A figure crawled into the dim light on his hands and knees, wearing only a pair of torn pants. Blood trailed down his right forearm, joining the other stains on the floor.

When the prisoner lifted his face to greet his visitor, the Scorpion resisted the urge to step back in disgust. Vittorio Rossi hadn't been inside the cell very long, but this place was designed to break bodies and minds. The Scorpion hardly recognized the man beneath his swollen cheeks, bruised eyes, and bloody lips.

His hair was still short, but the stubble across his jaw made the bruises look darker, more ominous. Even in the small cell, Rossi's six-foot frame appeared shriveled.

The Scorpion clicked his tongue several times. "They did a number on you, didn't they?"

"Please." Rossi clasped his hands in front of him. His hoarse voice was too quiet to echo off the walls. "Please, I did everything you told me to."

The Scorpion slipped the bronze key back into his pocket. "You did."

Rossi scooted forward on his knees. "I lied to everyone. Even my own men."

"You've protected our secrets well," the Scorpion agreed.

"I gave them the name of the archbishop, just like you asked me to."

Rossi's arm continued to ooze blood. He was missing a finger on his left hand, but he appeared to have forgotten about it for the time being. His eyes were so swollen, it was a wonder he could see the Scorpion at all.

Rossi moved forward another few inches. "No one will ever know. Your identity is protected."

The Scorpion looked down at the man, his lip curling at the sight of him so close to his leather shoes. The smell emanating from his weakened body was rancid. When Rossi reached out to grab hold of his visitor, the Scorpion stepped back. Rossi tilted forward and fell, his arms too weak to catch him before his face smacked against the concrete floor. He howled in pain.

"We appreciate your dedication to the cause," the Scorpion said over him. He reached into his pocket, wrapping his fingers around his handkerchief, not wanting to spend a second longer in this hellhole than necessary. The circumstances cast a shadow over his anticipation of what came next.

Rossi pushed himself off the floor and rested back on his haunches. One of the cuts on his face had opened again. "I haven't told you everything I know yet."

The Scorpion pulled his gun from his shoulder holster and pointed it at the beaten man. As far as bargaining went, Rossi was doing a poor job. He'd given them everything they'd needed days ago.

Rossi shook as he stared down the barrel of the gun. "I think you—"

BANG.

The Scorpion watched Rossi's body slump to the floor, half his head now splattered across the back wall of the cell. Ears ringing, the Scorpion returned his gun to its holster, hidden beneath his suit jacket. He hadn't bothered to silence the weapon.

Warmth on his hand drew his attention. He shifted his body until the dim lighting revealed the culprit. A few drops of blood had landed on the fingers of his left hand. With a grunt, he pulled a handkerchief from his pocket and wiped away the other man's bodily fluid.

He'd need to ensure that none had landed on his clothes. But that would have to wait until he stepped back out into the sunlight.

The Scorpion scrutinized the ring on his little finger. He used the corner of the cloth to clear away a droplet that sat on the head of the silver snake, making the reptile appear as though its eyes glowed red.

Then he tossed the bloody handkerchief onto the dead body and walked away.

He had so much yet to accomplish.

2

Bear followed Mandy off the crowded train and into the crisp Venetian air. They each carried stuffed backpacks draped over their shoulders. The chill of the midmorning breeze refreshed his senses after several hours in cramped quarters. He'd sprung for upgraded tickets, but no public transportation ever had enough room for him.

Bear did a preliminary scan as they followed the crowd away from the tracks. He'd been to Venice a few times, but it felt novel with Mandy by his side. Traveling the world with his kid had become his favorite pastime. The people and places seemed brighter and more vibrant.

Mandy stepped away from the bustling throng of people and leaned against a pillar. Her fingers blurred as she typed a message into her phone. Bear didn't need to see her screen to know it was to Marcus. Despite living halfway across the world in Upstate New York, he was the only one of Mandy's friends she kept in touch with. Their lifestyle didn't make it easy to stay in contact with most people, but at least Mandy had one person her own age to talk to.

He gave her a few seconds, then walked over and nudged her with his hip.

"Hey. Phone away." He peeked at the screen and confirmed his suspicions about who she was texting. "Eyes up."

Mandy finished her sentence and hit send before she tucked her phone back into her bag. Bear felt a swell of pride that she hadn't argued with him. Sometimes the guilt of bringing Mandy into his world ate at him, but moments like these reminded her that she was still here, still alert, seeing everything for what it was.

Mandy fiddled with the strap of her bag while she looked around. Bear followed her gaze, trying to imagine what she saw and how it made her feel.

The signs were in Italian, and while Mandy had picked up a few words from their time in San Gimignano, most would be impossible to decipher. She'd at least know where to go for more information if she were ever on her own.

The people breaking away and heading in different directions were nothing more than a blur of color and a cacophony of noise. Bear detected half a dozen languages he recognized, plus a few he didn't. Skin tones ranged from bright alabaster to rich ebony. Most of the faces were sun-kissed and bronze with dark hair and even darker eyes, but every once in a while, a fair-haired, blue-eyed tourist wandered by.

No one paid them any attention. Mandy's shoulders relaxed and her fingers stilled against the strap of her bag. They'd garnered enough notice in San Gimignano, and neither of them would soon forget what had happened there. The ancient tunnels under the city. The mystery of Lucia Moretti. The vast conspiracy they'd stumbled upon.

Here, in Venice, they were just another pair of tourists.

Mandy kept her gaze on the flowing mass of people. "How far away is our hotel?"

"Just across the Grand Canal." Bear waited for an opening in the crowd, then stepped forward into the current. "We can walk."

Mandy hummed in acknowledgement. When they stepped outside of the train station, they both stopped, blinking against the sunlight, until their eyes adjusted. It was a beautiful day in the mid-fifties with a cool breeze, and the only clouds looked like they belonged in a Renaissance painting. Fluffy, white, and ethereal.

Bear crossed the plaza in front of the train station with Mandy on his heels, then turned and walked along the street until they reached the first stone bridge across the canal. Most of the people here were tourists, some standing around and taking pictures. The Americans were easy to distinguish from the Europeans. Bear felt a pang of homesickness at hearing a Southern drawl from a man wearing a cowboy hat.

Mandy kept close as they made it to the other side of the canal. The atmosphere was different from what they'd experienced during their visit to Italy so far. Rome had been big and flashy. San Gimignano had been steeped in history. Venice offered a little slice of both.

After leaving the walled city behind, they'd gotten off a bus at Poggibonsi before hopping on a train to Florence. Bear had booked them a room for two nights, then they'd gotten on another train to Bologna. They'd spent three nights there before heading toward Padua. The views from the train were spectacular, the countryside lush and verdant this time of year, but Bear had been most excited for their final destination.

Mandy had been excited for Venice, too, but for an entirely different reason.

She believed the answers were here. Bear wasn't so sure—he'd learned the hard way not to lock himself onto a path before knowing where it ended.

They reached the hotel and checked in, confirming with the desk clerk that they'd only be staying a couple nights as Bear took a key to their room. Mandy bounced on the balls of her feet, energy radiating from her like sunlight. Bear forced back a smile, remembering a time in his life when he struggled to contain the adrenaline coursing through his body with every new adventure. Those were simpler days, back before the aches and pains greeted him before he even opened his eyes in the morning.

The narrow stairwell that led up to their room forced Bear to walk sideways. Reaching the landing, they paused halfway down the hall. Bear slid the key into the lock, the metallic click loud in the stillness, before he pushed the door open.

A light citrus scent greeted them, mingling with the warm brightness pouring in through the open curtains. He'd opted for two king beds which filled up a majority of the space. A desk occupied the opposite side of the room, large enough for Mandy to spread out her books while she read. Bear peeked into the bathroom, a pleasant surprise rippling through him at the size of the shower.

Mandy crossed to the far side of the room and tossed her bag onto one of the beds. She turned and watched Bear inspect the size of the closet, thankfully they didn't need a ton of space for clothes, before he turned to study an artistic aerial view of Venice hanging on the wall. It had all the major landmarks labeled.

"This is neat," he said.

"Bear."

He didn't need to turn around to see the look of exasperation on her face.

"Don't you like it?"

"It's great." The words snapped like a taut wire. "Can we look at it now?"

Bear chuckled but decided not to needle her anymore. She'd already been far more patient than he'd expected.

Slinging his bag off his shoulder, he set it down on the bed with care, then unzipped the largest compartment. He reached in and pulled out the small wooden box, turning to place it on the desk where they could both get a good look at it. Sunlight streamed in, sharpening every detail and casting crisp edges on the room around them.

The mottled brown wood looked richer in the bright room. He

already knew every grain that adorned the box but seeing it like this confirmed his suspicions that it had been carved from a single piece of wood. The way the edges dovetailed together revealed the maker's expertise, as did the ornate carvings across the surface.

When he'd first picked it up in the tunnels beneath San Gimignano, he'd noticed the stars and moons scattered across the surface, inlaid with gold and silver. But he'd missed the tiny animals galloping along its edges, and the fine gemstones embedded between them.

The snake head on top of the puzzle box demanded the most attention. Inlaid silver adorned its edges, the scales highlighted with a burnished gold. Two rubies sat where the eyes should be. With the way the sun hit them, they looked like they were glowing from within.

The woman they'd known as Lucia Moretti, but whose real name was Agent Isabella Fabrizio of L'Agenzia Informazioni e Sicurezza Esterna, had told them that the Order of the Iron Serpent created the puzzle box. Bear still thought the name "Order of the Iron Serpent" sounded pretentious, but Isabella's willingness to risk her life for the puzzle box had erased any doubt about the danger they posed.

And he'd stolen it out from under her nose.

She'd left him dozens of voicemails over the last week. He hadn't returned a single one. The deception wasn't personal. He wanted answers first, and partnering with an officer of the law would only complicate matters. He and Mandy didn't always do things by the book.

"Can I pick it up?" Mandy asked once they'd both gotten their fill of looking at the box.

Bear nodded. "Be gentle."

"I know." She exhaled through her nose, still locked on the box as though it held the only answer worth hearing.

Mandy lifted the box from the desk and tilted it just so, the way she'd discovered days ago. From that precise angle, the once-random engravings aligned into a single, continuous shape—Venice's Grand Canal.

Mandy ran her finger over the tiny rubies that dotted the path. They seemed important, but neither of them had evidence to support the theory.

In the silence of the room, Bear heard a distinctive *click*.

Mandy froze as a small side compartment popped open. She stared at Bear, wide-eyed. He didn't move a muscle, not even to breathe.

On more than one occasion, Bear had suggested they smash the box to see what might be inside. Mandy had been appalled. She'd argued the box itself could be as important as the contents. Maybe she'd been right.

He unfroze, reaching for the box. "What'd you do?"

"I'm sorry." Mandy handed it over with shaking hands. "I think I pressed one of the gems."

Bear's voice softened. He met her eyes and gave the faintest nod, a hint of a smile tugging at his mouth. "I think you just figured out how this thing works. Good job, kid."

Bear took the box and turned it to peer down at what was inside the drawer that had popped open. It looked like a flower, with each petal split into two different colors, one half opalescent and white, while the other was as black as night.

"What is it?" Mandy asked.

"A piece of jewelry." Bear picked it up and flipped it over in his palm. There were no distinguishing marks on one side, but it did have a pin attached to the other. "I think it's a brooch of some sort. Looks old."

Mandy twirled the silver ring on her finger as she stared at the item in Bear's palm. It was the same design Signore Bianchi had given her right before they left San Gimignano, the one that bore the face of Minerva, the warrior goddess. She hadn't taken it off once.

"It's pretty," she said, still staring at the brooch.

"Which gemstone did you touch?"

She pointed to one near the end of the path. "Pretty sure it was that one."

Bear held the box close to his face. Sure enough, the miniscule gemstone sat flush with the surface of the wood now. He pressed the other gems along the path, but nothing happened.

"You think it's important?" Mandy asked.

"Must be, considering how it was hidden away."

Bear crossed the room and stood before the map of Venice hanging on the wall. He traced his finger along the canal until he came to the spot where the ruby sat on the box. A grin spread across his face.

"Hey, kid. You fancy going to church?"

3

BEAR CROSSED A SMALL BRIDGE AND STEPPED INTO THE SHADOW of the Santa Maria Della Salute Basilica after letting a family of five pass him. Mandy stayed close, one hand gripping his arm so she could look up at the ornate building without running into anyone.

He'd seen the church before, but it was still a sight to behold. It wasn't the largest or even the most opulent building they'd seen on their walk over, let alone during their time in Italy, but that didn't make it any less incredible.

They navigated through the crowd of people standing around the plaza, some chatting in various languages, others taking pictures of the imposing structure. Mandy's hand slipped from Bear's arm. He stopped and watched as she pulled out her own camera, stepping back and to the right to frame it properly.

The main doors were a beautiful deep green, a splash of color against the pale stone of the façade. He recognized some of the figures adorning the outside of the building. The prophets around the entrance were easy to pick out, as was the figure of the Virgin Mary atop the larger of the two domes.

Mandy lowered her camera but didn't take her eyes off the basilica. "Can we go inside now?"

Bear guided her through the crowd and toward the smaller doors where they could enter. A chorus of murmurs emanated from inside, and Bear felt that familiar change in atmosphere when crossing into a space as old and venerated as this one.

People milled about the main area. Some pointed up at the high domed ceiling. Others studied the detailed carvings etched into the walls. Pillars loomed all around them. The space felt smaller than it had looked from the outside. But even the air itself felt sacred.

A tiny gasp from Bear's right drew his attention. Mandy stared down at the floor, her mouth hanging open and her eyes wide. When she tore her gaze away to meet his, her eyes sparkled.

"Do you see that?" she asked, pointing to an area of the floor just in front of them.

Bear had to wait until a large group passed. When the area cleared, he sucked in his own breath. The marble tiles created a beautiful mosaic consisting of black, white, red, and yellow shapes. The center of the patchwork's design spun in dizzying motifs. It demanded attention. Yet Mandy stared at the outer ring and the various circular patterns spaced along the perimeter.

They looked similar to the small brooch Bear had placed in his pocket before they left the hotel.

"You see it, right?" Mandy asked, her voice hushed.

"I see it," Bear said, his tone matching hers.

Together, they stepped forward. Bear drew the small pin out of his pocket and held it out. The pattern came close, but wasn't exact. Mandy pointed at the next circle on the floor, and Bear turned to peer down at it. The black and white alternating pattern beneath his feet wasn't as shiny as the one he held in his hand, but it was a clear match.

"What do you think it means?" Mandy whispered.

"That we're in the right place. Come on. Keep your eyes peeled."

"For what?"

Bear side-stepped a couple walking in their direction before he answered. "Anything that looks like it might not belong here. Or anything that reminds you of the box."

Mandy noticed every detail as they made their way around the room. Every other circular mosaic along the perimeter matched their brooch, so they had to walk slowly to ensure they didn't miss any hidden signs.

Bear still had no idea what this all meant and why the Order of the Iron Serpent was such a big deal. The internet only held vague speculation, and Mandy hadn't found any mention of it in her books. Marcus had even done some digging, but to no avail.

Instead of being a deterrent, however, the lack of information spurred them on. *Someone* had to know something about the group and their cause.

"Bear," Mandy hissed.

He followed her gaze to one of the pillars standing beside the main altar. He had to bend over to see it, but once he did, the etched serpent along the base of the column became clear as day. It was nothing more than a shallow indent, carved with a crude tool. Even without it being silver with red eyes, there was no denying it as the symbol of the Order.

Mandy snapped a few pictures. When she lowered the camera, she looked up at him, eyes searching for a clue or answer. "Now what?"

Before Bear could answer, he felt someone slide close to him. The touch on his forearm was light, the hands wrinkled with age, but he stiffened at the figure's proximity.

"You're looking for it too, aren't you?" the woman asked.

Bear faced her, placing his body between the stranger and his daughter. The woman was shorter than Mandy, which made Bear feel about eight feet tall. She slipped her hand from his arm and tucked a piece of silver hair behind her ear. A gold wedding band on her ring finger caught the light as she moved.

"Looking for what?" Bear asked, stalling while he assessed the people around them. No one else took notice of their hushed conversation.

"The Order," the woman answered. Despite her thick Italian accent, she spoke in smooth, deliberate English. "We should work together."

The hair on the back of Bear's neck stood on end. He glanced around again, feeling as though dozens of pairs of eyes watched them. But not a single person looked in their direction.

He peered back down at the woman. "Who are you?"

"My apologies." She placed a hand on her chest. "My name is Giulia Vasari."

Her movement drew Bear's attention to her clothes. Her simple blue dress was clean but faded. A delicate bracelet encircled her wrist, dull and tarnished.

When Bear didn't respond, Giulia pressed on. "I saw your girl taking photos of the symbol on the pillar." She dropped her hand from her chest as she leaned forward and lowered her voice. "You search for the Order of the Iron Serpent. Just like me."

"I don't know what—" Bear began.

"Please." Giulia took hold of Bear's arm again. She squeezed, her grip frail. "I have information that may help you."

Bear's curiosity tugged him forward. "What kind of information?"

"Not here." Giulia turned away, waving for them to follow. "Come."

Bear exchanged a look with Mandy. Her body vibrated with the effort it took to keep her feet planted.

"What do you think?" she asked, gaze locked on Giulia's retreating figure.

"I think it's awfully convenient she's here at the exact same time we are."

"She's old. We shouldn't have any trouble."

Bear scratched at his beard. "I also think distractions come in many shapes and sizes. Stay alert."

Mandy nodded. With one last glance around, Bear trailed after Giulia. The old woman led them to a small alcove where there'd be less chance of being overheard, yet still in plain view of everyone else inside the basilica. Was that for his and Mandy's sake, or hers?

The woman wore an expectant look as they approached. "What can I call you?"

"I'm Riley. This is my daughter, Mandy." Bear positioned himself so he could still see the rest of the room, even while he kept an eye on Giulia. "Why are you looking for the Order?"

"My husband disappeared two months ago. And the deeper I dig, the more I'm convinced the Order's behind it."

Giulia reached into the folds of her dress and pulled out a small notebook. She unwound the string from the front and let it fall open in the palm of her hand. Thin, slanted writing covered the pages. A silver paperclip held several pictures in place.

"It has been his dream for many years to restore one of the crumbling buildings here in Venice," Giulia continued, pulling a picture free and handing it to Bear. "He purchased a small apartment above a shop. During the renovation, he realized one of the walls in the back bedroom was untrue."

Bear furrowed his brows. "Untrue?"

"False," Mandy said. "You're saying it was a false wall?"

Giulia bobbed her head up and down, giving Mandy a grateful smile. "Yes. Behind it lay a mural. It was very old. Very cursed."

Giulia pulled another photograph free and handed it to Bear.

"Cursed?" Bear asked, taking the photo but studying the woman some more. "What makes you say that?"

"The trouble this apartment brought us has been unending. It has been all we could do to keep our heads above water." Tears gathered in the corners of Giulia's eyes. "A week later, my husband disappeared."

Boisterous laughter caught Bear's attention, and he scanned the crowd inside the basilica once more. Several adults gave a group of teenagers dark looks, and the kids quieted down. Despite the continued feeling they were being watched, Bear couldn't see anyone paying any attention to them.

Mandy tugged the photo out of Bear's hand, turning his focus back to Giulia.

"Could your husband have left?" Bear asked. "Voluntarily, I mean."

Giulia scowled. "No. We have been together since we were young. He would not leave me unless he had no other choice."

"What does this have to do with the Order?"

Before the woman could answer, Mandy tugged on his sleeve.

"Bear?"

He looked down at her, taking in the ghostly sheen on her face. "What's wrong?"

"The girl in the mural," Mandy said.

Hand shaking, Mandy passed the photograph back to Bear. He glanced down at it, his heart stuttering in his chest.

Bear could hardly hear Mandy when she spoke again.

"She looks just like me."

4

MANDY SAT ON A STONE STEP NEAR THE WATER, AWAY FROM THE main crowd gathered around the basilica. After Bear saw the resemblance of the girl in the mural, he'd led Mandy and the old woman outside, to a spot where they could talk without fear of being overheard.

Gentle waves masked Bear and Giulia's hushed tones. Mandy stared down at the photographs from the old woman's notebook. The sun warmed her shoulders, but it glared off the pictures in her hands. She hunched over and held them close to study the details.

The mural appeared to be about the size of a standard bedroom wall. The cracked plaster crumbling in places, and most of the paint had faded long ago. The reds and oranges stood out the most, but the deep green of the girl's dress remained just as bold as the day it had been painted. The folds of her garment were as realistic as any Renaissance painting Mandy had seen in a museum.

Finding a hidden mural by a long-dead master behind a false wall? Mandy could wrap her head around that. But staring into the painted eyes of a girl who looked exactly like her? That was something she couldn't begin to make sense of.

Tearing her eyes away from the familiar figure on the right, she scanned the rest of the mural. An explosion of symbols and figures spread across the entirety of the image—so much so that she had trouble focusing on one area. Her gaze narrowed in on a section along the bottom that featured several smaller figures wearing masks. Each guise created in the shape of a different animal, all of them painted red.

Mandy flipped to the next picture, a closeup view of the top left corner of the mural. She had no idea why Giulia or her husband had focused on this area, given how faded it was. The symbols were impossible to distinguish, and after a few moments, she gave up and moved onto the next one.

A breeze combed its fingers through Mandy's hair. She pushed several locks back behind her ears and out of her face. Children shouted from the stone steps in front of the basilica, but she didn't waste more than a quick glance in their direction. Behind her, Bear's voice rose above the noise of the ocean as he asked Giulia about the history of the apartment. Mandy tuned them out as she searched the photographs for clues that could point them to some answers.

The next picture focused on a different section along the bottom edge of the mural. Twining symbols created an intricate boarder. Some looked familiar, like she'd seen them in a book somewhere, but she couldn't decipher them. None looked like the symbols she'd discovered in the tunnels beneath San Gimignano, which meant they weren't Etruscan. To her untrained eye, there was no telling if they were older or newer.

A cloud passed over the sun, and the sudden darkness sent a chill down Mandy's back. In this lighting, she could see the next photograph in greater detail. It captured the middle of the mural, and she sucked in a breath when she caught sight of the reptiles centered in the picture. A pair of dull silver snakes wrapped around a man's forearm, their red eyes glowing.

Mandy scrambled to her feet, careful not to slip and fall into the water. Boats bobbed nearby, docked until their owners returned. The urge to climb into one and explore the Grand Canal was nothing compared to the pull she felt when she looked at the photographs of the mural.

"Dad?"

Bear turned to her with a searching gaze. "What is it?"

She handed him the photograph and tapped a finger against the snakes in the middle.

Giulia stepped closer, peering down at the picture. She clicked her tongue. "The Order of the Iron Serpent."

"They're just a pair of snakes," Bear countered, his eyes fixed on the image.

Giulia scoffed. "They represent the Order. Just as the serpent carved into the pillar inside the basilica represents them." She paused, looking between Bear and Mandy. "How did you come to know about them?"

Bear kept his mouth clamped shut, but Mandy had never been good at that.

"We found something with a snake on it that looks just like those." Mandy ignored the glare Bear shot in her direction. "Someone told us it belongs to the Order."

"What was it?" Giulia leaned toward Mandy, her gaze feverish now. "One of their puzzle boxes?"

This time, Mandy did keep her mouth shut.

Bear crossed his arms over his broad chest. "What makes you say that?"

"I have a friend. He knows more about the Order than anyone I've ever met. He hears rumors. One of them was about the puzzle box discovered south of here. The same day it was found, it disappeared again."

"Who's your friend?"

Giulia reached back into the pocket of her dress and drew out a pen. She flipped the notebook open to one of the last pages and scribbled something along the top. Then she tore it off and handed it to Bear. Mandy caught sight of a name and address.

"His name is Luca Ferrara," she said. "A local historian. He knows about more than just the Order. Go there tonight. After dark. He will be able to answer your questions better than I can."

Bear glanced down at the slip of paper, then stuffed it in his pocket. He looked up at the church looming above them. "Why were you at the church today?"

"It is the only place I know of with a tie to the Order. I have been coming every day, hoping someone will approach and tell me what they want with my husband."

"Why do you think the Order has your husband?"

Giulia pursed her lips. "After we discovered the painting on the wall, we received a message. A warning. It told Antonio the painting was for him and to abandon the restoration. The stamp on the bottom was in the shape of a serpent."

Mandy felt herself leaning forward, trying to absorb the woman's words as soon as they left her mouth. The familiar itch to solve a mystery plagued her, just like it had in San Gimignano. The memory of all that had happened there forced Mandy to take a step back and regain her composure.

"Do you still have the note?" Bear asked.

Giulia shook her head. "Antonio threw it away. He did not take it seriously, and now he is gone." She looked up at Bear, her eyes wide and glistening. "Please. No one else will help me. I am an old woman. We never had any children. My husband is all I have."

Bear glanced at Mandy, and she could see the hesitation on his face. She didn't bother hiding her excitement at the prospect of finding out more about the Order. They'd come to Venice for answers, but they hadn't anticipated finding a connection so soon.

"What was your husband doing when he disappeared?" Bear asked.

"Investigating the symbols within the mural." Giulia pulled the photograph from Bear's hand and placed it on top. She tapped one of the masks Mandy had noticed earlier. It was in the shape of a lion.

Wings stuck out like ears on either side. "This symbol is everywhere in Venice. He thought that might be a good place to start."

Bear peered down at the photograph, his expression blank as he studied the animal. When he looked back at the old woman, he hesitated for just a moment before he spoke.

"I can't make any promises, but we'll do what we can to find your husband."

Tears leaked down Giulia's face as she clung to Bear's arm.

"That's all I ask. Thank you. *Thank you.*"

5

BEAR STAYED CLOSE TO MANDY'S SIDE AS THEY FOLLOWED THE old woman back to the apartment with the mural. He kept one eye on Giulia and one eye on their surroundings. The woman's story seemed sincere and her emotions genuine, but he'd been led astray by far more innocent looking people in the past.

They crossed the Ponte dell'Accademia, veered toward San Marco, then wound through a tangle of alleys. Giulia stopped at a small shop, slipped around back, and led them up a narrow staircase to a locked door.

Dust swirled in the rush of air from opening the door, highlighted by shafts of sunlight filtering through the windows. Bear rubbed his nose to keep from sneezing. Despite the open windows, it smelled musty and stale, the scent embedded in the floors and walls.

He stepped aside to let Mandy in, then closed the door behind them. The small, rectangular living room was empty except for a toolbox that sat to one side, along with a heap of cleaning supplies. Giulia led them through a tiny kitchen, decorated in a variety of greens and yellows, and down a short hallway to the back bedroom.

Once they entered, Bear's gaze was drawn to the far wall where the mural stood out from the rest of the room. Just like in the pictures, the plaster crumbled in spots, and most of the paint had faded to dull hues. The figure of the girl on the right side insisted on being seen, and Bear felt himself sucked into her unrelenting gaze.

It wasn't Mandy, he knew that. And yet, he could see her in all the fine details. The slope of her nose. The shape of her eyes. The way her mouth turned down a little at the corners when she was deep in thought. The girl in the mural had hair a few shades lighter than Mandy's, but even a passing stranger would say they looked alike. Sisters, perhaps. Or a long-forgotten ancestor.

Mandy stepped forward, her gaze roaming over the mural. Bear scanned the rest of the painting too, noting the sections where Giulia had taken pictures and the area that hadn't gotten the same attention.

"Why didn't you have closeups of every part of the mural?" he asked.

Giulia stepped up beside him, each hand grasping the opposite elbow. Her voice shook a little. "Antonio, my husband, was studying some of them when he was taken. I only had what he left behind."

Mandy uncapped her camera and held it up. "Do you mind if I take some of my own?"

Giulia gestured toward the wall. "Please, be my guest."

Bear looked down at the old woman. "I'd like to see the rest of the apartment."

Her eyebrows scrunched together as she looked up at him, but she nodded. "Okay. Follow me."

The click of the shutter echoed in the empty room as Bear followed Giulia back into the kitchen.

"I take it you live somewhere else," Bear said.

Giulia shook her head, silver strands falling around her face. "We had another home not far from here, but Antonio's obsession got the better of him. We took what we could and moved in here not long after he discovered the mural."

Her voice carried no trace of bitterness. Bear suspected that any anger she felt toward her husband had been replaced with the desire to have him back again.

They stepped into the kitchen. There were no decorations, but it did have a toaster and a small coffee pot. He reached out and pulled open the refrigerator door. It held a jug of water, a small carton of milk, and a handful of oranges. The shelves were bright and clean, even if the fridge itself looked yellowed and dated on the outside.

He shut the door and gestured for Giulia to head back out into the living room. She tilted her head for a moment, but she pursed her lips and led him back out into the larger space.

"Why did your husband choose this apartment? Did he know the mural was here?"

"I don't think so." Giulia had her arms wrapped around herself again. She stared at the tools with longing, like she was imagining her husband walking through the front door, picking them up, and getting back to work. "This one was the most affordable we could find. It needed work, but Antonio has always been handy. He could do most of it himself and save money. A lot of upside."

Bear walked around the perimeter of the room, looking for anything out of place. "What did he plan to do once he restored it?"

"Rent it out. Many tourists will pay top dollar to stay in a historic apartment rather than one of the crowded hotels." She gestured toward the front door and the street down below. "We are not far from Piazza San Marco. It is a good location."

Bear stepped into the only room in the apartment they had yet to visit. It was larger than the back bedroom and had a small bathroom off to the side. A mattress and a pile of blankets sat in the corner. A book lay open face down on the floor, with a half-used candle next to it.

He knelt and picked up the book, placing a finger in the spot where it had been open as he flipped through the pages. He read off the title, "Il Nome della Rosa."

The Name of the Rose.

"His favorite," Giulia said.

Bear replaced the book and stood to his full height. "You said your husband was taken while investigating symbols in the mural. Specifically, the winged lion. Do you know where he started?"

"The Lion of St. Mark became a symbol of Venice. It is very famous here and can be found all over the city. The lion in the mural has a halo over its head and carries a sword in its paws. This is in contrast to the more traditional version of the lion holding St. Mark's Gospel." She walked across the room and peered out the window. "He was sure he had found a church with its exact likeness. I will give you the address."

"Is there anything else I need to know?" Bear kept his tone even. "If I'm going to help, you can't keep any secrets from me about this."

Giulia's shoulders stiffened. She turned to look at him. "I have told you everything I know. More than I should." Her eyes were huge as she peered at him. "The Order is dangerous. I wouldn't have asked this of you if you hadn't already been looking for them. What would be the point in me keeping secrets? I want to find my Antonio."

Bear studied her, searching her expression for any hint of a lie. Once again, she seemed earnest in her plea. But there was still a sense of unease in his gut. Before he could question her further, Mandy walked in, slipping the cap back onto her camera.

"I think I got as much as I could." She let the device dangle around her neck, then shook hair from her face. "Lighting wasn't the best, but I can tweak that on the computer. The resolution will be much better, too. I'll be able to zoom in on each part and see if there's anything we missed at first glance."

"Thank you," Giulia said, her smile soft.

"Do you have a number where we can reach you?" Bear asked.

Giulia nodded and rattled off her phone number. Bear programmed it into his phone and gave her his. Then she gave him the address to the church her husband had last visited. With a nod at the older woman, he led Mandy back through the living room and out the front door.

"You find anything else?" she asked, once they were back under the Venetian sky.

"No." Bear followed her down the rickety outdoor staircase, grimacing as it groaned beneath his weight. He let out a sigh once they reached the ground. "Apartment was clean, aside from the renovation stuff. He seemed pretty obsessed with the mural. You spot anything new?"

"Lots of things." Mandy waited for Bear to start walking before she fell into step beside him. "But none of it makes sense. There's so much to look at, and I don't know what any of it means."

"We'll start with the winged lion and the church Antonio visited. Then we'll go visit the historian Giulia mentioned."

"Sounds like a plan—*oomph.*"

He'd come to a halt, and Mandy had run straight into him. He reached out an arm to steady her, never taking his eyes off the man across the street.

"What is it?" Mandy asked, peering around him.

Bear held her back. But he felt her stiffen as soon as she spotted what held his attention.

The man wore a tailored charcoal suit, and shiny black shoes. He held a cellphone to his ear, his mouth moving at a rapid pace. From this distance, Bear couldn't tell what language the man spoke. If he had to guess, he'd choose Italian based on the man's bronze skin, aquiline nose, and dark hair.

He looked no different than any of the other men in suits wandering through the city, but the way he glanced around, stopping on seemingly inconsequential details, caught Bear's attention as soon as he'd stepped off the curb to head in their direction. When the man spotted Bear, however, he'd taken a step back onto the sidewalk, never taking his eyes off him.

Bear stared him down, and after another few seconds, the man turned and walked away.

"Not exactly subtle," Mandy said. "We gonna follow him?"

If Bear had been alone, he would've done exactly that. But

chances were high this was a member of the Order, or someone who worked for them, and he had no interest in going up against them without more information.

"Not today." Bear typed out a message to Giulia, telling her about the man and to keep her doors locked. Then he took off in the opposite direction. "I think it's time we do some sightseeing."

6

BEAR AND MANDY WALKED THE STREETS OF VENICE FOR several hours, soaking in the bright Italian sunshine and stopping at any landmarks or shops that caught their attention. Against Bear's better judgement, Mandy ate her weight in gelato, and he drank enough coffee to fuel a fleet of airplanes.

He kept his head on a swivel, whether they were standing in line at a checkout counter or peering up at the ornate façade of yet another basilica. He saw no sign of the man in the suit that had been watching him before, but that didn't mean there weren't still eyes on them.

If someone was following them, they were being discreet.

The sun had dipped below the roofline and shopkeepers were closing their stores by the time Bear felt comfortable enough to go back to their hotel. They circled the block three times before heading inside, walking up the narrow staircase and letting themselves into their room. It remained untouched from earlier that morning.

Mandy stalked straight over to her bag and pulled out a thin laptop. Bear crossed the room and peered out the window while Mandy uploaded her photos of the mural. She focused on the task at hand, sticking her tongue out between her teeth as she adjusted the lighting, saturation, and various other components to make the mural as vivid as possible.

The hours slipped by like this, Bear taking turns watching out the window and peering over Mandy's shoulder as she inspected each photo. He ordered them room service, making Mandy take a break from the computer while she ate. As soon as she had slurped up her last noodle, she was right back at it. He couldn't help but smile at her determination.

Bear emptied a few of the less important items from his backpack and replaced them with the puzzle box, wrapped in one of his clean shirts. Then he had Mandy put the photos of the box on a flash drive that he slipped into his pocket. He wasn't about to hand over the box to some stranger to inspect.

Giulia's contact, Luca Ferrara, lived east of Piazza San Marco. They walked by Giulia and Antonio's apartment, but the lights were out. She'd texted earlier that day that she was safe with a friend. Satisfied that Giulia wasn't in immediate danger, Bear led Mandy along the Venetian streets at a lazy pace. As far as he could tell, they'd dropped their tail hours ago.

Darkness had taken hold and there was a slight chill in the air. The cool breeze brought the smell of saltwater, and Bear inhaled the scent hungrily. It reminded him of being a kid back in North Carolina. Little Riley Logan would be amazed at all the adventures he'd gone on as an adult. Bear smiled at the thought.

Distant music added to the night's ambience, a tune Dean Martin had made famous, performed by a trio of street performers. A weight lifted from Bear. Mandy hummed to herself, bouncing as she walked. It was like they'd never even met Giulia or seen that strange mural on the wall in her apartment.

They stopped in the shadow of a tall building, the peace of the moment draining from the air like the tide going out around them. Four floors sat stacked on top of one another, two sporting ornate wrought iron balconies. A rainbow assortment of flowers cascaded from boxes along the banisters.

Bear reached out and pressed the buzzer for Luca Ferrara's address. They could hear an echo of the sound from one of the higher floors. Thirty seconds went by, and then Bear pressed the button again.

The crackle of static preceded a sharp phrase spoken in Italian. "Who is it?"

Bear pressed the button for the speaker and replied in English. "Riley and Mandy. We're friends of Giulia and Antonio Vasari."

Silence followed. It went on for so long, Bear thought he might've scared the man away. Or perhaps he didn't know English? Bear was just about to reveal his hand and make his reply in Italian when he heard the buzzer sound.

"Third floor," the man replied in English. "Be quick."

Bear checked to make sure the street was empty before he hauled open the door and held it for Mandy to follow in his footsteps. The entrance was tiny, as was the staircase heading upstairs.

"They really don't make places around here for people like you, huh?" Mandy said.

Bear chuckled but didn't reply, too keen to get to the third floor.

The man in question waited for them on the third-floor landing. Despite being taller than average, Bear still had a few inches on him. And at least a hundred pounds. He wore slacks and a dress shirt, which were at odds with the pair of slippers on his feet. Thick glasses perched on his nose, yet he looked over the top of them to study the newcomers. His short hair looked like he'd been combing his fingers through it, and his sharp jawline held a few days' worth of stubble.

"Did anyone see you come in?" Luca asked.

Bear kept his face passive. "No."

"Good, good." He held out a hand. "You may call me Luca."

Bear shook it, careful not to squeeze too hard. It was like shaking the hand of a skeleton. "Riley. And this is Mandy."

Luca shook Mandy's hand, then gestured for them to follow him inside.

If Luca felt embarrassed by the state of his home, he didn't show it. He led them through the front living room to his study in the back, winding around piles of books, odd statues and plaques, and the occasional forgotten plate. It smelled like cigars and ancient tomes. Bear didn't find it all that unpleasant.

Luca cleared a space on the couch for them, revealing faded green upholstery beneath a pile of papers that he neatly stacked on the floor. Then he gestured for them to sit.

"Coffee? Tea?" He looked at Mandy like he couldn't figure out how old she was. "Wine?"

"We're okay," Bear answered.

Mandy pouted like her last experience with wine hadn't been terrible.

While Luca poured himself a glass of red wine from a decanter he'd picked up from the floor, Bear cast a glance around the small room. Like the rest of the house, it was covered in bookshelves stacked two deep, with papers strewn everywhere. Takeout containers and forgotten plates were in strange places, like beneath the side table or balanced on top of a lampshade.

Luca swirled the wine in his goblet, took a deep sniff, then sighed with his eyes closed. He took a small sip, set the glass on his desk, then met Bear's gaze.

"Giulia told me you might stop by. I assume this has to do with the mural?" His gaze flickered to Mandy and then stayed there. His jaw went slack. "You looked so familiar when I first saw you, but I couldn't place you. But you—look just like the girl in the painting."

Mandy shrugged like maybe she hadn't noticed.

"What can you tell us about it?" Bear asked.

Luca stared at Mandy for a moment longer before returning his focus to Bear. "Not much." He took his glasses off and rubbed at one eye before replacing them. "I haven't had time to do a proper investigation to determine the mural's age or narrow down potential candidates for the artist."

"What about the subject of the painting?"

Luca's gaze settled on Mandy again.

"Not her." Luca twitched at Bear's tone and tore his focus from Mandy. "The snakes. The people in the masks. What do you know?"

Luca lifted his wine glass and took another sip. His eyes distant. When he finished, he placed the glass back down on his desk and leaned back in his chair, clasping his hands in his lap.

"What do you know about the Order of the Iron Serpent?"

"Let's say nothing."

Luca nodded. "Not much is known about the Order. I have looked for answers for decades, and most of what I know is conjecture."

"Start with the facts."

Luca ticked the items off on his fingers. "They're a secret society. They've been around for half a millennium, at least. Their signature motif is a silver serpent with red eyes."

The silence stretched on while Bear waited for more.

"That's it?" he asked.

Luca dropped his hands back into his lap and shrugged. "If I knew more, I probably wouldn't be around to tell you about it. They're secretive. Powerful. Paranoid."

"What a great combination," Mandy muttered.

"All right, give me your best guess as to what they want," Bear said.

"What all secret societies want, I suppose. Money, power, influence."

"By the sounds of it, they have all of those in spades."

Luca nodded. He grasped his chin in thought, rubbing his fingers along the stubble on his jaw. "But it is never enough for people like them."

"You have any idea who belongs to the Order?" Bear asked.

Luca tipped his head back and laughed. "Of course not. Their identities are secret, of course."

Bear bristled at his tone. "What *kinds* of people are in the Order then? The Vatican?"

Luca stilled. "It's possible, I suppose." He removed his glasses and swiped at the corners of his eyes before replacing them. "But as far as I can tell, that is simply rumor. The Vatican holds an enormous amount of power. The Order would benefit from letting slip they have members of the papacy amongst their ranks. I have found no evidence to indicate it is true."

"That doesn't mean it's not," Mandy argued.

Luca nodded in her direction. "Exactly."

Anger rose up inside Bear like a wall of flames. Talking in circles was a waste of time. "The mural," he said through gritted teeth. "What do you know about it?"

Luca cleared his throat and sat up a little straighter. "Not much. It likely has several meanings or purposes, hidden in layers amongst the various symbols and figures. I can tell you, however, that the people in the red masks along the bottom of the mural are significant. They represent La Velata Rossa."

"What's that?" Bear asked.

"The Red Veil. They are the masked council rumored to control Venice's criminal underbelly. It is my belief that they are an elite branch of the Order of the Iron Serpent. The mural is, most likely, a message, but to whom and for what reason, I cannot say."

Bear narrowed his eyes. "Can't or won't?"

Luca frowned. "Signora e Signore Vasari are my good friends. We have known each other for many years. She asked me to tell you everything I know. That is what I have done. It is not much, but it is all I have. I take great risk in sharing this information with you. If the Order finds out, I will disappear without a trace. I have no one to look for me."

The tension eased from Bear's shoulders. "All right. Last question. Have you ever seen one of the Order's puzzle boxes?"

Luca's eyes lit up. "Not in person, no." He leaned forward, placing both hands on his desk on either side of his half-empty wine glass. "You have it, don't you? The one that was discovered in San Gimignano and lost the very same day."

"How did you know it was found and lost again?"

Luca waved away the question. "Do you have it with you?"

"No," Bear lied. "But we brought you pictures. We were hoping you might be able to help us figure out how to open it."

Luca nodded, reaching out a hand. Bear dug the flash drive from his pocket and deposited it into the man's open palm. Luca curled his fingers around it and held it to his chest like it was a precious gemstone.

Bear stood, towering over the other man. "We'll be in touch. Don't tell anyone about this."

Luca shook his head. "As you can tell, I am quite adept at keeping secrets."

As Bear motioned for Mandy to stand and follow him out, he couldn't help but think that what Luca said was no reassurance at all.

7

BEAR STEPPED OUT ONTO THE COBBLESTONE STREET. A crescent moon hung high in the sky, dispersing its silver light amongst the soft golden glow emanating from various windows and streetlamps.

Mandy stepped up beside him. She looked both ways ensuring they were alone before she spoke. "You think we can trust him?"

"Not sure." Bear swept his gaze up and down the street too, lingering on the areas where the shadows were the darkest. "From now on, we keep the box on us at all times."

Mandy nodded once. "What now?"

"Time for church."

Mandy groaned. "Again? How many churches does this city even have?"

Bear chuckled. "Less than it used to. Come on, stay close."

It didn't take long for them to arrive at the address Giulia had provided. The church looked like a simple white chapel you might find back in the States. It was tucked between a pair of taller build-ings on a side street a few blocks from Piazza San Marco. Two plain columns bracketed a bronze door, which stood out against the white façade. The windows were devoid of any color or decoration.

Perched at the church's peak, the winged lion gripped a gleaming sword as if guarding the city itself. Light flared from below, casting fierce shadows across its face and wings, giving it the unsettling illusion of breadth and muscle, like it might leap down at any moment, blade raised to meet them.

"It looks just like the one in the mural," Mandy whispered.

Bear made a quiet noise of agreement. They'd passed other churches bearing the symbol of Saint Mark, but this was the only one that looked like an exact replica of what they'd seen inside Giulia and Antonio's apartment a few hours ago.

A subtle breeze ushered the evidence of city life through the air around them. Laughter and music mingled with the scents of roasting meat and coffee. A different world compared to where they were, half-shrouded in darkness and completely alone. Bear had seen no sign that they'd been followed from Luca's place, but his eyes still darted along every shadow before approaching the church's entrance.

As he stepped up to the door, he leaned in and strained to hear any sign of movement inside, but Mandy's steady breaths at his back were louder than the interior of the church. On a whim, Bear reached out and tugged on the handle in front of him.

The door swung open on silent hinges.

Mandy's eyebrows lifted in surprise when Bear peered over his shoulder at her. With a shrug, he slipped inside, grateful that his eyes didn't need to adjust to the dim lighting. Mandy closed the door after her, wincing when the click of the latch echoed in the chamber around them. They held their breath, but no one emerged to investigate the sound.

Bear stepped forward into the nave. The interior was nothing compared to the basilica they'd visited earlier that day, but it was more ornate than most small churches back home. Statues of the twelve apostles stood above simple columns, separated by small arches along the outer walls. The vaulted ceiling was unadorned, but more sculptures sat at the ends of the ribs where they reached the walls. He could just make out the altar at the far side of the chamber. Candles burned along the front, scentless except for the subtle smoke wafting from their flames.

Mandy's voice was strained as she whispered from behind him. "Bear, look."

He glanced over his shoulder at her, then followed her gaze to the two rows of wooden pews in front of them. They formed a wide aisle atop the blue and white mosaic floor, each one of them lined up perfectly behind the next—except for the first two on the right side.

"Stay behind me," he said.

Mandy's silence was agreement enough, and Bear made his way forward on light feet. The darkness inside the church put him on edge. If someone lingered in the shadows, they'd be able to follow his movements easily enough. Even still, the church remained silent around him.

Bear reached into his pocket and pulled out a small hunting knife, opening it up with a flick of his wrist. It wasn't as efficient as a gun, but it was quiet—and in his hands it was more than a little dangerous.

As he crept down the aisle, Bear searched for anything else out of place. The faded mosaic tiles beneath his feet and the worn seats on either side of him spoke volumes about the history of this church and the devotion of its congregation. It might not be as showy or well-kept as the Santa Maria della Salute Basilica, but it was no less well-loved.

He stopped a foot shy of the disturbed pews. His gaze landed on a spot of blood splattered across several tiles just a millisecond before Mandy lifted her hand to point it out. He nodded, scanning the area for any additional signs of a struggle. More blood adorned the wooden corner of one pew and the leg of the other.

Bear held his knife pointed down along his leg, hidden by his bulk, but at the ready. Stepping around the blood by the pews, he followed its trail to the altar. Several candles along the right had been tipped over, their flames dashed by the action.

"Lucky they didn't burn the place down," Mandy whispered, coming to stand next to him.

Bear stepped up into the sanctuary and peered around the pulpit and the altar. An ornate cross had been knocked over, the filigree along one side misshapen, likely where it had smashed against the hard floor. A golden urn lay next to it, its lid about a foot away. Both appeared to be priceless artifacts, yet they'd been abandoned like they were nothing more than cheap knockoffs.

Mandy approached the urn with her phone out and flashlight turned on. She'd taken one of the long-handled matches from the front of the altar, sliding it into the container's opening and lifting it gently to peer inside.

"Empty." She set it back down where it had fallen. "Think something was inside?"

"Might've been."

"What were they looking for?" she asked, straightening up and scanning the sanctuary.

"Not sure." Bear peered over his shoulder at the dark blood splattered across the tile flooring. "Must've been important enough to hurt someone over. Maybe even kill them."

Mandy walked toward the back of the sanctuary. "No dead bodies."

Bear pointed to a door that led to the back. "Doesn't mean there aren't any."

"We gonna check it out?"

The back of Bear's neck prickled with awareness. He let his gaze roam around the church, searching for anything that didn't belong. But there was no movement. No sounds. Nothing that could've caused the sensation.

Still, he'd learned long ago to listen to his gut.

Bear shook his head. "Not a lot of blood. Nothing leading to the back. Don't think it was serious. We shouldn't stick around. Don't want to risk getting caught at the scene of a crime."

"Just wish—"

Bear looked back at her to see what had caught her attention. She had her phone out in front of her, the light shining down on the urn. She squatted down, careful not to touch anything as she inspected the bottom of the upturned container.

"What is it?"

"Another symbol." Mandy looked up at him, her eyes bright. "It looks like a weasel." She glanced back down at the urn, tilting her head. "Holding a ring?"

Brows furrowed, Bear made his way to her, mirroring her posture as he looked at the animal carved into the metal. Sure enough, a small weasel holding a simple band, like a wedding ring, stared back at him. A random piece of Venetian history floated to the surface of his mind before fading away again, as though it had been swept back out to sea with the tide.

"This reminds me of something, but I can't put my finger on it."

Mandy held out her phone and took a few pictures. "Maybe it'll match something in the mural."

Bear straightened, his knees groaning in protest at the movement. That prickling discomfort creeping back up his neck.

"Come on." He gestured for Mandy to follow him. "Take a couple pictures of the pews too, then let's get out of here."

"What do you think it all means?" she asked, stopping long enough to snap a few photos before scurrying after him.

Bear gripped his knife harder.

"That we're not the only ones trying to decipher the mural."

8

MANDY WOKE UP AS SOON AS BEAR STIRRED IN THE BED NEXT TO hers. The sun had just peeked over the horizon, illuminating the room with its golden glow. The faint citrus scent that had hung in the air when they'd first arrived had disappeared overnight.

Stretching her arms over her head, she let out a heavy sigh when her back popped.

"You're up early," Bear said.

His voice was deep and gruff this early in the morning. When Mandy spoke, hers sounded just as rusty. She turned to him, a sheepish smile in place.

"I woke up every couple of hours. Couldn't stop thinking about the mural and the puzzle box."

Bear chuckled as he sat up and swung his legs over the side of the bed. "I had some weird dreams last night."

Mandy followed suit, standing up and stretching again. The burn in her muscles felt good. She glanced at Bear's backpack on the desk. "Can I go through my pictures now?"

Bear leveled her with a look, likely assessing the shade of the bags under her eyes and how many times she yawned per minute. Last night, after they'd left the church and returned to their room, he'd forced her to go to bed and get some sleep instead of opening her laptop.

She'd never admit it, but she was glad he'd done that. Despite her interrupted sleep, she felt much better today. More alert. Ready to tackle this strange puzzle and figure out what it all meant.

Bear stood too. "Go ahead. You want coffee?"

"Yes, please."

Mandy crossed the room and plopped herself down into the chair at the desk. She opened her laptop and pulled up the photos she'd taken when they'd visited the mural in Giulia's apartment. After adjusting the lighting, saturation, and contrast, more details emerged from the background of the mural than she'd noticed with her naked eye yesterday. And the ability to zoom in close made it so much easier to study everything new.

The smell of coffee preceded Bear's arrival at her side. He set a steaming paper cup down next to her laptop and leaned in over her shoulder. "Find anything interesting?"

"Lots of stuff." Mandy chewed on her thumbnail as she swiped a finger across the trackpad. "But I don't know what any of it means."

Bear straightened and took a sip of his coffee. "I figured out why that engraving on the urn felt familiar."

Mandy looked up at him, her eyes wide. "Really?"

He nodded, blowing over the top of his coffee cup and taking another sip. "There's a well-known Venetian ceremony involving a wedding ring. It's called Festa della Sensa. The feast of the ascension. It celebrates il sposalizio del mare. The marriage of the sea."

Mandy turned back to the computer, zooming out from the mural and scanning the masked figures along the bottom. Her heart jumped when her gaze landed on a mask that looked like a cross between a raccoon and a fox.

Without taking her eyes from the screen, she said, "This one kind of looks like a weasel, don't you think? And look, he's holding a wedding ring and standing in a boat."

"Not a weasel. An ermine."

Mandy looked back up at him, brows furrowed. He held his coffee in one hand and his phone in the other. He nodded to the device, a sly smile on his face.

"The Marriage of the Sea ceremony took place every year until the Republic of Venice fell in 1797." He paused as he continued to scan whatever article he read from. "These days, the mayor of Venice reenacts it. He throws a ring into the lagoon to symbolize Venice's marriage to the sea. There's a parade of boats beforehand, and afterwards, a boat race. It's a pretty big deal."

"What does it have to do with weasels?" She reached out for her cup as her gaze returned to the figure in the mural. Instead of sipping her coffee, she held it against her chest with both hands, allowing it to warm her. "Or whatever you said it was."

"An ermine is a type of weasel. The Doge of Venice—"

Mandy sighed. "What's *that*?"

Bear chuckled. "The Doge of Venice was basically the city's leader. They were like the head of state. It was the highest role of authority within the Republic at the time. During the ceremony, he'd get all dressed up in silk, embroidered with silver and gold thread, and ermine fur. It was very fancy."

Mandy took a dainty sip of her coffee. "If you say so."

"Want to know the most interesting part?"

Mandy glanced over at him, noting the sparkle in his eye. She couldn't stop herself from leaning closer. "Yes."

"La Festa della Sensa is taking place *today*."

Mandy's coffee cup almost slipped from her fingers. "Seriously?"

Bear nodded. "The mayor sails across the lagoon to reach the Lido port. Then he stands in front of the San Nicolò Church and throws the ring into the sea."

Mandy set her coffee cup on the desk, picked up the puzzle box, and crossed the room to look at the map of Venice on the wall. "Where's the church?"

Bear came to stand beside her. With his pinky finger, he pointed to a tiny spot on the map. "Right there."

Mandy held up the puzzle box, comparing the spot on the map to details carved into the wood. She frowned when she didn't find what she was looking for. "There's no gemstone there. But this has to be about the festival, doesn't it?"

Bear leaned in to look at the box in her hands before staring at the map again. "There's one here." He pointed to a spot a little inland. "That's Piazza San Marco. And they start on this side of the basin before heading over to Lido."

Mandy couldn't contain her grin if she tried. "That must be it then."

"Two churches. Two gemstones. One secret compartment with a pin." Bear took another long, slow sip of his coffee. "Two symbols carved into objects found in ancient churches. Now an ancient Venetian festival and a famous Venetian plaza."

"Plus the mural." Mandy looked over her shoulder at the picture still up on her screen. "It's like we have to use the puzzle box and the mural to decode whatever this is." Her heart rate kicked into high gear. "Like a treasure hunt!"

Bear frowned as he spoke. "Except we don't know who buried it. Or why."

"We're going to the festival, right?" She couldn't hide the hope and anticipation in her voice. "We have to go!"

Bear didn't say anything, just turned and dropped onto his bed, the mattress groaning under his weight. Mandy blew out a sharp breath, dragging the puzzle box to the far corner of the desk, away from her coffee, away from her reach, before jabbing at her laptop trackpad to zoom in on the one part of the mural she couldn't stop thinking about.

"We have to figure out why it looks just like me." Mandy peered over her shoulder at him. "Don't you want to know?"

Bear sighed. "Of course. But it's not that simple."

Mandy wanted to beg and plead with him, but that rarely

worked. Instead, she forced down her emotional response and tried to think through the situation rationally. "We promised to help Giulia find her husband. Going to the ceremony is the next logical step."

Bear brought his cup to his lips, staring at her over the top of it. He knew exactly what she was doing, but that wasn't going to stop her.

"We're involved whether we want to be or not," she argued. "We should get ahead of whoever else is searching for clues so we don't get left behind. That feels like it might be even more dangerous."

Bear nodded his head. "You're not wrong."

Mandy couldn't help but smile.

"But I still don't like it. Feels like we're digging a hole while the tide is coming in."

Mandy looked back at the mural, gazing into eyes that looked so much like hers.

"Then I guess we better dig faster."

9

THE CERULEAN SKY STRETCHED OVERHEAD, A FEW GOSSAMER strands of cirrus clouds drifting lazily above the rooftops. Sunlight spilled in from the east, warm against Bear's face. If only the breeze off the water could carry away the press of bodies and the sour tang of sweat.

They stood along the water looking out on St. Mark's basin, the procession about to start. Bear hiked his backpack up his shoulder, all too aware that he'd wrapped a priceless artifact in a pair of dirty shorts and shoved it inside. The puzzle box was safer with them, and there was no telling when they'd need to reference it. He'd also stuck the pin from the secret compartment in his pocket, just in case.

Mandy shielded her eyes with her hand, standing on her tiptoes to see past the throng of people in front of her. He could hear her grumbling over the crowd around them. Bear had no problem seeing the water, and if Mandy had been ten years younger, he would've put her on his shoulders like old times.

The crowd shifted, and Bear caught sight of a man and woman gesticulating wildly, a pair of children crying between them. The woman pointed back toward the plaza behind them, and the man threw up his hands in defeat.

Bear nudged Mandy with his elbow. "Follow me."

"Where are we going?" Mandy asked, as she trailed after him.

He didn't bother answering. Backing out from their spot, Bear circled the edge of the crowd before spotting the opening made by the family as they left their position at the edge of the water. Bear ignored the disgruntled looks and annoyed murmurs as he made his way forward, bringing Mandy around to stand in front of him once they were close enough. He was going to block someone's view one way or another, so he might as well make sure his kid had the best vantage point possible.

Once they were settled, she looked up at him with a bright smile.

He nodded and peered out across the water. Spotting dark silhouettes coming their way, he reached an arm over her shoulder and pointed them out. "There are the boats."

Mandy stood on her tiptoes more out of excitement than a need to see better. A strong breeze ruffled her hair, and Bear inhaled the scent of the salty ocean. If nothing else, at least it smelled better over here.

The crowd pushed forward as the boats drew nearer. Bear repositioned his pack until it hung it from his front so it wouldn't get crushed. The conversations around him grew louder as people pointed at the boats. Children clapped and jumped up and down. Couples held each other, soaking in the sights and the sun.

Bear leaned down to whisper in Mandy's ear. "The ceremony took place on the Doge's boat, called a Bucintoro. The mayor's boat is called the Serenissima. You can see him standing there at the front, dressed in those robes."

"He's wearing ermine fur, just like you said," Mandy whispered back. "Who are the other people?"

"City officials and other dignitaries. Once they get to the other side, the mayor will throw the ring into the sea. They started doing this more than a thousand years ago."

Mandy's eyes grew wider. "Whoa."

Bear's mouth stretched into a toothy smile. As complicated as their lives were most days, moments like these made up for it. He loved being the one to show his kid how big and interesting the world was. How many other sixteen-year-olds from the United States got to witness something like this?

Mandy's gaze drifted from the boat at the head of the procession to the ones surrounding it and trailing behind. "What about the rest of the boats?"

"It's like a water parade." Bear watched as each boat passed them. The people who didn't have oars in their hands waved to the crowd. "Many of them are residents of Venice and the surrounding areas. See the way they're rowing? That's a special, traditional technique developed in Venice a long time ago."

"Is there usually a boat with people in masks?"

Bear furrowed his brow, thinking back on everything he'd learned since this morning. "I don't think so. Masks aren't—"

"Because that boat is full of people wearing masks. And they're the only ones."

Bear followed her line of sight, his gaze landing on one of the smaller vessels. It was long and narrow, with silver flourishes on the front and back, and along the sides. Bright red paint covered the interior to match the cloaks and masks of the six rowers—strikingly similar to the ceremonial garb of *La Velata Rossa*.

As the boat drew closer, Bear noticed the shape of each mask, an ermine, identical to the one in the painting. He heard Mandy inhale sharply and knew she had spotted it too.

A splash of black at the back of the boat drew Bear's attention. The figure sat so still, he could have been a statue, black cloak matching the rowers' red ones. But instead of wearing an ermine mask, he wore one with a long beak protruding from the center of its face. A wide-brimmed hat sat atop the figure's head.

"Is that a bird," Mandy asked, "wearing a hat?"

He would've laughed if the gears in his brain weren't turning at full speed, the familiarity of what he saw clicking into place. "It's a plague doctor."

"What's that?"

"A doctor who treated people with the bubonic plague back in the Middle Ages. They wore masks like that because they thought it would keep them safe from disease. They'd stuff herbs and flowers inside the beak, thinking the good smells would keep away the bad air full of disease."

Mandy snorted. "That's stupid."

"To you, maybe," Bear said. "But back then, they had no idea where the plague came from or how to keep it from spreading."

Mandy lifted her camera off her chest and started scrolling through her pictures. She tugged on Bear's arm. "Look. Just like in the mural."

Bear finally tore his gaze from the boat and looked down at the screen of her camera. Sure enough, he saw a small figure in the corner wearing a plague doctor's mask. Its cloak was even black, just like the one in the boat.

"Bear." Mandy craned her neck to look at the boat full of masked figures. "Do you see what's painted along the side?"

Bear didn't have to stretch to catch a glimpse of what she was looking at. He'd been so focused on the people inside the boat that he hadn't taken the time to look closely at the vessel itself. When he spotted what held her attention, his stomach clenched.

"A pair of silver snakes," he said.

"That's not a coincidence," Mandy murmured.

"And look." He nodded toward the boat as it drifted farther away. "It's not going with the rest of the procession."

Mandy was on her tiptoes again "Where's it heading?"

"Looks like it's docking farther up the coast."

She gave up trying to find it through the sea of people around them. "What are we going to do?"

Bear was already turning away from the shore and the rest of the procession.

"We're going to follow them."

10

MANDY GRIPPED THE BACK OF BEAR'S SHIRT AS HE LED HER
through the crowd, letting him take the brunt of jostling elbows and
wandering feet. Not nearly as many people grumbled about their
departure as they had at their arrival, but she ignored them anyway.
Her mind raced to put together the new information they'd received
during the procession.

The silver serpents undulating across the side of the boat were a
dead giveaway this had something to do with the Order of the Iron
Serpent. The people in red masks made sense too, but something
bothered her about the one dressed in black. He matched the figure
in the mural, but was there a reason he wore black instead of red?
And why was someone dressed up like that during today's ceremony?
She'd never heard of a plague doctor before, but as far as she could
tell, that wasn't a normal occurrence.

Bear made a final push to exit the crowd around the basin. As
soon as they were free of the unrelenting press of bodies, he swung
his backpack up on his shoulder and glanced down at her.

"All good?"

She nodded but didn't say anything. A million questions swirled in her head and she couldn't keep up with them. If she spoke now, she'd never stop. And none of her words would make any sense. Better to let Bear take the lead.

He did just that, striking out toward where he'd seen the vessel make landfall. It was easier to move now, but there were still way too many people. Despite being out in the open, it felt like invisible walls were closing in on her. They pressed against her chest, making it hard to breathe. Hard to focus on anything but putting one foot in front of the other.

So that's what she did. Gaze locked on Bear's shoes, she followed in his footsteps, trusting that he would keep an eye out while she gathered herself. He wasn't a fan of crowds either, but most people moved out of his way, whether they wanted to or not. Mandy didn't garner the same reaction. If he were her biological father, maybe she'd end up growing to his height. She had no idea how tall anyone in her family had been, but she wasn't holding out hope for a miracle.

Bear stopped suddenly, and it was only because Mandy was watching his feet so closely that she knew to swerve around him before she ran into his back.

"Damn."

Mandy looked up in time to catch a glimpse of the boat bobbing up and down in the water before the crowd blocked it out again. And it was empty. "Now what?"

Bear scanned their surroundings. Mandy could tell the moment he found what he was looking for because his body coiled tight, like it was preparing for a fight. "I see them. Come on, stay close."

They headed toward Piazza San Marco, the crowd growing thicker with each step. The scent of grilled meat and fresh fruit was almost enough to overpower the stench of so many warm bodies in one place.

Sandals and sneakers turned to boots and strange heels with buckles. More women wore long dresses. Some of the men were in tights. Those that were dressed differently wore funny hats.

Mandy pressed closer to Bear. "What's going on?"

"Locals dress up to participate in historical reenactments." Bear's gaze fixed on something in front of them. "They're in period costumes. Some of them will recreate famous moments from Venice's past."

"People used to dress like this?" she asked, eyeing a woman in an elaborate dress. The neckline plunged down the front of her chest, outlined with frilly lace, and a huge collar that fanned out from the back. Her hair sat on top of her head like two curly horns. "Weird."

"You've seen nothing yet," Bear said, glancing at the woman before looking back out across the crowd. "Trust me."

"Do you still see them?"

"The ones in red disappeared."

He stopped short as a little boy bounced off his leg and went sprawling across the cobblestones. Before the kid could even make a sound, his mother scooped him up into her arms and walked in the opposite direction. Mandy could hear her reprimanding the child in rapid Italian.

Bear let out a low growl. "I lost the doctor."

Mandy peered through the crowd, but she struggled to spot the robed figures now that so many more people wore period costumes. A man and a woman holding hands passed between her and Bear, and she had to step back to avoid getting trampled.

As she did, she spotted the edge of a rippling black cloak.

"Over there!" She didn't wait for Bear to confirm he was following as she chased after him. "Hurry, before he gets away again."

"Mandy, wait—"

Mandy stopped, but someone jostled her from behind. For a moment, she felt like a ping pong ball, getting knocked around and sent flying in different directions. When she finally came to a stop, she looked back in the direction she'd come from. Bear was farther away than she would've guessed. The crowd had swept them in opposite directions. Someone elbowed her in the side, and she stumbled. A hand gripped her arm, helping steady her.

She let out a slow breath. Mandy turned to thank the person

who'd helped her. But when she opened her mouth to speak, the words died on her lips.

A person in a red mask and robes stood over her. Their grip tightened around her bicep, sending searing pain down her arm. Sunlight bounced off something silver as their other hand emerged from beneath their costume. She didn't need to see it fully to know it was a knife.

Despite the masked figure being bigger than her, Mandy managed to yank her arm free from their grasp. The person froze in surprise. She didn't hesitate as she kneed them in their crotch. A man's voice cursed in Italian as he doubled over. Mandy took the opportunity to knock the knife from his hand, then spun in the opposite direction- where she'd last seen Bear.

Another figure in red barreled toward her, shoving people out of their way.

Mandy ground her teeth together and angled her body away from the newcomer. The crowd surged around her, but she didn't have time to be polite. Shoving her way between couples and families, Mandy kept her eyes off the ground and on the people around her. Whenever she spotted the color red she spun in the other direction.

Eventually, she made it to the edge of the plaza. Looking over her shoulder, she saw three masked figures heading toward her now. She wanted to search the crowd for Bear, but if she waited any longer, one of her pursuers would end up getting their hands on her. She'd escaped once because they hadn't expected her to fight back. She doubted that would work a second time.

Mandy sprinted down a cobblestone street, her shoes slapping loudly against the ground. With more space to dodge between people, she picked up her pace. Her breaths grew ragged the more she ran and the further she got from Bear.

If she couldn't find him, she'd have to make her way back to their hotel on her own. Thankfully, she had her phone. But she'd also have to make sure she wasn't being followed. They'd both be in trouble if she led the masked figures to their doorstep.

Between one rasping breath and the next, a large man stepped out from a side street and snagged her by the elbow. She yelped and whirled on him, her fist already raised. Then she registered the back-pack straps on his shoulders. The large beard. The worried eyes.

"Bear," she wailed, throwing herself into his arms.

"I know," he said, squeezing her tightly before he set her down and grabbed her hand. "Are you hurt?"

Mandy did a quick mental scan of her body before she answered. "No. The one guy grabbed me, but I surprised him and got away."

Bear pulled her along the street, farther from the main square. "You sure it was a guy?"

"Positive." She couldn't help the grin that spread over her face. "He swore at me in Italian after I kneed him in the crotch."

Bear chuckled. "Good job, kid."

Mandy's grin slid away as reality of the situation took hold, knot-ting her stomach. "Why were they coming after me?"

Bear's voice dropped into a deep growl. "No idea, but if they think they're the ones hunting us, they've got another thing coming."

11

Bear kept a gentle arm around Mandy's shoulders as they left the plaza. The crowds thinned the farther they walked, but he didn't let his guard down. From the outside he looked calm. He even made it a point to nod at the locals standing outside their shops. But his thoughts were much too dark for this bright, sunny day.

Despite his rumbling stomach, the mouthwatering scent of authentic Italian food was background noise in his brain. The image of the red-robed assailant grabbing Mandy's arm flashed repeatedly in his mind. She'd reacted quickly and efficiently, choosing to run instead of fight. Pride filled his chest, but anger still swelled alongside it like a crimson wave. It was as much for himself as it was the masked figures. He'd been too far away to help her. It didn't matter that she could take care of herself. That was still his job. And he'd failed.

He fought the urge to take Mandy by the hand and drag her to the nearest airport. Leave this mess with the Order of the Iron Serpent behind. She'd hate him for it, but she'd get over it eventually. And if she didn't? Well, at least she'd be safe.

But Mandy was too much like him. They both had a pathological need to solve whatever puzzle they found. Giulia might have been the latest victim of the Order, but she was far from the only one. If their power reached as far as he'd been led to believe, there would be nowhere they could run. It was best to stay put and join forces with those who wanted to take down the secret society.

Mandy looked up at him from where she walked at his side. "You're blaming yourself, aren't you?"

"I should've been there." Bear hated the anger in his voice. "You shouldn't have had to fight him off on your own."

"I shouldn't have run off through the crowd like that." Mandy looked forward, her gaze distant. "I'm sorry. It was impulsive."

A deep ache filled his chest, like his heart had cracked in two. Mandy was a good kid who sometimes made rash decisions. "I'm proud of you, though. Running away was the smartest choice. You did a good job."

She smiled up at him, some of the shadows behind her eyes dissipating.

They were quiet for the rest of the walk back to the hotel. Bear kept to the major streets, even though it took them longer. The dense crowd made it difficult to spot a tail. The reverse was also true—they'd be lost among the tourists.

Bear was looking over his shoulder when Mandy tugged on his shirt. He looked down at her, then followed her gaze to the front of the hotel. He hadn't expected to see a familiar face, especially not the one belonging to the man waiting for them.

Luca Ferrara stood at the entrance, dressed in another button-down shirt and pair of slacks. This time, at least, he wore a pair of leather shoes instead of slippers. He shifted from foot to foot, running his fingers through his hair half a dozen times. As they watched, he took his glasses off, pulled a cloth from his pocket to polish them, then set them back on his nose.

When he looked up and spotted them, he stuffed the cloth back in his pocket and rushed across the street. The lighting in Luca's office the night before had been dim, but Bear thought he looked a shade or two paler today.

"There you are." Luca's breaths were ragged. "I need to speak with you."

Bear kept a firm hand on Mandy, who stuck to his side. "How did you find us?"

Luca wrung his hands together. "I spoke with Giulia. She gave me your address."

Bear stilled. "I didn't tell her where we were staying."

"Then she must have found out somehow. Giulia knows many people in Venice." He waved away Bear's concerns with a flap of his hand. "But that is not important. What I must tell you is a matter of life and death. *Your* life, to be exact." He swallowed. "Maybe mine as well."

Bear took a moment to scan their surroundings. There were enough people coming and going that there'd be at least a dozen witnesses to whatever happened, except most people didn't give them more than a cursory glance.

He returned his gaze to Luca. "What is it?"

"Your names have been spoken at a council meeting. The Order knows who you are."

That much was obvious after their encounter that afternoon, but he wasn't going to tell Luca that. "How do you know this?"

"I also know many people in Venice." Luca took his glasses off his nose and cleaned them. When he replaced them, his eyes looked wider than they had before. "I have my own contacts who trade in information. As long as I provide them with what they're looking for and don't get in their way, the Order leaves me alone. Whether it's because of my contacts or pure luck, I can't say."

"Why bother warning us, then?"

Luca scowled at him. "You are trying to help my friend. To betray you would be to betray her and Antonio."

It was a legitimate reason. Was it the only reason he had for coming to warn them? "Do you know who mentioned our name? What they said about us?"

Luca shook his head. "La Velata Rossa is even more mysterious than the Order. All I know is that you two are now marked targets."

"We saw masked figures at Festa della Sensa today." Bear studied Luca's face for any minute reaction. "Some of them were dressed in red."

Luca took a step back. "That was La Velata Rossa. You are lucky to have escaped after having your name marked." He shook his head. "They are more dangerous than you can even imagine."

He looked over his shoulder before glancing down at Mandy and then back up at Bear. "I do not say this lightly, given what you are doing for Giulia, but you should leave Venice. Leave Italy, if you can. Return to the United States."

Bear started shaking his head before the man finished speaking. "That's not going to happen."

"Then you are a fool."

Bear shrugged. "I've been called worse."

"Your daughter—"

"Can take care of herself," Mandy finished, standing straighter. "Did you look at the pictures we gave you?"

Luca closed his eyes, clenched his fist, arms curled at his side, as though having a silent argument with himself. When he opened them again, he looked defeated. "Yes. La Velata Rossa views the mural as a sacred artifact. It is not just a painting or symbol—it is a map of the Order's future. It is meant to be used in conjunction with the puzzle box to unlock their secrets."

Bear had figured as much, but it was a small reassurance that Luca agreed with him. "What secrets are we talking about here? And why would they want someone to unlock them?"

Luca let out a short huff, reminding Bear of an angry bull. "If I knew that, I would not be here, now would I?"

"Do you at least know why one of the masked figures was dressed like a plague doctor?" Mandy asked.

Luca tilted his head to the side. For a moment, his wringing hands stilled. "That is quite interesting. Venice has its history with the plague..." He shook his head as if to dislodge the thoughts. "But it is a suicide mission. You need to leave this place. Go into hiding."

Bear thought of Isabella Fabrizio and how long she'd spent pretending to be Lucia Moretti. "I've spent an entire lifetime looking over my shoulder. Worked too hard to leave that life to go back to it now. We're staying."

Luca nodded, a frown tugging at his lips. "Then I wish you the best of luck." He sighed heavily before turning to go. "Even though it won't do you any good."

12

Bear insisted Mandy remain at his side as he did a full circle of their hotel before heading up to their room. Between the obvious tail outside of Giulia's apartment and the run-in with the masked figures, he was feeling more paranoid than ever. His eyes darted around so quickly he feared missing something. Add in Lucas' warning, and it was about time they packed up and moved on.

They headed up the stairs to their room, each cautious of what could be around every corner.

"You sure you don't want to take Luca's advice and leave Italy?" Mandy asked.

Bear almost tripped over his own feet as he peered over his shoulder to look at her. "Surprised you're even asking that."

Mandy pursed her lips, brows furrowed. "I don't want to go, but everything we've heard so far makes me think we might be in over our heads."

"Might?" Bear chuckled. Then he paused at the top of the stairs, dropping his smile as he turned to his daughter. "We can go if you want. We don't have to do this."

Mandy came to a stop in front of him. "But we're getting so close to some answers."

"It's not worth our lives. Today in the piazza—"

"—was a mistake." Mandy scuffed her shoe on the step before looking up at him. "I learned my lesson. But them trying to hurt me in broad daylight surrounded by thousands of people was reckless. Something doesn't add up."

Bear stared down at her, proud that she was so attuned, but also a little worried to see her taking this so seriously. "That's not exactly an argument for staying, though."

"I don't want to run scared, Bear. I'm tired of being afraid." Her shoulders slumped, like the weight of the world was on them. "If they're as powerful as people say they are, we both should've disappeared by now. This feels like some sort of test. Maybe it wasn't originally intended for us, but we've got the puzzle box now. I want to see it through."

Bear felt the same way. If it was just his life on the line, he wouldn't hesitate to throw himself into the fray. But with Mandy at his side, he had to tread carefully.

"We'll keep digging," Bear started. When Mandy broke out into a grin, he held up a hand. "But the second I feel like it's become too dangerous, we're out of here. And I don't want to hear any arguments from you."

Mandy nodded fiercely, her eyes wide . "No arguments. Got it."

Bear had his doubts, but it was a start.

He gestured for her to follow him to their door. Once they'd arrived at their room, he stepped close to listen for any sounds on the other side. When he didn't hear any, he unlocked it and slipped through the opening, clearing the space in a matter of seconds.

He swung his bag off his shoulders and onto one of the beds. "Doesn't look like anyone was here."

Mandy strode across the room and sat down at the desk in front of her laptop. Her fingertips flew over the keyboard at a rate Bear found astonishing.

"Luca said Venice has its history with the plague." She hit enter on the keyboard, then leaned forward to read what popped up on her screen. After a moment, she sucked in a breath. "He wasn't kidding. According to this, about fifty percent of the population died in 1348 due to an outbreak of the Black Death."

Bear crossed the room to look over her shoulder. "Probably because of all the ships coming and going from all over the world. Venice was a huge trade hub, and it's not like people were great with their hygiene back in the day."

"It says Venice implemented strict quarantine measures. Anyone suspected of being infected would be sent to designated islands. They also built columns to give thanks for the passing of the outbreak. There's one in Piazza San Marco and another in front of the Santa Maria della Salute Basilica." Mandy looked up at him. "That can't be a coincidence."

Bear pointed to the screen. "What's it say there about the plague doctor masks?"

Mandy turned back to her computer and skimmed several paragraphs. "Pretty much what you already told me. They filled the beak of the mask with aromatic herbs. It also had glass eye pieces. The doctors would wear long, flowing robes and gloves to protect their skin."

Bear returned to his backpack where he'd left it on the bed and pulled out the puzzle box while Mandy kept talking.

"Did you know the word quarantine comes from the Italian quaranta giorni, which means forty days? The Venetian Republic required all arriving ships to anchor offshore for forty days before the people were allowed to come into the city."

Bear held up the puzzle box, turning it so he could see the uninterrupted groove that represented the Grand Canal. "I don't think it's a coincidence that Festa della Sensa features a procession of boats heading out to one of the islands."

"And the figure in the mural wearing the bird mask was standing in a boat." Mandy pulled up the photograph she'd taken of the painting and zoomed in on the plague doctor. "It's also the only one surrounded by a thin gold border."

Bear looked over at the screen. "Is that the shape of a bell?"

Mandy switched windows and typed in the words *Venice, plague, boat,* and *bell.* She scoffed at the results. "Holy shit, I can't believe that worked."

"Language," Bear chided, a smile tugging at his lips. "What's it say?"

"The island of Poveglia," she said, mangling the pronunciation. "Well it's *actually* one island in a group of three. There's a belltower on one of them. It's the most recognizable building there."

Bear glanced at the picture on the wall, but it only included the mainland. He crossed back over to her. "Pull up a map."

Mandy clicked around a few times, then zoomed in until Venice and the islands could be seen together. She could barely sit still as she peered up at the puzzle box in his hands.

Bear tilted the wooden contraption until he found the Grand Canal again, then glanced between the box and the screen to orient himself. He used a finger to draw a trajectory from the coast to where the island should be in the ocean.

When he lifted his finger, a gleaming red gem winked back at him.

He showed Mandy the spot on the box. "Poveglia must be the right place."

Mandy took a deep breath and turned back to the screen. "It went from being used for customs control to plague control. A pair of ships that stopped there had several cases of the plague, and from then on, it was a quarantine site, especially when the two other plague islands, Lazzaretto Nuovo and Lazzaretto Vecchio, were both full. In the twentieth century, they even built a psychiatric hospital there. Apparently it's pretty haunted, but most people aren't aware of its existence for some reason."

Bear lowered the puzzle box. "I'm much more worried about the living than the dead."

Mandy turned and waggled her eyebrows. "What about the *un*dead?"

He shrugged like the idea wasn't out of the question. "I've seen enough zombie movies to know what to do. And what *not* to do."

Mandy grinned and returned her attention to the article. "There are a lot of ghost stories about the island, which makes sense because researchers estimate about 100,000 people died there. Oh, gross. They would just throw them all into big holes called plague pits."

"Does it say anything about people visiting?"

Mandy scrolled a bit farther down the article. A moment later, she groaned. "This says the island is closed to visitors because it's been abandoned and isn't safe. We'd need special permission to visit it, and that's only for things like filming, photography projects, or research."

Bear set the puzzle box on the desk, then fished his phone out of his pocket. "Pack up your stuff. We're finding a new place to stay. Later tonight, we'll head to the island."

Mandy's jaw dropped. "Really? How?"

Bear pulled up his short contact list and tapped on one of the names. "I think it's about time we call in some backup."

"Brandon?" Mandy asked as the phone rang. Then her eyes went wide. "Mr. Jack?"

Bear hesitated and looked back at her. "I was thinking of someone a little more local."

A moment later, a woman spoke from the other end of the line. Her words clipped. "You've got a lot of nerve, Riley Logan."

Bear grinned as Mandy slapped a hand to her forehead.

"Hello, Agent Fabrizio. Hope you don't mind, but I need to call in a favor."

13

Mandy leaned over the side of the boat and peered into the dark water, seeing only the reflection of the silvery moon hanging overhead. Fog clung to the surface like a funeral shroud. A shiver slithered down her spine like a snake, but she couldn't look away. The harsh breeze tangled her hair around her face, and she had to gather it in one fist to hold it back. Even the windshield on the boat wasn't enough to break the onslaught.

Bear sat next to her, keeping his eye on the man driving.

On the phone, Isabella had read Bear the riot act for stealing the puzzle box, disappearing off the face of the planet, and ignoring all her calls. Mandy got bored after a while and returned to her laptop to study the mural. She tried making other connections, but nothing stuck. She hoped by going to Poveglia 'they'd be able to figure out the next step.

By the time Bear hung up with Isabella, he'd secured them private transport to the island. Agent Fabrizio had wanted them to wait for her to arrive before they visited the area. Bear had convinced her there was no time, but that they'd meet up with her as soon as she reached Venice. And he'd promised to answer her phone calls from then on.

As Mandy tried peering through the fog to the dark horizon, she let her thoughts drift to the woman she'd met in San Gimignano. Isabella had seemed like a good person, but she was also a foreign intelligence agent, and there was no telling if she'd hold a grudge against them after they'd disappeared on her.

Still, she'd agreed to set them up with one of her contacts so they could visit the so-called plague island of Poveglia after Bear had caught her up on everything they'd learned and experienced since arriving in Venice. Isabella's anger had seeped away the more he'd talked, and by the end of the call, her words came quicker, edged with anticipation.

The boat hit a small wave and Mandy had to grip the side of her seat with her free hand. She glanced up at the man driving. After Bear had found them a new place to stay, they'd waited until nightfall to make their next move.

They'd met their driver an hour ago. He looked older than Bear, but by how much, Mandy couldn't tell. Years of being out on the water in the bright Italian sun had likely aged him. He gripped the wheel with dirty nails and scratched at a patchy beard. The cap on his head sat slightly askew, but it had been that way since before they'd taken off. A pipe sticking out of the corner of his mouth wouldn't have looked out of character.

The man had introduced himself as Luigino and had only spoken a few words in Italian to Bear. He stood in front of the wheel, peering over the windshield and out into the dark water. The engine hummed beneath their feet. The lights remained off because of the thick fog. As the boat dropped into a lower gear, the wind that had been buffeting Mandy calmed to a gentle breeze. She let go of her hair and started the herculean task of unknotting it.

They were probably breaking a dozen laws, but Bear had handed over a stack of bills when they'd met the man at his private dock.

Mandy didn't think he was another agent, just a local willing to look the other way. She wondered how Isabella knew him.

Bear nudged her with his knee. "Heads up."

She glanced at him, then followed his line of sight when he nodded toward the front of the boat.

Mandy's eyes had adjusted to the darkness, and the moon shined bright enough to see the outline of the island ahead, even through the mist. As they approached the dock, she scanned the area and saw mostly trees peering back, coils of fog slithering over their roots like vines. A bell tower rose above everything else, nothing more than a silhouette against the night sky.

Luigino said something in Italian. Bear leaned forward and replied, but the old man shook his head and gestured to the island. Bear grunted in response, then stood and hiked his backpack over his shoulder. He didn't even sway as the old man hit reverse to bring them to a halt along the dock, before he reached over and grabbed a rope to keep the boat in place.

Luigino looked over his shoulder. He didn't tie them off.

"Come on, kid." Bear hopped over the edge of the boat and landed on the dock with a dull thud. He held out his hand for her. "We've only got a couple hours before he comes to pick us up, and if we're not back within five minutes of him docking, he'll leave us till morning."

Mandy stood, securing her own backpack in place. She didn't move to take Bear's hand. "He's not coming with us?" She hated the high pitch of her voice. "He's leaving us here?"

"It'll be fine." Bear gestured for her to hop out. "He only gets the other half of his payment if we return to Venice unharmed—and not in police custody."

Mandy took Bear's hand and let him lift her up and out of the boat. She landed on the planks of the dock as it swayed in the water, small waves breaking against its frame. Out here, away from the city's constant hum, the quiet pressed in on her. No voices, no footsteps, no distant rumble of vaporetti—only the faint lap of water and the creak of wet wood. After hours surrounded by Venice's chaos, the stillness felt strange, as if the island itself were holding its breath. The trees along the shore loomed like silent sentinels, their shadows bleeding into the fog that swallowed everything it touched.

"Bear." She didn't bother hiding her shaking voice. "I don't like this."

Luigino tossed the rope back onto the dock and put his boat in reverse. In a matter of seconds, he'd disappeared back into the night.

Mandy felt lightheaded. The dock swayed harder under her feet now. Fear crawled up her throat and out of her mouth in the form of a strangled cry.

Bear's warm palm landed on her shoulder and squeezed. "Look at me."

Mandy forced her gaze up to his. Her eyes felt like they might pop out of her skull.

"We're gonna be okay." Bear's voice carried all the warmth and security she associated with him. It seeped into her skin and relaxed her muscles. "I doubt anyone's here but us and maybe a flock or two of birds. We get in, find what we're looking for, and get out."

Mandy took a deep, calming breath. The dock felt solid under her again. "Okay."

"If you want, you can stay here. Make sure our driver doesn't leave before I'm back."

Somehow, that sounded worse.

"No, I'm okay. I just needed a second." She forced her lips into a smile. "Besides, you might need me to recognize the symbols from the mural."

Bear grinned down at her, then swung his backpack off one shoulder and retrieved a couple of flashlights. "I'm definitely gonna need you for that." He handed her one and clicked on his own. "Any idea what we might be looking for?"

Mandy turned her light on too, shining it toward the tree line. It reflected off the mist, but it looked thinner farther from the water. "If I had to guess, I'd say we're either looking for something related to the plague or the bell tower. Out of the three islands, this is the only one with buildings on it."

Bear glanced at the map on his phone. They were standing where the old housing used to be. Beyond that lay the prison, and further still, the asylum. No wonder the place felt creepy.

Mandy groaned. "Nothing good ever happens in an abandoned asylum."

"The church with the bell tower is on the far side, so if we don't find what we're looking for in the other buildings, we'll have already started to head there anyway." He checked his watch. "We better get moving. No telling how rundown this place is or how difficult it'll be to navigate."

Mandy fell into step beside Bear as they walked down the dock and stepped onto the island for the first time. She half expected a gust of wind to blow through, carrying with it the sounds of the dead and dying.

"Hey, Bear?" she asked.

"Yeah?"

"Why didn't Luigino want to stay here and wait for us? Why wouldn't he step foot on the island?"

Bear glanced down at her. "You don't want to know."

Mandy gulped. "Was it because of the ghosts?"

Bear answered right before the forest's shadows engulfed them.

"Yeah, it was because of the ghosts."

14

Whisps of fog drifted over the ground as Bear stepped around exposed tree roots and under low-hanging branches. Vines crawled up the trunks, reminding him of the serpents they'd found on their journey to track down the Order.

Mandy stayed close, the beam of her flashlight bouncing in time with his.

Doubts crept in like shadows. What the hell were they doing on an island with such a tragic past, in the middle of the night, hunting for a secret society more powerful than any he'd heard of before? Bear didn't believe in ghosts, but he'd seen the way Luigino had cast a wary look at the island. He hadn't even tied off his boat while they disembarked.

The crack of a branch had both Mandy and Bear spinning in that direction, searching for the source of the noise. The fog muffled most sounds. Except for that damn branch. He'd gotten used to the raucous sound of the city within a day, but the island lacked most of the usual noises they might encounter out in the woods back home.

A flutter of movement caught his attention.

"Just a bird," he said.

Mandy blew out a breath. "For a second, I thought—" She shook her head.

For the span of a single breath, he'd also wondered if the island could be haunted. The Order posed enough of a threat that they didn't need to borrow trouble from local legends.

Bear faced forward, his flashlight illuminating a pale shape up ahead. It stood tall and wide, unmistakable despite being half-hidden by ivy and fog.

"There's the first building." Bear gestured to it with his flashlight. "That was the main area for housing, I think. Then the next building after that was the prison."

Mandy shuddered but didn't say anything.

"Once we make it past the prison, we'll be right on top of the hospital." Bear started forward. "We'll keep our eyes open as we move through the other buildings, but I don't want to waste too much time if we're sure what we're looking for is either in the hospital or the church."

"Or the asylum," Mandy muttered.

Bear didn't want to go in there anymore than she did. "Given the plague doctor mask, I don't think we'll have to step inside that one. But if we don't find anything in the other buildings, we'll do what we have to do."

Mandy side-stepped a sapling. "I wish I knew what we were looking for." She paused, her gaze drifting as if weighing the words before speaking again. "Saying we're looking for a needle in a haystack isn't a spooky enough saying for this place. Maybe looking for a bone in a graveyard?"

Bear snorted. "Yeah, that works."

He stopped when they reached the wall, shining his light along the brick. A couple yards down the edifice, there was an opening where a door used to be. The few steps leading up to the building were crumbling and covered in ivy.

Gesturing for Mandy to follow, he walked over and peered inside. Darkness swallowed the beam of his flashlight the further inside he looked. Wood and stone debris littered the floor. Colorful graffiti covered the walls. Several cigarette butts lay piled up in the corner.

"This place has been abandoned for a long time." He looked down at Mandy, his voice steady but serious. "There's no telling how stable any of it is. Follow in my footsteps. No wandering."

Mandy nodded, her eyes wide as saucers. "Don't have to tell me twice."

"Good." Bear peered back inside. "We move quickly but safely. If we get separated for any reason, meet back at the dock. You know what direction that is?"

Mandy turned on the spot and pointed back the way they'd come.

Bear nodded. "It'll be easy to get turned around while we're inside but try to keep your orientation the best you can. You ready?"

Mandy took a deep breath. "No, but let's get it over with."

Bear felt the same way. With one last look at the trees around them, he stepped through the open doorway and into the darkness.

Mold and mildew assaulted his senses as they passed close to the walls. Dust hung in the air, tickling his throat and chest with each breath. Was that a result of the wind moving through the building, or had someone just been here?

Mystery and rumors haunted Poveglia. Some said half the island was made of human ash. Others spoke of experiments done on prisoners and patients. Even without the exaggerated fabrications, it was evident this place had seen its fair share of horrors. Walking through these buildings now, he felt the weight of the island's history weighing on him.

Both he and Mandy remained silent as they made their way through various rooms and corridors. Rubble lay strewn across the floors. Bear counted them lucky that most of it didn't impede their forward movement. Some of the areas were easy to recognize for what they were—old plumbing indicated a former bathroom; rusted bedframes revealed shared living spaces.

They reached the other side of the building and plunged back into the overgrowth. A pair of birds took off not three feet from them, and he swore loudly enough that another pair abandoned their perches somewhere off to their left.

Even without a trail to follow, Bear had seen enough from the map to know the prison would be dead ahead. They stumbled into it a few minutes later, crawling through a hole in the wall.

Jail cells lined the walls, the iron bars dark with grit and grime. He spotted a few manacles on the floor but didn't point them out to Mandy. Her breathing remained steady, but she stuck closer than usual. He didn't blame her. They'd been on the island for less than an hour, and he wanted to crawl out of his own skin.

It took longer to navigate broken floorboards and collapsed walls than it would have to wind their way through the trees outside. But they couldn't risk missing something out of the ordinary by taking an easier route.

By the time they approached the old hospital, Bear's anxiety ticked higher with each passing minute. So far, neither building had contained anything odd. They hadn't spotted any symbols carved into the walls or any unusual patterns in the rubble. He wondered if maybe he was going crazy as they looked for the strange signs. But given everything they'd come across so far, he knew anything was possible.

They climbed through another hole in the wall to enter the hospital, this one small enough that Bear's arms scraped against the sides. When he stood up, dust and tiny chunks of brick and mortar cascaded from his shoulders. Mandy's hair was pale in the dim light. And covered in a layer of grime.

Bear checked his watch. "Halfway through our time here. Let's get going."

Mandy brushed her hand along the crumbling wall as she nodded, sending a small plume of dust into the air. Bear tried not to breathe it in as he walked forward, sweeping the beam of his flashlight across the room. The rubble in this building was identical to what they'd encountered in the other two, and yet the air held a heaviness to it, like something tragic had happened here.

Metal bed frames had been shoved into the main room, what might've once been the lobby now resembled a makeshift sick ward. Hundreds, if not thousands, of people had died here. As much as Bear fought the wave of images bombarding him, he couldn't stop from picturing their emaciated bodies, covered in sores and bruises. He could've sworn he heard their rattling breaths and wracking coughs.

Bear didn't share his thoughts with Mandy. They kept to the outside of the room, choosing to go counter-clockwise to reach the door on the opposite side of the hall. He was just about to step through the opening when he heard Mandy gasp behind him. Her hand clamped down on his arm and pulled him to a stop.

Heart in his throat, he turned and followed her gaze upward to the second floor. He expected to see a figure looming over them. He wasn't sure if he'd be more or less surprised if they were noncorporeal.

But when he searched the balcony above, he found it abandoned. A banister ran along the overlook. A grand staircase had once connected the two floors. Now, most of the steps were broken and cracked, like broken teeth protruding from the wall. A crooked smile glaring back at them.

"Do you see it?" Mandy whispered.

He cast his eyes and flashlight upward again. A flash of gold twinkled. He stepped to the side, bringing more of the far wall into view. Splashes of color made him first think it was just more graffiti. But no, this had a different style. A different purpose.

"We have to go up there," Mandy said.

When he turned, she was already stepping onto the first stair, one hand out to keep her balance. Bear grasped her arm and pulled her back to solid ground, scowling down at her. She huffed but didn't argue.

He studied the stairs again. Enough of them were left that they'd be able to walk up to the second floor without too much trouble, so long as they didn't crumble beneath them.

"I'll go first." He placed a tentative foot on the first step and found it strong beneath him. "If it holds my weight, it'll hold yours."

Mandy vibrated with excitement, but she waited until Bear was two or three steps ahead before following behind. They both kept one hand on the wall beside them to steady their movements, while the other held their flashlight out for balance.

There were about two dozen steps to get to the landing. Bear kept his eyes on his feet instead of the wall in front of him. Any distraction could spell the end for either one of them.

When they made it to the second floor, Bear had to hold out an arm to keep Mandy back. Her eyes had been on the painting across the room and not on the floorboards. He pointed to a spot about five feet in front of them, and she gulped when she noticed the boards were sagging.

Bear inched forward, keeping close to the wall, where the planks were more likely to hold his weight. When he felt safe enough to stop, he lifted the beam of his flashlight to the opposite side of the room, illuminating the intricate painting someone had left there.

They'd finally found what they'd been looking for.

15

BEAR STUDIED THE PAINTING IN FRONT OF HIM AS A BREEZE whistled through the open room, kicking up dust until it floated down like snow. He held his breath, not wanting to inhale the particles. On the plus side, the stench of mold was less overpowering up here.

Unlike the graffiti on the other walls, the illustration in front of them had been meticulously created using fine paint brushes. The artist had created the illusion of a three-dimensional mask on a two-dimensional surface. They had outlined the white paint in black to make it stand out from the wall. The eyes were dark pits, lifeless, yet all-seeing. Gold filigree decorated the face, with a thick silver line that ran from the right ear, up and over the forehead, and then down the center of the face along the right side of the nose. Metallic gold lips shimmered in the beam of his flashlight.

The shutter on Mandy's camera interrupted the silence.

"Another mask," she whispered.

Bear bobbed his head, unable to take his eyes off the wall in front of him. "Venice has a long history with masks. It was a major part of the Venetian Carnival, and they were sometimes seen as a status symbol. It also allowed people of different social classes to rub elbows, since there were strict rules regarding that during the Republic."

"Do you think that has anything to do with the Order? Are they trying to tell us something?"

Bear leaned forward. The floor creaked beneath his weight. "This is a volto mask. Worn by commoners." He'd seen them displayed in shop windows all over the city. His gaze traced the silver line bisecting the face, widening at the bottom. The shape clicked into place in his mind, cold and undeniable. A snake. His gut tightened. "This isn't just connected to the Order... it belongs to them."

"Bear." Mandy's voice lost its usual lightness, dropping low and deliberate. Her expression hardened, eyes fixed on his as though weighing every word. "That's a map of Venice. That line is the Grand Canal."

He peered at the gold filagree, noticing how they crisscrossed across the forehead, around the eyes, and down onto the cheeks. They could easily be streets running parallel and perpendicular to each other, forming city blocks. Thin gilded bands crossed the silver streak down the center, exactly where the bridges spanned the canal.

As Bear's gaze swept along the face of the mask, he noticed a gouge had been taken out of the wall just above the left eye. That wouldn't have been strange given the state of the building, but from his vantage point, he couldn't see any paint inside the hole.

"Wait there," Bear said. "I'm getting closer."

"What? No." Mandy's voice came out like a squeak. "What are you doing?"

"Just give me a second. I'll be careful."

Bear kept his attention on the floorboards in front of him, testing each spot before putting all his weight down. The wood bowed beneath his boots but held firm.

It took him a full minute to go a couple dozen feet, but he eventually reached the mask, looking up at it as it stared back down at him.

This close, he could see the individual brushstrokes within each color. The white paint still bright and opaque. The gold and silver sparkled with metallic accents. Unlike the mural in Giulia's apartment, this looked like it had been created within the last couple of days. Only a thin layer of dust clung to its surface. And the faint scent of paint still permeated the air beneath the foul smell of dust and mildew.

"This is fresh," he called out. "And those are definitely the streets of Venice. There's a hole here just above the left eye. No paint on the inside."

"They did it after the fact," Mandy mused. "Anything inside it?"

Bear held the flashlight up and peered into it, wincing when the floor shifted underneath him. "No. It's deep, but empty. The shape is weird."

"Weird how?"

He studied the hole, the way it started broad and narrowed to a point. It was wide but thin. "It's from a knife. Probably a dagger. The blade was symmetrical. Both edges were sharp."

"Did it fall out?" Mandy asked. "Could it be on the floor?"

Bear lowered the beam of his flashlight, pointing it at the spot where the wall met the floor. Like everywhere else, rubble littered the space surrounding the mural.

The floor shifted again, but Bear hadn't moved. A creak emanated from somewhere behind him. Where Mandy had been standing. He peered over his shoulder, not trusting the integrity of the building enough to turn on the spot.

"Mandy—"

"Bear, look." She had walked forward a few steps, leaning over to look at something on the floor. "Do you see—"

Her words cut off as the floor gave out beneath her.

Bear forgot how to breathe. His heart dropped into his stomach. The room grew dark around him as his gaze narrowed in on Mandy as she slipped through the hole that opened under her feet. His arm shot out as if to grab her but found nothing but air.

Mandy's words transformed into a scream, then a grunt, as one of the straps of her backpack caught on a jagged board and stopped her fall. She held out her arms and braced them on either side of the hole, her legs dangling through the opening. The whole floor groaned beneath them.

What little bit of logic he could hold onto told him to stay still. If he moved too much or in the wrong direction, he'd make everything worse. The best thing he could do right now was keep his head.

"Bear!"

"You're okay." He said it as much for his benefit as he did for hers. "Try not to move too much."

"I'm going to fall."

"Mandy, look at me." He waited until her wild gaze met his. "You're not going to fall. I won't let that happen. But I need you to hold still and stay calm, okay? Your straps are caught. I can pull you up, but we have to be smart about this."

Her arms were already shaking, but she nodded. "Please hurry."

He'd already started moving, retracing his steps over floorboards that had been, more or less, sturdy beneath his feet. He stopped when he was parallel to Mandy, shining his light along the floor to see if he could find the weak spots.

Mandy's breaths were ragged. Even in the dim lighting, he could see the perspiration gathering on her forehead. Her hands slipped an inch. They were probably slick with sweat. A whine escaped her mouth even as she bit her lip to keep it inside.

Bear circled wide, inching back toward the stairs he knew were secure, before he turned and picked a path forward. Every step felt like waiting for a landmine to trigger, each creak of wood, the ticking of a time bomb.

"I'm a foot away," he told her. "Just hang on."

"Please," she said. The word sounded more like a sob.

He went to take one more step forward, and the soft wood groaned beneath him. He lifted his foot and placed it slightly to the right. When he shifted his weight forward, a crack shot through the air like someone had pulled the trigger on a gun.

Mandy gasped in surprise, sucking in a lungful of dust. She coughed, her body spasming. The floor around her cracked again.

Then it gave way.

Mandy shrieked.

Bear lunged forward.

He grabbed the handle at the top of her backpack, groaning with the effort of supporting her weight with one arm.

The hole grew wider. Debris fell through the opening beneath them, clattering against metal and stone.

Bear kept a firm grip on Mandy's backpack. She grunted as she slammed into the jagged pieces of wood along the opening. He pulled as she twisted, kicking her feet for added momentum. She scrambled against the rough floor, finding purchase and dragging herself forward. Bear hauled her away from the hole, not stopping until they were back at the top of the stairs. The concrete support beneath them strong and steady.

Mandy's whole body shook. "Holy shit, holy shit, *holy shit*."

Bear pulled her into his arms and squeezed until she squeaked in protest. When he finally let go, he held her at arm's length and looked her over.

"Are you hurt?"

She shook her head, dislodging several chunks of wood that had gotten caught in her hair. "Maybe some bruised ribs and a couple splinters, but I'll be fine."

For the first time, Bear noticed how hard his heart hammered in his chest. He wanted to shake her as much as he wanted to pull her back into a hug. He tried and failed to keep the growl out of his voice. "What were you thinking?"

"I'm sorry." Tears cut a line through the dust that clung to her skin. "I saw something on the floor. It was a drawing. Like a crown made out of leaves and flowers."

Bear stilled. "You're sure?" His chest grew tight as Mandy nodded. "What kind of flowers?"

"Sort of like this." Mandy knelt to the floor and drew a symbol in the dirt.

"That's a fleur de lis." He looked to the hole a few feet away. "Stay here."

Mandy kept her hand clasped in his as he inched toward the opening in the floor, as though she were big enough to be his anchor and keep him from falling through. Bear appreciated the thought, especially as the wood beneath his feet protested with every step.

Once he'd pushed his luck to the edge, he leaned forward and pointed his flashlight into the abyss below. There was no sight of what Mandy had described, but he didn't doubt her. What she'd seen must've been left on purpose. The boards had been ready to give way on their own, but the tracks in the dirt below revealed that someone had recently dragged the pile of rusted hospital beds and placed them beneath the weak spot above. They'd been flipped so their bent and broken legs pointed skyward.

If Mandy had fallen, her injuries would've been fatal. Whether from the initial impact or lack of medical care on the island, she wouldn't have lived through the trek back across the island or the boat ride returning to the mainland.

Gritting his teeth against the acrid swell of rage rising in his throat, he backed up to the top of the staircase.

"Did you see it?" Mandy asked.

"No." He turned away from the hole. "But it's time to go."

Mandy didn't argue as she followed him back down the stairs and through the jungle. They bypassed the other buildings in favor of taking an easier path through the trees. Even so, by the time they arrived at the dock, Luigino sat there waiting for them. He looked as if he'd been ready to shove off and leave them for dead.

Bear had half a mind to tell the man that ghosts were the least of their worries.

Someone was one step ahead of them.

And knew they were being followed.

16

Bear woke as dawn broke over the horizon. Soft sunlight illuminated their new room, filtering through the thin curtain hanging over the single window and highlighting the two twin beds. The room was plain, with bare walls, a shared nightstand, and a small chest of drawers. A stark reminder that they were no longer in their cozy hotel. A private room in a hostel was better than shared accommodations, but he missed having a bathroom to himself.

Flipping back his blankets, he swung his feet over the side of the bed, wincing when he touched the ice-cold floor. This particular hostel had been converted from a 10th century church, and while the front gates were a wonder to behold, the walls did a shit job of keeping out the night air. Even in late April, Venice got downright chilly at night, once the stones lost all the heat they had soaked up during the day.

Suppressing a groan as he stood, Bear dug through his backpack until he found a fresh pair of socks. He took a few minutes to stretch out the tight muscles in his neck, shoulders, and legs. It wasn't all that long ago he'd gotten shot in the shoulder, and he was slower to heal these days. Not to mention the island adventure they'd had last night. Plus the cheap beds. And the fitful night's rest.

He'd had several dreams involving Mandy slipping through the hole in the floor of the hospital back on the island. Each time, he'd missed her fingertips by mere inches. Forced to watch, over and over again, as she plummeted to her death. Powerless to prevent his worst nightmare from coming true.

Each time he'd woken up, sweating and panting, he'd looked over to find Mandy asleep in her bed. Her face smooth and carefree. Knowing she remained untouched by these terrors made it easier for Bear. Not that she couldn't handle it.

Bear padded over to the window, ignoring the bite of the cold that still permeated his socks. He parted the curtain and looked out onto the orchard below. This early in the morning, shadows still covered every inch of greenery contained within the stone walls. The only movement came from a gentle breeze. The wind sighed as it passed through the tiny openings in the stone walls, but otherwise, the former church remained silent.

Bear turned back to the room, his gaze falling on Mandy's sleeping form. He wished he didn't have to wake her just yet, but they had a meeting to keep.

Last night Bear had reached out to Luca Ferrera. He'd told the man what they'd seen on Poveglia, including a description of the drawing that had almost sent Mandy to an early grave. Bear would've preferred to have had the conversation face-to-face, to study Luca's reaction in person, but his instincts to keep Mandy safe and secure behind literal stone walls outweighed any desire to show up on the man's doorstep unannounced.

Luca hadn't known anything about the mask they'd found, or the area marked as their next target. When Bear pressed for more, Luca admitted he knew someone who might be able to help them. Bear wasn't keen on bringing anyone else into the mix, but he'd been unable to find anything connecting the point on the map, hidden in the design of the mask, with anything that could help them track down the next clue. As far as the satellite images were concerned, that spot marked a newly renovated shop and pair of apartments.

Besides, Isabella would be arriving sooner rather than later, and Bear wanted to gather as much intel as possible before they met up with her.

Mandy groaned and sat up, her hair sticking straight out in places. Her bleary gaze landed on him. "Morning already?"

"Afraid so."

"When are we leaving?"

"As soon as you're ready." He crossed the room and pulled off the shirt he'd slept in, then replaced it with a new one. "Luca's contact is an early riser."

"Apparently," Mandy grumbled, but she swung her legs out from under her covers. When her feet touched the floor, she hissed like the stone had jumped up and bit her. When Bear chuckled, she leveled a glare at him. "Warn a girl next time."

"You might want to put some socks on. Floor's cold."

Mandy mumbled something else, but Bear didn't catch it. He busied himself with rearranging his pack, making sure everything was in its rightful place. Mandy reached for her own bag without touching the floor, pulled on a pair of socks, and set about gathering her belongings.

Within minutes, they were packed up and ready to go. Bear had reserved the room for a few nights, but depending on how today went, they might not return. Losing out on a few bucks was nothing compared to losing their lives.

A few people stirred behind closed doors as Bear led Mandy through the former church and out into the courtyard. The sun rose higher in the sky, warming the salty breeze that greeted them. Bear pulled up the address Luca had given him the night before and headed in that direction.

They were silent while they walked. Bear wanted to soak in as much of the still morning as possible. Neither of them knew what the day would bring, and he'd learned long ago to take advantage of quiet moments like this.

The scent of fresh coffee coaxed them into a tiny café. At this hour, there were only a few people out and about, and they both took advantage of the outdoor seating to wolf down a cup of coffee and a pastry.

Ten minutes later, they rounded a corner and spotted Luca pacing back and forth along the stone steps leading up to a wide doorway. An array of red and pink bricks made up the church's façade, differentiating it from the paler surrounding buildings. A large rose-shaped window sat in the center, reflecting the golden sun that was now higher in the sky. The bell sitting atop the tower looked miniscule from their vantage point on the ground, but Bear was sure it'd be much more impressive up close.

Luca came at a clip, the customary wild hair and, today, a shirt that had clearly surrendered its fight against wrinkles. He reached for Bear's elbow and thought better of it. "We must hurry."

"Where's the fire?" Bear asked.

Luca tilted his head to the side, then glanced around. "There is no fire."

"He means what's the rush?" Mandy asked. "We're only a couple minutes late."

"Father Benedetto is a busy man." Luca turned and strode toward the entrance he'd been pacing in front of. "We must not keep him waiting."

Bear looked to Mandy and shrugged. Luca hadn't said much about Father Benedetto when they'd spoken the night before, other than the fact that the man knew about the Order of the Iron Serpent and may be able to provide insight into the group's motivations.

Bear glanced around, then followed Luca into the church. Red-and-white marble gleamed underfoot as they moved down a side aisle. There, Luca pushed through a door into a narrow hallway. A robust wooden door stood like a sentinel at the other end. With a sharp, quick knock, their guide announced their presence. A voice called from the other side, and Luca swung open the door, gesturing for Bear and Mandy to enter first.

Bear took in the room at a quick glance, noting the two windows on the opposite side. The rest of the walls were covered in bookshelves, so laden with tomes that they sagged in the center. A small couch and armchair sat opposite a stately wooden desk. The man behind it watched as Luca followed Bear and Mandy inside the office and shut the door behind him. Only then did the priest stand to his full height.

Father Benedetto was a tall, thin man with a shock of white hair combed back from his face. Large glasses sat atop a long, hooked nose and beneath a pair of bushy eyebrows. His irises were such a pale shade of blue, they appeared translucent. The look wasn't just curiosity. It was the kind people gave to a storm cloud on the horizon, uncertain if it would pass them by or break overhead.

Luca introduced them in Italian. Father Benedetto nodded and gestured to the couch. In English, he said, "Please. Take a seat."

Bear ushered Mandy to the sofa, swinging his backpack from his shoulders and setting it on the floor between his legs. As he sank into the cushions, Mandy eased down beside him with a soft sigh, melting into the plush fabric as though it had been waiting for her all day. "Coffee?" Father Benedetto asked.

"No, thank you." Anticipation crawled up Bear's spine and settled in his chest. "I don't want to take up too much of your time. Luca tells us you're aware of the Order?"

Father Benedetto lowered himself into the chair beside them, leaning back and placing his hands on the armrests. His fingers curled into the fabric, and it took him a moment to answer. "Yes. I have studied the Order at great length, particularly their ties to the church. Not many believe they exist, and those of us who do know better than to speak of them amongst mixed company." He glanced at Luca, who had remained standing. "But I have been assured that this meeting will remain between the four of us."

"Of course." Bear held the man's gaze. "We're grateful for your time and knowledge."

Father Benedetto's smile was sad. "I am no expert on the Order. They have spent centuries burying their secrets. It is my belief that those which have surfaced were uncovered intentionally."

"Why would they do that?" Mandy asked.

The man didn't glance past her or cut her off. He met her eyes, listening as if every word mattered. His voice stayed even, measured, as he answered, and Bear found himself leaning back slightly, a quiet respect settling over him. "The Order believes in cyclical prophecy. Do you know what that means?" When Mandy shook her head, he continued. "It is the belief that time and history are not linear but rather circular in their construct. There are periods of renewal and decay which repeat throughout the ages. Within these periods, there is a pattern. The Order looks to take advantage of these particular sequences, believing they are a roadmap for political and social manipulation."

"So, what you're saying," Mandy said, drawing out the words, "is that they want to use the knowledge that history repeats itself to, like, take over the world?"

The corner of Father Benedetto's mouth quirked up, even as his eyes remained serious. "Something like that." He looked at Bear. "Luca says you have been to Poveglia but would not say what you found there. I would like to hear about it directly from you."

Bear shifted under the priest's intense gaze. "Someone painted a mask on the wall in the hospital. The patterns decorating its face were a map of Venice. It looked like someone had stuck a dagger over the left eye, but it was missing when we got there."

"Someone left a drawing," Mandy said before Bear could stop her. "A crown made of laurel leaves and the fleur-de-lis."

Father Benedetto glanced between the two of them, his mouth pulling down into a frown. "I know nothing of this crown. But masks are an important part of Venetian history, as I'm sure you've come to realize. Of course, they were used to hide one's identity, but also their social status. The Order employs them for the same purpose. They do not care whether you are a baker or a politician. As long as you prove to be a benefit to the group, they will allow you within their ranks." He folded his hands under his chin. "Where was the dagger located in relation to the city?"

Bear retrieved his phone and pulled up a map of Venice. When he located the spot, he handed it to the priest. "We've found multiple symbols so far, and each of them led to another at a new location. Each made sense within the context of the Order. But this one leads nowhere."

Father Benedetto stilled as his gaze landed on the map in his hands. "Not nowhere." His voice was no louder than a whisper. "Ca' della Maschera."

"House of the Mask?" Bear asked. "It didn't say that on the map."

"It is a forgotten palazzo." Father Benedetto stood and passed Bear's phone back to him. "Once buried beneath rumors and now hidden beneath stone and water. It should stay there."

Bear stood as Father Benedetto walked over to the door. "Why?"

The man paused, his hand on the doorknob. He didn't look at them as he spoke. "It is a place of horror and bloodshed. Do not go searching for it. If not for your sake, then for your daughter's."

With that, Father Benedetto pulled open the door and strode from the room, leaving a heavy silence in his wake.

17

Bear followed Luca back out into the morning air, Mandy on his heels. In the streets, shopkeepers were propping open doors, the clatter of carts echoing between buildings. A fisherman hauled his morning catch from a small truck, calling prices to an early customer. Church bells chimed the quarter hour, cutting through the hum of a city waking in earnest. Locals and tourists alike now flooded the streets. The three of them paused outside the church, watching squabbling couples and shrieking families walk by. Suited businessmen spoke rapid Italian into their cellphones. Old friends greeted each other with enthusiastic hugs and friendly ribbing.

The world had continued to spin despite Father Benedetto's ominous warning.

Mandy looked up at him, squinting against the bright sunlight. "What now?"

Bear turned to Lucas, who hovered nearby. "Have you heard of Ca' della Maschera before?"

Lucas's gaze swept the waterfront, eyes lingering on anyone who wandered too close. Then, as if satisfied, he motioned for them to follow toward the Grand Canal, where the bustle of heavier traffic would swallow them from view. "I have heard of it," he admitted. "But I always thought it was nothing more than a rumor."

Bear turned sideways to let a small child slide past him. "Why's that?"

Luca took a moment to respond, chewing on the inside of his cheek as though he were tasting the words in his mouth. By the look on his face, they were bitter. "There is not much about the palazzo in the readings I have done, but what I have found aligns with Father Benedetto's words. It is a place of violence and death. They used this place for a ritual I do not understand. I believe it is meant as a test for its newest members. To see what they are willing to sacrifice and what they desire to gain."

"A ritual?" Mandy asked, jogging a little to keep up. "But so many of the symbols were in churches all over the city."

Luca wore a patient smile as he looked down at her. "Rituals are not reserved for pagan religions. Your morning routine is a ritual. A wedding, whether or not it has religious undertones, is a ritual. Christianity itself is subject to a great many rituals—baptism, taking the sacrament, burial rights."

"Do you know anything about this ritual?" Bear asked, stepping around a pair of tourists who had stopped in the middle of the path to look at something on one of their phones.

Luca led them from the street to the Ponte di Rialto. The ornate stone bridge was congested this time of morning, forcing them to walk single file. Bear caught his eye once, silently pressing for answers, but Luca only gave the smallest shake of his head and kept moving. Whatever he had to say would have to wait.

Once they crossed, Luca descended the stairs to Riva del Vin, weaving through the press of tourists and vendors. Tour boats and gondolas crowded the bank, the air full of calls, splashing oars, and the clink of glasses from nearby cafés—perfect cover for the kind of discussion they needed to have. Luca stepped out of the way, pressing his back into the building behind him. "I know nothing concrete about the ritual. As I said, it is clouded in rumor. Until this morning, I did not realize the palazzo was even real. But, from what I understand, time and weather have had their effects. It is not what it once was."

Bear waited until a loud group of giggling girls passed before he spoke again. "Does the ritual say anything about a dagger?"

"No, I'm afraid not." Luca watched several groups walk by before he continued "I think I have done all I can for you. The Order has you in their sights. I wish you and your daughter no ill will, but I have stayed off their radar for a long time by knowing when to take a step back into the shadows." His gaze was imploring as it landed on Bear. "I suggest you do the same."

"That's not really an option for us," Bear said.

Mandy gazed up at him with a wry smile.

Luca opened his mouth, but a deafening boom drowned out his response. He covered his head and ducked. Mandy screamed and slapped her hands over her ears. Bear whipped his head in the direction of the sound—just in time to see a fireball erupt into the sky.

He could feel the heat of the flames from where he stood, scorching his face and arms. His ears rang, and his eyes burned from the sudden, bright flash. Pitch black smoke billowed into the sky. A swift breeze changed the direction of the wind, and the acrid stench of the plume drowned out the smell of the sea around them. Chaos erupted as people screamed and ran away from the blast.

Bear turned back to Mandy, making sure she was unharmed. Her eyes were wide and her jaw had dropped open, but she appeared uninjured. He cast a quick glance over Luca, who trembled as he pressed himself back against the brick wall behind them. People ran past, jostling into them with elbows and stepping on their feet in an attempt to get away.

Bear placed his considerable bulk in front of Mandy, blocking her from any oncoming blows. He focused on the thick cloud still billowing into the air. The explosion had been on a tour boat halfway down Riva del Vin, docked in front of a rooftop bar. The bar patrons who were brave—or stupid—enough to peer over the edge of the building had their phones out, filming the aftermath.

Someone shoved an old woman out of the way, and she stumbled into Bear. He helped steady her before she dove back into the stream of people without uttering her thanks. Parents hugged children to their chests. Couples clasped hands, one dragging the other forward. The steps they'd come down just minutes before were clogged.

Mandy clutched his arm. "Bear?"

He looked down at her, fear making her eyes impossibly wide. The urge to help the people around him battled with his urge to keep her out of harm's way. "It's okay. Let's get out of here before the police come."

She nodded, shoulders squaring with purpose. Luca plunged ahead, swallowed by the press of bodies. Bear drew Mandy in front of him, his hands firm on her shoulders—not just to guide her, but to keep her anchored. The crowd surged, their cries and shouts blending into a restless roar that pressed in from all sides, a reminder of how quickly control could slip away. Calle del Gambaro was the only side street that veered off this road, a slit of shadow between weathered stone walls. Bear slowed at the sight of it, instincts pricking. If trouble waited, there'd be no room to move, no easy way out. People crowded around the entrance to the bridge ahead. There'd be more room on the other side as the bottleneck dissipated. He shouted at Luca to keep going straight, but the man either couldn't hear him or didn't listen. When Mandy tried to follow him, Bear steered her forward.

The crowd around them started to thin. A woman tripped and fell in front of them. Bear pulled her up by the elbow. Blood poured from her temple. He grabbed a cloth napkin from one of the tables at a nearby restaurant and pressed it to her head. She took it in a daze and let the crowd carry her away.

At the top of the stairs, Bear grabbed Mandy's hand and pulled her behind him, using his bulk to shoulder them through the last knot of people. A sharp elbow caught his ribs; a heel clipped his shin. He shifted Mandy up beside him, keeping her out of the crush. By the time they broke free a block later, the press of bodies had thinned enough that he could move without bracing against someone else's weight. He still caught the bitter tang of smoke in every breath. People milled about, half turned in the other direction in case there was another explosion. Sweat made his grip on Mandy's hand slick, but he refused to let go. She jogged to keep up but didn't complain about the pace.

He only stopped when they were tucked under the shadow of an umbrella at a café on the corner. He looked Mandy over again, giving her more than a cursory glance this time. "Are you okay?"

"Yes." Her voice was quiet but steady. "My ears are still ringing a little, but I'm not hurt. What about you?"

"Same." Bear glanced around them, cataloging faces and body language. They were getting some curious glances, but Bear assumed it had more to do with the direction from which they'd come than anything else. "We should keep moving."

Mandy held her ground, gazing up at him until he met her eyes. "I don't think that was an accident."

"I don't think so either," he admitted. "I heard someone say the French consulate was right around the corner. Like we need that on top of everything else—"

Mandy shook her head; gaze trained on his face. "That's not what I mean. Didn't you see the name of the boat that exploded?"

Bear furrowed his brows, thinking. "No, I don't think so. Did you catch it?"

"Il Orso." She said it with a slight Italian accent, just like he'd taught her. "Doesn't that mean—"

Bear didn't want to finish her thought, but he forced himself to do exactly that.

"The Bear."

18

MANDY SAT CROSS-LEGGED ON HER BED, HER LAPTOP BALANCED on her knees. She was back in their room at the hostel. Afternoon clouds had rolled in on the breeze, dimming the sun for the time being. For the moment, she was alone.

After the boat exploded, she and Bear had walked the streets of Venice with no particular destination in mind. When he was certain they weren't being followed, he headed back to the hostel and called Isabella. It'd been good timing, too, because she'd just arrived in the city. He'd left to meet her, after giving Mandy strict instructions not to let anyone into the room but him.

It was strange to be left alone like this, but she wasn't complaining. She could use the downtime after the early start, the cryptic warning from Father Benedetto, and an honest-to-goodness explosion. As much as Bear seemed to agree the blast had been the Order's way of sending a message, Mandy doubted they'd expected him to be right there when it happened. No one could have known they'd head that way after meeting at the church, and the quick flash of surprise on Luca's face looked too real to be fake.

Just as she dragged her finger across the trackpad to study more of the mural, someone rapped their knuckles on the door. Three quick knocks, a pause, a singular knock, another pause, and then one last knock.

Mandy set her laptop aside and crawled off the bed. When she reached the door, she asked, "Who is it?"

"Me," Bear said. "I've got Isabella with me."

Mandy pulled the slide lock back, then undid the deadbolt. When she opened the door, Bear's face was as unreadable as a blank page—no flicker of thought she could catch. That, more than anything, told her their company had put him on guard. "All good?" Bear asked.

"All good," Mandy answered, stepping aside and letting them in.

Isabella's gaze swept across the barren room before landing on her. "Hello, Mandy."

"Hello."

Mandy offered a faint smile that never reached her eyes, her tone pleasant but measured. She kept her posture open, though her fingers tightened imperceptibly around the edge of the nightstand, a quiet anchor in case the conversation turned. It was bad enough Isabella was an Italian foreign intelligence agent, but they'd also stolen the puzzle box from her. Bear had said Isabella was more interested in working with them than against them, but Mandy would play it safe, just in case.

Sliding the locks back into place, she returned to her bed and pulled the laptop back into her lap. Bear stood next to the window, leaning against the wall with his arms crossed. He gestured for Isabella to take a seat on his bed. She did, but she kept both feet planted on the floor, ready to bolt at any second.

The mural remained forgotten on the screen as Mandy glanced between the two of them.

"Well, this is awkward," she said.

Bear chuckled. Isabella's mouth pulled down at the corners, her expression unreadable—cool, measured, with no heat in her eyes. "Did you guys hear about the tour boat?" she asked.

Bear's laughter died away. "We were there. Saw the whole thing."

Isabella said something in Italian. Mandy didn't know what it was, but she could guess if she were to repeat it, Bear wouldn't be pleased.

"Are you okay?" Isabella glanced between the two of them. "You're not hurt, are you?"

Bear shook his head before answering. "No, we're fine. We were far enough away."

"Did anyone else get hurt?" Mandy asked. She'd been wondering since the explosion, but there was nothing confirmed online yet.

Isabella looked to Bear, who nodded. She turned back to Mandy. "Three people died. Several injured. Two in critical condition. The explosion happened as they were disembarking. It could've been worse. Much worse." She paused, then looked back to Bear. "Did you notice the name of the boat?"

His face remained impassive. "Mandy did."

"A warning."

"Most likely."

Isabella tipped her head back, eyes on the ceiling, and let out a slow, controlled breath. "This is getting serious." "It's been serious."

She returned her gaze to his. "I could've been here sooner if you'd answered my calls."

"How do we know we can trust you?" Mandy asked. Isabella wouldn't be here if Bear wasn't certain, but he had yet to explain what had changed his mind.

Bear locked eyes with Isabella. "Go ahead. Tell her what you told me."

Isabella turned her whole body to face Mandy. "You know the name of my agency, yes?"

Mandy said it with what she hoped sounded like an air of confidence. "L'Agenzia Informazioni e Sicurezza Esterna."

Isabella's eyes lit up. "Very good. Yes. This means I'm a *foreign* intelligence agent. We do not normally work inside Italy. In fact, it is against the rules."

Mandy scrunched her face. "But you've been in Italy for years, pretending to be Lucia Moretti."

"I had special permission from L'Agenzia Informazioni e Sicurezza Interna. It is our domestic intelligence agency. Do you remember my colleague?"

Mandy pictured the woman with unruly curls dressed in a sharp suit and nodded. "Agent Maya Santos."

"Yes. She was my point of contact for this other agency, AISI."

Mandy cocked her head to the side. "Was?"

Isabella looked down at her hands, picking at some skin along her thumbnail. "She was killed not long after you left San Gimignano. It was made to look like an accident, but I don't believe that. Only other AISI agents knew where she was located."

"You think it was an inside job," Bear said.

The woman nodded. "She was a good agent." Isabella's lips pressed into a thin line before she continued, as if forcing the words past an ache lodged in her chest. "A good friend. I'd known her for a long time." Mandy studied Isabella, noting the tension in her shoulders. Whatever the reason, it was carved deep into her. "My undercover mission started as a ploy to draw out the powerful people who wanted to make Lucia Moretti disappear."

She continued to pick at her finger as she said, "Lucia had overheard people speaking about the Order during a trip to Vatican City. They'd mentioned the puzzle box, and when she saw an opportunity to take it, she did. I think she understands now that this was a mistake, but at the time, she'd only wished to use it to help her family, perhaps to pay off debts, or to secure the kind of future they'd never had."

"Blackmail," Bear supplied.

Isabella shrugged. "More or less. Once she'd realized the Order would stop at nothing to obtain her and the box, she hid the object and then herself." Isabella's words were soft. "When I took on the role of Lucia's double, I didn't know anything about the Order of the

Iron Serpent. Once I transferred to the sanctuary in San Gimignano, my superiors revealed the truth and gave me my new mission."

"Retrieve the box." Mandy's blood froze in her veins. "Did someone kill Agent Santos because we stole it?" She swallowed the bile rising in her throat.

Isabella studied her hands again. "I don't know for sure. Most likely, as I almost suffered the same fate."

Mandy's eyes almost fell out of her head. "They tried to kill you too?"

Isabella pulled at her neckline, revealing a bandage across the top of her shoulder. "Tried and failed." Her voice carried a hint of pride. Then her eyes went cold. "I would like to know why this box is worth killing good agents."

"They're looking for you," Bear said, studying her from across the room. "Both AISE and AISI. And half a dozen other agencies. If you're spotted by the wrong person, you'll be arrested."

"It's almost funny." Isabella's sad smile twisted up one side of her face. "That I feel more comfortable trusting two strangers than my own people, my own colleagues."

Bear shrugged. "Yeah, we get that a lot. It's part of our charm."

Isabella sobered. "I would like to help, if you'll let me. This has become personal."

Bear looked to Mandy. She studied his face and the way his eyes asked her a dozen silent questions. Could they trust Agent Isabella Fabrizio? Was this all an elaborate ruse? Would bringing her into the fold make things more, or less, dangerous? Mandy wasn't one hundred percent certain about any of her answers, but if Isabella was telling the truth—and Mandy thought she was—then having another highly skilled member on the team meant they might have a better shot at getting the upper hand when it mattered most. She thought it was worth the risk.

Holding Bear's gaze, Mandy gave him a slight nod. He returned it, then turned back to Isabella.

"Let me catch you up to speed," he said as he crossed the room and grabbed his backpack. "A lot has happened since we last spoke."

Mandy tuned them out, returning her focus to her laptop screen. She'd been absently zooming in and out of certain areas of the painting during their conversation. Right now, several masked figures filled her screen, smaller than the others in the portrait, almost as if they were meant to be overlooked They all had on green robes that matched the shade of the dress her doppelganger wore. Unlike the others, most of these faced away from the viewer. The last one wasn't even wearing his mask.

In fact, they almost looked like they were all the same person. There was something familiar about the set of the man's shoulders and the width of his bulk. The way he stood tall in each position.

It took a few minutes for her to outline each figure using the software's tools. She copied them into a second program, layered them, and aligned the backgrounds. Seconds later, the program animated the sequence. She set it to loop and hit play. Holding her breath, she watched as the figure in the green robe, wearing a plain silver mask, moved in real time right in front of her eyes. It bent and straightened, pulled a knife from behind its back, then held it aloft. It brought the knife down once, twice, three times, and then stood triumphantly with its back to the viewer. One arm reached up and pulled off its mask before turning back to its audience. Mandy bit back her gasp.

His dark eyes stared back at her, and his mouth, buried beneath a beard, was set in a firm line. It wasn't an exact replica, but Mandy had seen that look on Bear's face too many times to believe this was anything other than a representation of him. She hadn't noticed it before, tucked into a shadowed corner of the canvas, easy to miss unless you were looking for it.

Could the knife in his hands be the missing dagger from the hospital on Poveglia? Was this the ritual Father Benedetto had warned them against? Would it take place in the forgotten palazzo?

As Bear and Isabella solidified their plans for the rest of the evening, Mandy saved the short video to her computer, her hands shaking, and hid it in a folder deep within the recesses of her hard drive. A dark, creeping sensation clawed its way out of her gut. Her instincts screamed that this was important, but her rational mind told her it was impossible.

The man in the painting wasn't Bear, just like the girl wasn't Mandy.

No, something else was going on here. Better not to waste Bear's time, considering everything else going on. She'd figure it out on her own, and they'd laugh at her hairbrained theories once the dust settled and everything was back to normal.

There had to be a logical explanation for all of this.

But the longer she tried to find it, the more she feared the truth was far worse than she could imagine.

19

SWEAT FORMED ALONG BEAR'S HAIRLINE AS HE STOOD ON THE landing outside Giulia's apartment. The fluffy white clouds from that afternoon had knitted together to form a soft gray blanket that stretched from one end of the sky to the other. It kept the direct sunlight off their shoulders, but it also trapped the moisture in the air around them, leaving them sticky and uncomfortable.

He watched the street, looking for anyone that seemed a bit too interested in what they were doing. Mandy and Isabella waited in silence at the bottom of the stairs, their eyes mirroring his as they scanned the street.

A prickle of unease tickled the back of Bear's neck. He clenched his fist, resisting the urge to rub it away. He didn't regret the calculated risk of bringing Isabella on board. He'd double-checked her story, and the details about Agent Santos' death and her being wanted by several intelligence agencies all checked out.

He'd keep an eye on her, but he had to admit he could breathe easier knowing someone else was looking out for Mandy. Isabella might be the next closest thing to a stranger, but she'd been kind to his kid from the beginning. And unlike most enforcement officers, she'd given him the benefit of the doubt about his intentions regarding the puzzle box and the Order of the Iron Serpent.

A sharp breeze whipped around the corner of the building, cooling the sweat along his forehead and causing an army of goosebumps to march across his skin. A figure emerged before he had a chance to enjoy the sensation.

Giulia Vasari.

She pulled up short when she spotted Isabella. Bear watched as she wrung her hands together, searching their small group for anything else out of place. Her cheekbones looked more pronounced, and the bags under her eyes were puffier than they'd been the other day.

Giulia took a few steps closer but hesitated at the foot of the stairs . "Who's this?"

"A friend." He looked down at the Giulia, searching her face for any sign that she was up to no good. "You're late."

"Lost track of time." Her plain green dress fell to her ankles. Sandals coated in dust adorned her feet. Giulia used one hand on the railing to steady herself and another to lift her skirts as she started up the stairs. When she reached the top, she unlocked the door and gestured for them to follow. "Come in, come in."

The old woman stepped to the side and watched as the others filed in. Bear made quick work of checking that they were alone in the apartment. Isabella stood by the front window, checking the street. Mandy studied Giulia with appraising eyes.

Giulia locked the front door and turned as Bear reentered the room. "You were not truthful about this meeting."

He folded his arms across his chest. "You haven't been truthful about a lot of things, so it seemed only fair."

Giulia winced like he'd slapped her but recovered quickly. She gestured to Isabella. "Who is this?"

"A friend," Bear repeated. She didn't need to know more than that. "One who knows as much about the Order as we do. She needs to see the mural in person."

Giulia looked Isabella up and down, then nodded. She used a knobby finger to point past Bear. "In the back room."

Isabella offered the woman a polite smile, then slipped out of the room. She was light on her feet. The old floorboards didn't creak once when she moved across the room. It was a different story for Bear. They groaned if he breathed too deeply.

Giulia made to follow Isabella, but Bear held up a hand. "We need to talk."

The old woman stilled, her hand pausing mid-air as though bracing for something. Wariness crept into her eyes as she studied him. She flicked a glance at Mandy, but the kid only raised her brows, a silent I'm on his side. Bear had to fight back a laugh. "Mandy, why don't you keep Isabella company?"

Mandy cast one more look at Giulia before she walked out of the room.

Once they were alone, Giulia turned her attention back to Bear. "Have you found any new information about my Antonio?"

Bear frowned. As sure as he was that the old woman was keeping secrets, he was also certain she cared for her husband and was desperate to get him back.

"No." He didn't mean to be short, but the events of the day had gotten to him. Anxiety crawled over the surface of his skin like a horde of spiders. It made him twitchy. "And you won't get him back until you start being honest with me."

Giulia's jaw unhinged, her lips parting as if she'd been slapped. She stared at him like he'd been the one to kidnap her husband, her eyes narrowing, sharp with rage that seemed to coil through every line of her face. "I have told you—"

Bear slashed his hand through the air, cutting her off. He took a step forward, ensuring there was still plenty of space between them. He wanted to intimidate her, not give her a heart attack. "We've followed the clues, starting with the church your husband went to investigate. You know what we found there? Signs of a struggle. Blood."

Giulia paled. "Blood?" She stepped back to lean against the wall, hand clutching her chest. "Antonio's?"

Bear lifted one shoulder and then let it drop. "There's no way to tell. We also found another carving there. It led us to the procession for Festa della Sensa, which then took us to Poveglia."

If the old woman got any paler, she'd turn translucent. With the hand that had been clutching her chest, she made the sign of the cross. "That is cursed land. You should not have been there."

"Probably not, but we weren't the only ones." He pulled a slip of paper from his pocket. It was a close rendition of what Mandy had seen before she almost fell to her death. "Do you recognize this symbol?"

Giulia stared into his eyes for a moment—too long, like she was weighing what answer would serve her best. Did she think this was a trick? He held the paper out farther. She took a step forward and peered down at it, biting her lip. He noticed the way her eyes roamed over the crown, taking in all the details. After a moment, she stepped back and shook her head.

"I have never seen this before."

Bear slipped the paper back into his pocket. "Someone else has been one step ahead of us the entire time. You know anything about that?" When Giulia shook her head again, he pressed her harder. "Did you ask anyone else to find Antonio? Tell anyone else that we were helping you?"

The old woman's lips trembled and her eyes grew damp. "Only Luca. I have told no one else."

"A tour boat exploded today. Did you hear about that?"

She nodded, then muttered something under her breath. A prayer.

"We were there. I think the Order was sending us a message." He took another step forward. "My kid was with me. She could've been hurt." He lowered his voice. "She could've been killed."

"I did not tell anyone." Tears slipped from Giulia's eyes now, and she wiped them away. "But I think they are watching me."

Bear clenched his jaw. "Why?"

"The Order-" Her voice trembled, so quiet he could hardly hear it. "They wanted my husband to decode the mural. When he couldn't, he disappeared. They told me if I finished what he'd started, I'd see him again." Tears poured down her cheeks. "I thought you could help. I never meant for you to become a target."

"We were always going to be a target." That didn't excuse what she'd done. Or the secrets she'd kept. "What do you know about Ca' della Maschera?"

"I have not heard of this place before." Her eyes widened and she looked in the direction of the mural. "The painting is full of masked figures. Is this where my Antonio could be?"

Bear had wanted to get more out of the old woman. Hopefully Mandy and Isabella were having better luck studying the mural.

"I don't know," he said, turning his back to her. "But I intend to find out."

20

ONCE THE SHOPS HAD CLOSED FOR THE DAY AND THE STREETS were covered in darkness, they set out for Ca' della Maschera.

Bear stood at the back of the gondola, oar in hand, trying not to show how much he regretted their current circumstances. The lanterns reflected in the dark, choppy water. Five minutes after they'd stepped foot into their borrowed boat, which Isabella had procured from their superstitious friend Luigino, it had started to drizzle. That had soon turned into a cool spring shower. Then a torrential downpour.

Isabella and Mandy huddled side by side in the middle of the boat, holding their jackets over their heads to try and stay out of the storm. Bear wasn't so lucky. He'd volunteered to steer the boat, and it was hard enough to see through the sheet of rain without trying to keep himself dry at the same time. In a matter of minutes, his clothes were soaked and the once-gentle breeze was now strong enough to cause goosebumps to erupt all over his body.

Mandy turned in her seat and glared. He offered a lazy shrug in return. He should've known better than to leave their room without checking the weather first.

It was hard to think on the bright side in weather like this. The wind slashed at the canal, the rain needling against his coat in relentless bursts. Bear didn't mind that they were now the only ones traversing le Rio de le Do Torre—solitude in the storm suited him just fine. Like the roiling clouds above, he was restless, heavy with unspoken tension. Even with the lights glimmering off the water from the surrounding buildings, he knew they'd be harder to spot on a night like this. And maybe, deep down, he didn't mind being invisible. "Almost there," Bear shouted over the rain.

Neither of his companions turned around. He wasn't sure if they hadn't heard him or were ignoring him on purpose. Bear was no expert gondolier, but he did well enough to steer them over to the line of brick buildings bordering the water. There were no docks here, but he hadn't been expecting one. Father Benedetto had said the palazzo was hidden beneath stone. He hadn't told Mandy or Isabella his suspicions about what that meant, but as soon as they got close to their destination, he knew he'd been right.

Bear dragged his oar through the water and brought the boat to a stop next to a line of brick buildings sitting along the edge of the canal. Next to them, the mouth of a tunnel beneath the foundation yawned back. He pulled a flashlight from his bag and pointed it in that direction. The water was too high for him to see into the opening, but when he cast the beam over the peak of the arch, he spotted an engraving through the haze of the falling rain. Leaning closer, he could just make out its shape.

A Volto mask. Just like the one on the island.

Mandy's voice cut through the rain. "You've got to be kidding me."

Bear turned to her, unable to hide his guilty grin. "On the plus side, we're already wet."

She rolled her eyes. She might have crossed her arms over her chest too, if she weren't so busy holding her jacket over her head. "I'm not going in there. The water is disgusting. Plus, we have no idea what's on the other side. What if it's all collapsed? What if it's a trap?"

Bear's grin faded. Her concerns were valid. The water in the canal was not fit to swim in thanks to the wastewater regularly dumped into the lagoon. He also couldn't blame her for not wanting to navigate an underwater opening without knowing what was on the other side. He didn't like the idea either. "I won't hold it against you if you want to stay with the boat. Isabella and I can check it out."

Isabella looked as dubious as Mandy, but she didn't say anything.

Mandy studied the churning water for a moment. When she glanced back up at Bear, he saw the familiar glint of determination in her eyes. "You're gonna need me. I know the mural better than you."

Warm relief chased away the chill of the rain, at least for a few seconds. He wouldn't have made Mandy go if she didn't want to, but he didn't like the idea of letting her out of his sight, either. It was always better when they were side by side.

He swung his backpack off his shoulders and set it on the bench in front of him. They'd only brought the essentials, but since that included the puzzle box, he had never been more grateful to have gotten them a pair of waterproof bags. Mandy's sat on the bottom of the boat, between her feet.

"Stay here." If it hadn't been raining, he would've stripped off his shirt. "I'll check it out first. See what we're working with. If it looks safe enough, I'll come back for you both."

Mandy frowned. "What if you don't come back?"

Bear placed a hand on her small shoulder, waiting for her to look him in the eyes. "I'll always come back for you, kid. I promise."

Isabella stood up, dropping her coat on the seat where she'd been sitting. In a matter of seconds, her hair was plastered to her face with rainwater. "If you're not back in five, I'll come in after you."

He nodded.

Without another word, Bear turned toward the water and lowered himself over the edge of the boat. The smaller channels weren't as deep as the Grand Canal, so he didn't want to risk jumping in. Besides, the less he got the dirty water in his eyes and mouth, the better.

The channel was warmer than the rain pelting him from above, but being this close to the surface, the strange mixture of seawater and sewage, was unpleasant.

Without looking back, he dragged his hands through the water, cutting a line forward. The only thing he'd brought with him was his flashlight, which he held in his mouth as he approached the entrance to the tunnel. Once he was under the cover of the arch, he clicked it back on and took in the tunnel before him.

The bricks were darker under here than they had been along the sides of the building. A few had crumbled along the edges, but overall, the tunnel was solid despite its age and exposure to the saltwater. Father Benedetto had implied the hidden palazzo was old and forgotten, but these bricks looked like they'd been taken care of on a regular basis.

Bear used one hand and his feet to push forward, keeping his head and the flashlight above the surface of the water. The channel's stench clung to the stone around him. He swept the beam of his light back and forth but didn't find any more carvings.

Soon, he'd reached the end of the tunnel.

Steps rose out of the water beyond another arch. The water level was just low enough that he didn't have to submerge his head to duck under it. When he got to the other side, he placed his feet on one of the stone steps and climbed the staircase to the top. A chill ran through him as he stepped further out of the water.

The only sounds came from the lapping water along the walls and the beating of his own heart. The tunnel had transitioned from brick to stone, and he was able to stand to his full height as he ascended the stairs. At the peak, there was a small landing. He stood there, feet planted wide, as he took in another dozen steps leading to a small chamber with an arched ceiling. It was as ornate as the churches they'd visited over the past two days—arched ceiling traced with faded gold leaf, walls inlaid with intricate mosaics, and a stone altar carved with swirling serpentine patterns.

As much as Bear wanted to investigate the space and find out what lay in the tunnel on the other side, he knew he only had a minute or two left before Isabella came after him. Not wanting to worry Mandy, he turned and descended the staircase until he was up to his neck in canal water. This time, he sped back to the entrance of the tunnel. He could see where the water was open to the sky as fat raindrops bounced off its surface a few feet away.

Mandy's shoulders relaxed when Bear emerged from the tunnel, clicking off his flashlight and swimming over to the side of the boat. He didn't bother getting out.

"The entrance leads to some stairs. There's a chamber on the other side. That must be the forgotten palazzo. I saw another tunnel leading deeper under the foundations." Bear studied both of them. "Last chance to stay behind and guard the boat."

Both women shook their heads. Mandy dropped her coat onto the bench, then picked up her backpack to pull out another flashlight before strapping it on her back. Isabella had retrieved her own supplies before they'd ventured out onto the canal, and she came armed with a flashlight and waterproof pack, too.

"All right." Bear grabbed the front of the gondola and turned it toward the entrance. "We'll store the boat inside so it doesn't float away on us. The ceiling is low enough that you'll have to get in the water to navigate the tunnel."

Mandy looked down into the dark water and sighed.

"Lucky us."

21

SHE NEVER THOUGHT SHE'D BE HAPPY TO SEE THE LIGHT AT THE end of a tunnel, but if it meant getting out of this water, she'd take it. Even the slick, uneven stone steps glistening with runoff felt like a blessing beneath her feet. The warmth of the canal still clung to her skin, but it carried a faint, sour tang—like rust and rotting vegetation —that she didn't want to think too hard about. They couldn't hear the rain beneath all this rock, and there was no wind inside the chamber, but she still shivered in the still air. The stone and concrete hadn't let in any of the heat from earlier in the day.

"Don't stand still too long," Bear said, rubbing his big hands up and down her arms. "Stay warm and loose. Let's get in and out as quick as we can."

Mandy's teeth chattered as she nodded. The few minutes he'd been gone had stretched into an eternity. She and Isabella hadn't exchanged any words, just kept a close eye on the tunnel for Bear, and the surrounding water for anyone who might want to arrest them. Going for a swim in the canal waters wasn't strictly legal.

They crested the top of the stairs, and she looked down into the chamber he'd described when he'd returned to the boat. The chamber was more beautiful than she'd expected. Her steps slowed, one foot hovering above the next stone as her gaze swept the space. The floor held a mosaic of diamond-shaped stones, each a different shade of gray and blue, and for a moment she forgot to breathe. The walls had once been covered in paintings, the faint ghosts of color still clinging to patches of plaster. In places, the murals had flaked away entirely, leaving pale scars where time and damp had claimed the artistry. Ornate arches covered in delicate silver designs held up the domed ceiling. She would've bet Bear's life savings those designs were shaped like snakes. A plain stone table sat in the center. It looked out of place amongst the elaborate decoration.

Bear made it down the steps first. He swept the beam of his flashlight around the room. The first arc was quick, looking for anything or anyone hiding in the shadows. The second was slower, studying the remaining artwork around them.

"These are old." He stepped closer to one of the murals. "Damaged."

Isabella descended the stone steps and stopped next to him. "The damage only goes about halfway up the wall. Bet they built the staircase to keep this place from flooding. Between the city sinking and rising sea levels, it's been under water more than once over the years."

Mandy walked down the stairs and stopped in the center of the room, right next to the stone table. "In other words, we picked the worst possible time to visit this place, huh?"

The three of them turned and pointed their beams in the direction they'd come from. Every time a wave rolled in from the storm raging outside the tunnel, a little bit of water cascaded down the steps. Not enough to make them worry, but enough to be a reminder that their time was limited.

"Right." Bear pointed his beam up at the ceiling. "Let's see if there's anything useful in here. That dagger embedded in the painting of the mask must've been important. See if we can find anything related to that."

Mandy thought back to the mural and the figures of the man moving through space and time. The dagger he had in his hands. An ominous feeling washed over her, as heavy as the stone above their heads. She didn't know why she was keeping that information from Bear, but it still didn't feel like the right time to tell him. She needed more information first. Needed to understand what it meant. Once she had some possible explanations, she'd tell him about the figure that looked just like him.

"Those look like snakes, don't they?" Isabella said, her gaze locked on the spot Bear highlighted with his flashlight. The arches Mandy had noticed earlier.

"Sure do," Bear replied.

Mandy moved away from them, toward the far wall. Something else had caught her attention. The paintings here were in worse shape than the one in Giulia's apartment, but similar in style. They were also a lot more coherent, featuring only a couple figures per panel. They seemed to tell a story, but what moral it tried to convey, she wasn't sure.

The first one featured a group of four women gathered around a table, similar to the one behind Mandy, but the room looked less intricate. Perhaps inside some sort of castle or fortress. Papers sat in the center of the table, the writing illegible. One woman stood pouring out a jug of water onto the floor, peering up at the ceiling. A second woman knelt on the floor, inspecting the stones. The other two women drew the most attention. One sat on the back of a giant crab, looking back over her shoulder, and the other was a mermaid sitting on top of a large goat, pointing to something in the papers.

Mandy blinked, unsure of what it all meant. This had been made with a practiced hand. Time and effort had been poured into the painting, despite the strange scene. It must mean *something*.

Hoping there would be answers in the next mural, she stepped to the side and took in the second scene. She looked at a large field with a castle front and center. A man with a bow and arrow stood atop one of the turrets, his weapon at the ready. Beneath him, at the castle's gate, a man rode a ram and held a spear aloft. Further out from the castle, near the forest line, a minotaur and a man stood side by side, fighting a two-headed snake.

Mandy chewed on her bottom lip and leaned forward. There were little black creatures skittering across the ground at the man's feet. She would've thought they were spiders, if not for their elongated bodies and curled tails. Scorpions, then. They seemed to be attacking the serpent, too.

Mandy shook her head, trying to unscramble the questions she had yet to find answers for. She moved on to the last scene on this wall. All the way to the left, a woman sat on a throne, blindfold over her eyes as she held up a set of scales. On the opposite side, a bipedal lion whispered into the ear of a two-faced man. One face was serious while the other was animated, speaking to a faceless crowd. Along the bottom, a woman wearing a dress made of fish scales painted the picture before her.

Only, it wasn't an exact replica.

Instead of a blindfold, the woman wore a crown. And instead of scales, she held a scepter. The bipedal lion was just a regular man, dressed in a toga and carrying a book in his arms. The other figure only had one face, but he was still speaking animatedly to the crowd.

Mandy huffed. What the hell did any of this mean? Other than the two-headed snake, she had no idea what any of this had to do with the Order of the Iron Serpent or La Velata Rossa. Since it would bug her until she figured it out, she pulled her camera out of her bag and snapped a few pictures of each mural. It'd be something else to analyze later.

Bear stepped up next to her. "Find anything interesting?"

"Not sure. Taking pictures just in case."

He nodded his approval, then gestured for her to follow Isabella, who'd stepped into the tunnel opposite the entrance. "Come on. I don't want to stay for too long, and we've got more of this place to explore. We were led here for a reason, so we might as well find out what it is."

Mandy capped her camera and hung it around her neck before following in Isabella's footsteps. The stone tunnel reminded her of the network of chambers they'd found below San Gimignano. The space here, beneath the streets of Venice, was smaller. She didn't think it was meant to be a sanctuary like in the other city, but someone had still built it for a reason.

All these unanswered questions were starting to get on her nerves, each one like a marble in her head, a thought or theory based on their latest clue. Every time she added a new one to the mix, they bounced around her skull, crashing into each other and scattering in every direction. Bear would say that was just her ADHD. She would say that was just *annoying*.

The next chamber they came across looked like it was being used as a meeting room. It was small but crammed with at least a dozen chairs inside. They looked old to Mandy, but Bear said they were probably from the fifties or sixties. Wooden and sturdy, like what a grandmother might have in her kitchen. Mandy's chest ached at the thought. She'd barely known her mother and hadn't met her biological father. Never mind ever getting the chance to sit in her grandmother's kitchen like any other kid might have.

The second area was empty, but the deep grooves in the stone told her that something had been stored in there at one point. It must've been heavy to leave marks like that in the rock. Bear and Isabella debated what it could've been for a few minutes, but Mandy tuned them out. She needed to find something solid to work on, something that would give her the answers she was desperate to find.

Moving on, they came across two larger chambers across from each other. Isabella and Bear stepped into the one on the left. Mandy peeked in and saw masks tacked up around the wall, some of which looked like they could be straight out of the mural. There were old ledgers and other pieces of art on various surfaces and leaning up against the stone.

She itched to sit down and go through it all, but Bear and Isabella already had their heads bent over one of the books, and Mandy struggled to focus at the moment. She turned and walked into the other chamber, her eyes following the beam of her flashlight as it landed on what looked like more of the same.

She recognized a few of the masks around the walls, including the one in the shape of an ermine and another that was too similar to the plague doctor's disguise to be anything else. She wanted to step closer to get a better look, but a giant framed painting sat in the way. At first, she thought it was just as worn as the others she'd seen so far, but when she peered closer, she realized it wasn't faded at all.

It was unfinished.

Mandy held her breath as she leaned in, afraid that any disturbance in the air might make it all disappear. She couldn't believe what she was looking at, but the longer she stared at it, the more certain she became that this was an incomplete copy of the mural in Giulia's apartment.

From what she could remember, the figures were sketched out in the same spots, including the large one off to the right that looked like her. The artist had yet to complete their eyes and her hair lacked any depth. The colors were brighter than the one on the wall, but the lines weren't as crisp. Was this the original sketch for the mural, or had someone been in a hurry to copy it onto this framed canvas?

Mandy uncapped her camera and took a few pictures to compare with the ones she had on her laptop. Then she circled around the large frame and used her flashlight to illuminate the back of the canvas. Some artists signed their names back there, or perhaps they'd dated it. But all she found was something wrapped in brown paper, taped to the top right corner. She reached out and ran her fingers along the front, brushing something solid and cold, like it was made of metal.

"Mandy?" Bear appeared in the doorway.

She couldn't take her eyes off the package. Had someone left it for her? Is this why they'd been led here? "I think I found something."

"We're leaving."

Mandy peeked her head around the side of the frame to look at him. Something in his voice sent a tremor of warning down her spine. "Why?"

He looked over his shoulder, deeper into the tunnel than they'd explored, before turning back to her

"We're not the only ones down here anymore."

22

Bear's heart thundered in his chest as he watched Mandy duck behind a giant framed painting before stepping out again a second later. She stuffed her camera into her bag and zipped it up, then swung it up and around her shoulders. Had she said she'd found something? It didn't matter. They could talk about everything they'd found later.

The scuffing of boots against stone was like an alarm bell going off in his head. They'd gotten louder than when he'd first heard them. Closer. But he couldn't tell how many pairs there were. If it ended up being a fair fight, they'd come out on top. But the narrow tunnel walls would make it infinitely more difficult for him.

He met Isabella's eyes as she emerged into the hallway, and in them saw the same shadow of tension, the same wary calculation he felt tightening his own chest. It was the look of someone who knew these walls could hide anything—and that every step forward might invite danger.

Trapped, like a rat in a maze.

Isabella stopped in the doorway and looked deeper into the tunnel. "There must be another entrance."

"Seems like it." Bear steered Mandy back the way they'd come. "We might be able to get out of here before they even catch up to us."

"But there's so much stuff in here," Mandy argued. "It could help."

"Won't help if we're dead." He propelled her down the tunnel, away from the approaching footsteps. "No idea how many there are. Not worth the risk."

Mandy remained silent. He could feel the tension in her shoulders. He and Isabella hadn't found anything in the one chamber, other than some creepy masks and a few encoded ledgers. They seemed different—more intricate, the masks carved with symbols he didn't recognize, the ledgers bound in a material that looked older than the ones in San Gimignano. But once he realized they weren't alone, any thought of figuring out why went straight out the window.

Isabella slipped a knife from her side and held it in a reverse grip-spine pressed against her forearm. Bear copied her movements with his own blade. Would their pursuers fire a gun down here in the tunnel, and risk hitting one of their artifacts? He didn't think so, but he had no interest in waiting to find out.

His boots slapped against the stone floor. Answering echoes ricocheted all around them. No point in being quiet now. The approaching figures were close enough that he could hear snippets of their conversation, spoken in Italian. They knew there were intruders in their tunnels, and they intended to capture them at any cost.

Bear, Mandy, and Isabella were flat-out running now. Mandy entered the initial chamber first and stumbled to a halt. Bear opened his mouth to tell her to keep going, but a flash of red silenced him. Three robed, masked figures stood at the bottom of the stairs, soaking wet and guarding their exit out of there. Each carried a knife, the blades longer than the ones he and Isabella had. Silver handles covered in red gemstones glittered in the beam of his bouncing flashlight. They looked ceremonial, but still wickedly sharp.

The figure in the middle stepped forward, tall and broad and imposing. His mask sported ram's horns that curled back to sharp points. He spoke in a low, heavily accented voice. "You're surrounded. Give up now, and we won't hurt anyone."

Bear almost snorted. The Order of the Iron Serpent—and, by extension, La Velata Rossa—had proven they were not opposed to violence. He wasn't about to take their word for it.

Instead of wasting time talking, Bear charged forward at the same time Mandy and Isabella fanned out on each side. The other two guards also wore horned masks, but theirs looked shorter and less curved. Like a bull. They may have been smaller than the one in the center, but they moved with practiced ease.

The guards must've expected them to try to talk their way out of the situation. The one in the center only had his knife half raised by the time Bear planted a foot in the center of his chest, sending him flying backwards into the steps. He landed with a grunt and wheezed. It wouldn't take long for him to catch his breath again.

Knowing Isabella was armed and could hold her own in a fight, Bear turned to the guard on Mandy's side. Unlike the man in the center, he didn't raise his blade to attack Mandy. Instead, he reached out and tried to grab her. She spun off to the side, quick as a whip, forcing the man to turn his back on Bear.

Between one breath and the next, Bear grabbed the hand that held the knife and wrapped his other arm around the man's throat and squeezed. The guard choked and scrabbled with his free hand, but Bear's grip didn't loosen.

Mandy didn't hesitate, launching forward and delivering two quick punches to the man's solar plexus. What little oxygen he'd had in his lungs was forced out, and he sagged in Bear's arms. Letting the guard drop to the ground like a sack of potatoes, Bear spun to check on Isabella's progress with her target, only to see him writhing in pain on the ground.

Bear ran up the steps two at a time. "Let's move!"

When he reached the top, a fourth guard popped up from the other side and tackled him, sending them both reeling back down the staircase. Mandy and Isabella dodged out of the way to avoid being taken down with them.

"Dad!" Mandy shouted, scrambling after him.

Bear wanted to tell her to go without him, that he'd be right behind her, but he couldn't find his voice. The man on top of him wasn't as big as the center guard, but he'd landed square on Bear's chest.

Out of the corner of his eye, Bear could see more figures rush into the room. They all wore red, but he couldn't risk looking more closely than that.

Despite the burning in his lungs, Bear forced a huge gulp of air in through his nose and bucked his masked opponent off him. The guy landed with a thud, his bull's mask going askew before he righted it. Bear hadn't seen any identifying features, and as much as he wanted to rip the mask off every person in that room, they didn't have time.

"Dad!" Mandy shouted again.

Bear sat up just in time to see the first guard as he wrapped an arm around Mandy's neck. She could still speak, which meant he wasn't squeezing too hard, but Bear saw red. The man would lose both his hands if he hurt Mandy in any way.

But before Bear could move, Isabella launched herself at the guard, forcing him to let Mandy go so he could hold her off. They tumbled down the stairs just as the other masked figures descended on Bear. Fury filled his veins as he slashed at each of them, all while backing up the stairs and keeping himself between them and his kid.

"Get to the boat!" Bear yelled.

Mandy groaned but didn't argue. Isabella, now on her feet, fought side by side with Bear. Together, they reached the top of the staircase and fought their way down the other side. A few of the masked figures hung back, their bodies stiff with anger as they watched their escape.

When the water lapped at Bear's ankles, he pushed Isabella behind him and forced her to go first. The guards didn't come in after them. Still, he held his knife aloft, daring them to get between him and his daughter.

Mandy shouted from somewhere behind him. "Let's go!"

Bear didn't need to be told twice. He pushed off the stone steps and back into the warm water. Mandy sat in the boat outside the tunnel, helping to pull Isabella up.

It only took a few strong strokes for Bear to reach them. Kicking with his feet, he launched himself up and over the side, rocking the boat in the process. Mandy yelped and fell back into her seat next to Isabella. Bear shook the water from his eyes. Not that it made much of a difference considering the rain hadn't let up while they were underground.

He turned to Mandy, running his hands over her arms and turning her. "Are you hurt?"

Mandy pushed his hands away. "I'm fine, Dad." She looked to Isabella, her brows pinching. "But she's not."

Bear looked at the other woman, his gaze landing on the place where she had a hand clutched to her side. "What happened?"

Mandy answered for her. "When she grabbed that guy who had a hold of me, I think he got her with the knife." She frowned, glaring at Isabella. "You didn't have to do that. I don't think he wanted to hurt me."

Isabella let out a strangled laugh. Blood oozed from the slash in her side. She kept pressure on it, but within seconds, crimson liquid dripped from between her fingers.

"I'll be sure to remember that for next time."

23

Mandy hurried ahead of Bear and Isabella, gripping the key the other woman had given her just moments ago. Isabella's building reminded her of Luca's, but at least her apartment was on the first floor. It had also been much closer than where Bear and Mandy were staying. And considering how much blood Isabella had lost since emerging from the tunnels, they didn't have time to lose.

As Mandy pushed the key into the lock, she glanced over her shoulder, chewing on her bottom lip. Bear had an arm around Isabella's waist, his hand just above the knife wound in her side. To the casual observer, the two of them looked like they could be a little drunk, walking back arm in arm from some bar or restaurant. It was a good ruse.

Guilt ate at Mandy as she pushed open the door and stepped to the side, allowing the other two to enter first. Isabella was only hurt because she'd been protecting Mandy. The wound wasn't fatal, as long as Bear took care of it sooner rather than later, but the sheen across Isabella's forehead had nothing to do with the relentless rain outside. It told Mandy all she needed to know about how much pain must be coursing through the woman's body.

Bear led Isabella down a short hallway and sat her on a couch in the middle of a cramped room. Mandy shut and locked the door behind her and followed, hovering nearby. She didn't want to get in anyone's way but needed to know that Isabella would be okay.

"Med kit?" Bear asked.

"Bathroom. Under the sink." Isabella's voice was strained.

Bear disappeared deeper into the apartment. Mandy stepped forward, casting her gaze around Isabella's place. It was as barren as their hostel room. Gray walls and gray flooring, with a matching couch and chair. A small cot sat to one side, neatly made. There were no decorations on the wall, the curtains were drawn, and the fluorescent lights buzzed overhead with a glare that made Mandy squint. Within minutes, the harsh brightness had begun to throb behind her eyes.

AT LEAST BEAR would be able to see what he was doing as he patched her up.

"Promise I didn't decorate this place."

Mandy glanced at Isabella, who offered her a half-smile. The woman still clutched her side, looking pale beneath these lights, but Mandy noticed a spark in her eye. Either she was fine, or she was trying to make sure Mandy didn't freak out.

Little did Isabella know that Mandy had seen—and done—much worse.

"Guessing you weren't planning on being in town for long." Mandy stepped over to an open doorway and peered into the tiniest kitchen she'd ever seen- also decorated in shades of gray. She turned her focus back to the sitting room, glancing pointedly at Isabella's wound. "You know, there are less painful ways to add a splash of color to the place."

Isabella snorted and then groaned. "Shit. Don't make me laugh."

Bear entered the room, first-aid kit in hand. "Mandy," he chided.

"What?"

Bear shook his head. "All right. Lean back. Let me see how deep it is."

"Just don't try to harvest my kidneys, Logan."

Mandy let loose a laugh. After everything they'd been through, the knot in her stomach began to ease.

Seeing that Bear had everything handled, she strode across the room and plopped herself down in the chair nearby. It took all her willpower to calmly open her backpack and pull out the package she'd taken from behind the painting.

As soon as the paper crinkled, Bear looked up from where he hovered over Isabella. "What's that?"

"It was taped to one of the paintings. Figured maybe it could be useful."

Isabella turned to look over her shoulder, but Bear placed a firm hand on her arm. "Don't move unless you want these stitches to be as curvy as a country road."

"God, you're bossy," she replied.

"You don't know the half of it," Mandy added.

Bear responded, but Mandy only half-listened. She'd undone the paper around the object and let it fall into her open palm. It was a thick metal disc made of four concentric wheels stacked flat on top of each other. The outer rim was silver with a snake running along the entire edge. At the top, it was biting its own tail. A red gem sparkled from where it had been embedded as its eye.

The next three wheels alternated between gold and silver, each engraved with a variety of symbols. Some were in the shape of animals, others looked like letters from an ancient language. A few she recognized as symbols of the zodiac. A large red gemstone protruded from the center.

Mandy blinked down at the object. The three inner wheels spun creating different combinations of the symbols etched along the wheels. Would the symbols spell out a message? Maybe it would unlock something. She flipped the disc over, but the other side was blank. When she shook it, nothing rattled inside.

Just another puzzle they'd have to solve.

Mandy sighed and turned the disc back over to stare at the front. The snake along the outside represented the Order of the Iron Serpent. At least that much made sense. The gemstones in its eyes and the one in the center looked just like the ones on the puzzle box. But she struggled to determine the significance of the symbols etched into the silver and gold wheels. Symbols covered the mural, but at a quick glance, she didn't think any of them were the same. That didn't feel like the right answer.

Bringing the disc closer, Mandy studied each engraving in detail. She saw a lion, but it didn't look anything like the Venetian symbol they'd followed to the church the other day. Nothing on here looked like an ermine, either. She turned the wheels, searching for any birds, but nothing resembled the mask for the plague doctor.

The shape of a scorpion caught her attention, reminding her of the painted panels she'd seen in Ca' della Maschera. There was a crab, too, and a bull. There was also a goat, but instead of having hind legs, it had a tail like a mermaid.

Mandy sat up straight, staring down at the disc in her hands but no longer seeing it. The paintings she'd discovered in the chamber had been personifications of the zodiac. The woman on the crab was Cancer, the man with the bow on top of the tower was Sagittarius, the lion was Leo, and so on. Could the answer be there, in the frescos?

The wheels of the disc came back into focus. Nothing had been a coincidence so far, which meant the silver and gold wheels were also a clue. They had to be part of the sequence. The gemstones reminded her of the puzzle box, which was also inlaid with gold and silver. It even had little stars all over it—

Mandy launched herself to her feet and hurried across the room to Bear's backpack.

Isabella hissed in pain. "Watch where you're sticking that thing. Hurts worse than the knife did."

"I doubt that." Bear watched Mandy open his pack. "What'd you find?"

"Not sure yet." She struggled to catch her breath. "Give me a second."

Mandy pulled the puzzle box from Bear's pack, shoulders sagging in relief when she saw that none of the fighting had damaged the precious artifact. She'd known it was important the second she laid her eyes on it, but she never expected it to keep giving up its secrets after all this time.

Mandy sat on the floor, metal disc in one hand and the puzzle box in the other. There were groups of stars scattered across the box, some of them in silver and some of them in gold. She'd first thought they were random, but now she could see them for what they really were—constellations.

She easily spotted Scorpius, with three stars out in front, meant to represent the insect's head and pinchers. The rest of the stars curved around, like it held its stinger aloft, ready to strike. The stars were painted gold, which matched the symbol on the largest wheel of the disc.

She held her breath as she spun that piece until the scorpion sat beneath the head of the snake. Nothing happened. Mandy exhaled and squared her shoulders. Two more rings to go.

The next one she needed would be silver. There were several groupings across the box, but only one looked familiar. This one had always bothered her. How did early astronomers decide that a triangle looked like a goat with a tail? It didn't much matter now. She knew, without a doubt, that this one was Capricornus and swiveled the second wheel until the creature sat beneath the first one.

The last constellation would be in gold. She looked at the last wheel and identified the zodiac symbols. It could be Leo or Libra or Gemini. Mandy turned the box in her hands, searching for any patterns. With a quiet gasp, she found it—a large grouping of stars that looked like two people standing side by side. The twins. Gemini.

Mandy twisted the final wheel, pausing only for a fraction of a second before locking the last symbol in place. She had no idea what would happen, or if anything would happen at all. How would she know it worked?

Once Gemini slid in line with Capricorn and Scorpio, she heard a small *click*, and the jewel in the center of the device popped out and fell to the floor at her feet. Mandy's heart stopped. Was that the wrong sequence? Had she broken it?

But in the center of the disc, a prong stuck out of the hollow where the gem had been. It was made of gold and only a few millimeters in diameter. The tip was round, but the shaft had notches. Like a key.

Except she hadn't seen any keyholes on the puzzle box.

She looked again, turning the box every direction, trying to find a miniscule hole they'd missed during their other inspections. It wasn't until she flipped the box over that she found what she was looking for.

Dizzy with excitement, Mandy lined up the metallic device with the puzzle box until the prong slid into the microscopic hole. She could feel the ridges hitting something inside. When the two pieces were flush, it made another soft click.

Then nothing.

"Well, that was anticlimactic," Isabella muttered.

Mandy looked up to see Bear and Isabella staring at her. She flushed and returned her attention back to the combined object in her hands. She tried turning the metallic disc, twisting it like a key in a lock. But it didn't budge.

Mandy let out a low, frustrated groan, the kind that came from hours of trial and error, and yanked the box away from the disc. Maybe she had to switch it around, so it lined up the other way? But as soon as she gave the contraption a tug, it split in two. The bottom stayed stuck to the disc, and the box pulled free.

For a second, Mandy was horrified. But when she peered at the underside of the box, she saw it had remained unscathed. Only now, it lacked any designs.

"A false bottom?" Bear asked, standing up and stepping closer.

"What's that on the other side?" Isabella asked, planting her feet on the ground. Her wound had stopped bleeding, and Mandy could see the dark stitches against her skin. It was an angry red color along the outside, but Bear had done a good job keeping it neat.

It took a second for Isabella's words to sink in. When they did, Mandy looked at the bottom that had fallen off the box. The one still attached to the metallic disc. A small stone slab sat nestled on top of a velvet cushion. Mandy pried it out and looked closer. Two lines of symbols were etched into the top half, while the bottom bore letters of the English alphabet.

"I think it's the key to these symbols." Mandy's mind spun at a million miles a second. "We're meant to use this to decode them."

Bear knelt beside her, looking down at the tablet in her hand. "What symbols?"

For once, Mandy had the answer right away. A grin spread across her face as her heart hammered in her chest.

"The symbols on the mural."

24

BEAR'S EYES BURNED FROM THE BRIGHT OVERHEAD LIGHTS IN Isabella's apartment. It smelled stale in here, like there hadn't been a living soul inside in a long time. Stiff cushions and rough fabric scraped against his skin as he sat on the couch. It sounded like a horde of elephants had been directed to stomp across the apartment floor above them. He had to keep reminding himself to unclench his jaw.

It didn't help that he hadn't gotten a good night's sleep in the last couple days. Between the extra shots of adrenaline coursing through his veins, plus the nightmares of Mandy falling through the floor at the abandoned hospital, his sleep had been far from restful.

But every clue they uncovered spawned a dozen new questions, and Bear's patience wore thin. He wanted to solve whatever insane puzzle the Order had set up and—then what? Bring them down, once and for all? Unmask the people hellbent on attacking them at every opportunity? Save Antonio Vasari, even though they hadn't picked up his trail once since Giulia asked them for help?

They were in too deep to stop now, as much as Bear considered cutting their losses might be the best course of action. But Mandy would never go for that. She sat between him and Isabella on the couch, laptop resting on her knees, while she peered down at the mural on her screen like it held all the secrets to the universe.

Bear held the puzzle box's false bottom in one hand and the ruby that had fallen off the metal disc in the other. Despite everything, a swell of pride surged through him. Mandy had solved that cipher wheel like it was nothing. He would never understand the way she could connect seemingly random pieces of information and find the pattern. Whatever career she chose, he knew she had a bright future ahead of her.

"Okay, let's start at the top and go clockwise. I'll find the symbol, Dad can find the corresponding letter, and you can write it down. Hopefully whatever it says makes sense and we don't have to unscramble it or anything."

Isabella snorted. "That'd be just our luck."

"I know, right?"

Mandy's knee bounced as she zoomed in on the first symbol in the mural. Isabella had a pen poised above a pad of paper, her eyes also locked on the computer screen. Bear glanced down at the stone tablet in his hands. Dark gray with white flecks, and while it wasn't thick, it was surprisingly sturdy in his hands. A dozen questions bounced around his skull. How long ago had the rock been carved, and who had done it? But most importantly, *why* had they done it?

He didn't recognize any of the symbols on the tablet. Not that he was an expert or anything. He'd seen enough languages over the years to guess that this wasn't anything from the modern age. Maybe it was much older than anything he'd seen before, or maybe it was completely made up. It didn't really matter either way, as long as they could translate it.

Mandy nudged him with her elbow. "You paying attention?"

Bear grunted. "Sorry. Yeah. Go ahead."

Mandy gave him the kind of look usually reserved for people promising they'd "totally read the terms and conditions," but she didn't argue about it. It was well after midnight, and they'd had an eventful day. All three of them needed to get some sleep, but he knew Mandy wouldn't let this go until they figured out what the symbols spelled out. If he were being honest, he wanted to know, too.

One by one, Mandy described the symbols, and Bear relayed the corresponding letter from the alphabet. A few of them looked similar, and every once in a while, he had to double-check the image to make sure he'd gotten the right one. Even as his eyesight turned blurry and his brain sluggish, he forged ahead.

"All right, last one." Mandy couldn't keep the excitement out of her voice. "This is one we've already had. Looks like a triangle with two lines going through the right side and a single dot below it."

Bear ran his finger over the stone until he found what he needed. As soon as he read out the corresponding letter, Mandy set her laptop on the floor and leaned in closer to Isabella. They each studied the piece of paper with all the letters on it, mumbling to themselves as they tried to make sense of it all.

Bear stood and placed the stone on the cushion he'd just vacated. He needed to stretch his legs. As the girls studied the message hidden in the mural, Bear took a lap around the room, hoping to get his blood pumping a little bit.

He stopped at the window and parted the curtain, looking out onto the street below. It was still raining, though it appeared to have let up a little bit. As bad as Isabella's injury was, it could've been much worse. And she'd done it to protect Mandy. He wouldn't forget that, not for as long as he lived.

Through the rain, Bear saw a few people running from awning to awning, gripping umbrellas or holding their hoods in place. Not many people were typically out at this time of night or in this sort of weather, but like most cities, Venice was never truly asleep. Regret tugged at him, threatening to pull him deeper as he thought about what this trip could've been like if they hadn't been chasing after the Order. Mandy would've seen a whole different side to Venice.

It's not too late to pack up and leave.

That's what Luca had told him to do. But would they ever be able to return to Venice without the threat of the Order hanging over their heads? Would they even make it out of Italy if they tried? A strong contingent of members resided here in Venice, but from everything he'd learned so far, there were people all over the world who swore loyalty to the Iron Serpent.

He'd gotten used to looking over his shoulder, but Mandy deserved better than that.

Isabella's voice cut through Bear's thoughts. "It's not English."

He turned and watched as Mandy bit her lip.

"Is it Italian?" she asked.

Isabella shook her head. "Latin."

Mandy looked up at the woman, eyebrows nearly touching her hairline. "Can you read it?"

"I'm a little rusty, but I think so."

Bear walked over to stand behind the couch and peer over Isabella's shoulders. The letters on the page swam in front of his eyes, so he relegated himself to watching Isabella translate the text from Latin to English. She wrote the words beneath the letters already on the page. Mandy had her hands clenched tight in her lap, like she might snatch the paper right out from under Isabella's pen if she unclasped them.

"Can't promise this is a perfect translation." Isabella muttered to herself, double-checking her work. "But it's close enough. We can verify it tomorrow to make sure."

"What does it say?" Bear asked.

Isabella handed the paper to Mandy. "Want to do the honors?"

Mandy nodded, taking the note gently, as though it were as precious as the gemstone in Bear's pocket.

"Three masks. One truth." Her voice was steady, but her eyes flicked to Bear. "The Red Veil rises."

Silence hung in the air while they let the words sink in. Isabella leaned back into the couch, her eyebrows scrunched together. Whether it was in pain or contemplation, Bear wasn't sure. Mandy looked up at him, her mouth pulled down into a frown.

"What the hell does that mean?"

Bear's head swam with possibilities, but he couldn't catch a single one long enough to consider it. "Not a clue. Let's leave it for tonight. Fresh eyes and fresh brains in the morning will make all the difference."

Mandy opened her mouth, but Isabella cut in before she could argue.

"I agree. You two are welcome to stay here. My room is in the back, but the couch and cot are yours if you want them." She studied Bear, then glanced at the furniture. "Neither one will be too comfortable for you, but it beats walking back to your place in the rain. Especially if you're not firing on all cylinders right now."

"Appreciate it." Bear watched as Isabella made her way to the back bedroom and shut the door behind her. He looked down at Mandy. "Pack it up, kid. Time for bed."

Mandy huffed even as her eyelids drooped. "You want the couch or the cot?"

He didn't want either one, but their options were limited. The cot would be more comfortable.

"You take the bed. I'll take the couch."

A few minutes later, Bear laid back on the sofa, his head pressed up against one armrest while his feet dangled over the other. A spring poked him in his back, but he hardly noticed. Within seconds, his eyelids grew heavier.

If he could just get a solid four or five hours, he'd be back on his feet in no time.

25

BEAR HAD ONLY JUST CLOSED HIS EYES BEFORE A SHRILL RINGING jarred him from unconsciousness. He didn't remember any of his dreams from the night before.

Mandy moaned from the cot in the corner. Her speech slurred . "Turn it off."

Bear fumbled for his phone, hitting the side buttons until it stopped screaming. Within seconds, he'd slipped back into that dark, peaceful place where he didn't have to deal with secret societies or masked figures coming after him and his kid.

The ringing started up again. With a curse, Bear hit the answer button and brought the phone to his ear. He hadn't even bothered to open his eyes to see who was calling. His throat scraped like sandpaper as he tried to force words from his mouth.

"What?"

There was a pause. "Riley? Is that you?"

Bear didn't recognize the voice. He opened his eyes, blinking until the light trickling through the curtains was no longer a dagger hellbent on blinding him. He peered down at the phone. It was Giulia.

Bringing the device back to his ear, he sat up to dislodge some of his grogginess. "Yes. Sorry. It's me. What's up?"

Now that the lingering sleep had subsided, he could hear the tremor in the old woman's voice.

"Luca told me he took you to see Father Benedetto. That he answered some of your questions about the Order. About La Velata Rossa."

Bear pulled the phone away from his ear again to check the time. She rang him at seven in the morning to ask this? He cracked his neck from side to side to relieve some of the tension in his shoulders before he answered.

"Yes, that's right. Look, we got in late last night. Can I give you a call back when—"

"He's dead."

Bear froze, letting her words sink in. "Who's dead?"

"Father Benedetto." A sob punctuated the end of her answer. "And I am having trouble reaching Luca. I think something has happened to him."

"Okay, okay." Bear stood, letting the rest of his bleariness fall away with the motion. "Back up. Tell me about Father Benedetto. How do you know he's dead?"

Bedsheets rustled from the other side of the room. Mandy's voice was heavy with concern. "Father Benedetto is dead?"

Bear nodded. He didn't want to have this conversation in front of her, but the apartment was too small for there to be any real privacy. Plus, she'd find out sooner or later.

"He was found late last night. Many people are already talking about it. One of the crime reporters will tell you anything you want to know if you slip him some money. He has a gambling problem."

Bear shook his head, trying to sort through the relevant information. "How was he killed?"

"They found him in his home." Giulia took a few deep breaths before she continued. "His tongue had been cut from his mouth."

"Jesus." Bear ran a hand down his face. "Any idea who did it or why?"

"They aren't reporting this in the papers yet, but the reporter told me there was a message written in blood, found next to his body."

Bear hesitated before asking his next question. "What did it say?"

"The Scorpion comes to sever false loyalties."

A shiver ran down Bear's spine. He had no idea what that meant, but it was ominous as hell. "Any leads?"

"No." Giulia cleared her throat, but emotion warped her words. "But it must be from the Order." She took two heaving breaths. "Have you heard from Luca? Do you know anything about my Antonio? What if—"

Her words dissolved into sobs, but Bear didn't need to hear it to understand where her mind had gone.

"Hey, hey." He kept his voice gentle but firm. He watched as Mandy sat up in bed, studying him. He wanted to turn away from her, but he forced himself to stand tall. "Listen. It's going to be okay. We don't know for sure that it was the Order. See what else you can find from your contact and fill me in as soon as you can."

She choked on her words, but he could just about make out Giulia saying, "Okay."

"I haven't heard anything about Antonio yet, but I have no reason to believe he's been hurt. If they wanted to send a message, we would've found him by now." It was little consolation, but it was all he had at the moment. "I'll reach out to Luca to see if I can get ahold of him. I can even stop by his place later today. We'll find him, okay? Don't lose hope just yet."

The frailty had vanished from her voice, replaced by a commanding certainty. "Okay. Thank you, Riley. For everything."

"You're welcome. Keep your phone close. I'll call with any updates."

Giulia mumbled her goodbyes before hanging up. He caught the beginning of another sob before the line went dead.

With a deep sigh, Bear tossed his phone onto the couch and met

Mandy's eyes. Her throat bobbed as she swallowed. When she spoke, her words came slow and deliberate. Too steady for it not to be an act.

"How was Father Benedetto killed?"

Bear rubbed a hand down his face again. "Not sure of all the details. But his tongue was cut out. They left a message."

Mandy's voice cracked along with her act. "What kind of message?"

"*The Scorpion comes to sever false loyalties.*"

Mandy blinked back at him. "The Scorpion?" She looked over to where they'd left the puzzle box, the cipher wheel, and her laptop. "That can't be a coincidence."

Bear tracked her gaze but couldn't follow her train of thought. "What do you mean?"

"There was a scorpion symbol on the cipher wheel. And when we were in Ca' della Maschera, there was this series of paintings on the wall in that first chamber. In one of them, there was a man surrounded by scorpions."

Bear had no idea where she was going with this. "They were attacking him?"

"More like he was controlling them. Commanding them." Mandy stood and paced back and forth across the floor. "Each of the figures in that painting represented the twelve zodiac symbols. I found three constellations on the puzzle box that represented the three animals that solved the cipher wheel." She ran a hand through her hair, making it stick up even more. "Those people who attacked us were wearing masks with horns. They looked like—"

"Bulls." Bear finished. "Taurus. And ram's horns. Aries."

Mandy came to a stop, nodding. "It's connected, but I can't figure out how."

"Me neither."

Mandy's gaze softened as she studied Bear. "Is Signora Vasari okay?"

Bear didn't want to lie to her. "She's worried about Luca. He's not answering his phone. We may need to swing by his place and check on him."

Mandy's chin wobbled. "Do you think they hurt him too?"

"I don't know. I'm not jumping to conclusions yet. One step at a time."

"Right." Mandy stood a little taller. "One step at a time."

Bear caught the faint shift in her breathing, the way her shoulders loosened as if the weight on them had eased. She clung to his words like a lifeline. He wished he could do the same. For him, the air only seemed to grow heavier, the walls inching closer with every heartbeat.

26

BEAR KNOCKED ON ISABELLA'S DOOR AND WAITED FOR HER TO emerge from her bedroom. Somehow, the bags under her eyes were even worse than his and Mandy's that morning. The stitches in her side probably kept her awake all night. Bear let her shower as he made them all coffee. After he checked her wound and replaced her bandages, he got her up to speed.

When he finished explaining everything he'd learned from Giulia, Isabella tipped her head back and swore at the ceiling.

Mandy took a delicate sip of her piping hot coffee from where she sat in the armchair across from them on the couch. "That about sums it up."

Isabella had already finished one cup of coffee and got up to pour herself a second. From the kitchen she asked, "Did you reach out to Luca yet?"

Bear nodded, then realized she couldn't see him. "Yeah. Called him three times while you were in the shower. No answer."

"Did it ring or go straight to voicemail?"

"Right to voicemail."

She cursed again as she emerged with a steaming cup in hand.

"Even if I could reach out to someone and get them to track it, it won't do us any good."

Those were Bear's thoughts too. He had people, like Brandon, who could track anyone and anything. But if the phone was off, dead, or destroyed, it didn't much matter. "If Luca's in hiding, he probably ditched his phone."

Bear left the alternative explanation unsaid. None of them wanted to think Luca had been killed, much less in a similar fashion to Father Benedetto. Bear hadn't known either man well, but neither deserved that fate.

"Any updates from Giulia yet?" Isabella asked, sitting back down on the couch.

"No. Not surprised. It'll take some time for her reporter contact to get the information, and even more time for her to bribe him to pass it along."

Mandy clutched her mug while she let it rest on her knee. "So, what's the plan then?"

Isabella flicked out a finger for each of their options. "See what we can find out about Father Benedetto's death. Stop by Luca's apartment and try to track him down if he's not there. Dig up something on Antonio Vasari." She paused. "I suppose we could also go back to Ca' della Maschera and knock on the Order's door again, but on the long list of stupid things we could do, that seems to be at the very top."

"I've got another idea," Bear offered.

Isabella and Mandy turned their focus to him, silent as they waited to hear what he had to say.

With a shrug, Bear gestured toward the cipher wheel and the puzzle box. "I say we destroy it all."

Isabella blinked once. Mandy's jaw dropped open. She recovered first.

"Are you joking?"

"Not even a little bit." Bear took a sip of his coffee, debating the best way to convince them that this might be their best course of action. "All of our trouble started when we found the puzzle box."

"The word you're looking for is *stole*." Isabella had a glint in her eyes, but she didn't seem angry. "You *stole* the puzzle box."

"All I'm saying is that as soon as the Order got wind that we had it, they started coming after us. We've been finding trouble around every corner. The second we figured out the first clue, it led us to the basilica where we met Giulia. It's clear that the Order doesn't want us to have any of this information, so I say we destroy it. The cipher wheel, the puzzle box, the pin and the gem. Even the mural."

Somehow, Mandy's jaw dropped even lower. She sputtered for a moment before she found her voice again. "We can't do that."

"Yes, we can. I know you're invested in all this, kid, but sometimes you gotta know when to cut your losses."

Mandy stood so fast, some of her coffee sloshed over the side of her mug. She didn't seem to notice. "What about Signora Vasari, huh? We told her we'd tried to find her husband. And Luca! He's missing, and he could be seriously injured. And you just want to walk away from them?"

Bear took a slow, steady breath before he responded. He could feel the heat of her anger, a taut wire between them, and the wrong word would snap it. "I don't want to walk away from them, Mandy, but if I have to choose between them and you, I'm going to choose you. Every time."

Mandy's mouth snapped shut, and he could see her jaw clench When she spoke again, her voice flattened. "You don't have to choose between them and me. How many times do I have to prove that I can take care of myself before you start to believe in me?"

Bear glanced at the woman on the couch next to him. He didn't like having this conversation in front of her. It was like showing a home inspector a crack in the foundation.

"I know you can take care of yourself, Mandy. But you shouldn't have to. Not like this." He rubbed his eyes and let out a heavy sigh. "You're sixteen years old, and you've already seen and done more than most adults twice your age. I just want to protect you from all that for as long as I can."

"You've done a great job on that so far, haven't you, Bear?"

As soon as the words were out of her mouth, Mandy looked down at her feet. Bear recoiled like she'd slapped him. Of course, she was right. Adopting Mandy meant exposing her to danger. He found himself forever caught between shielding her from the threats of the world and showing her how to overcome them once he was no longer around.

"I didn't mean it like that," Mandy whispered. "I'm sorry."

"I know." Bear's voice was raw, the words dragging like they'd cost him to say them. Part of him wanted to cross the space and pull her into his arms, anchor them both. The other part wanted to retreat, to put a wall between them before she saw how deep her words had cut. "I just want to make sure we discuss all our options."

Mandy looked to Isabella. "You have any thoughts on this?"

It sounded more like a challenge than an honest question, but Isabella surprised them both with her answer.

"I agree with Mandy."

Mandy grinned. Bear turned and stared at Isabella, grinding his teeth.

Isabella held up her hand. "I'm not saying it's a bad idea to keep Bear's option on the backburner. If we torch the mural and everything else along with it, that could provide enough of a distraction for us to make our escape."

"But?" Mandy prompted.

"But that should be our last resort. I became an agent because I wanted to help good people and stop the bad ones. We still don't know what the Order ultimately wants, but I do know they're willing to go to extremes to get it. We can't abandon Giulia, her husband, or Luca. It might be too late for Father Benedetto, but we can still avenge him."

Mandy beamed. "Thank you."

"Easy for you to say," Bear said through clenched teeth. "Your kid isn't mixed up in all of this."

Isabella's head snapped in his direction, eyes narrowing. "I took a knife for your kid because I care about her. I've got literal blood in this game. Not to mention that they killed my friend. I don't want Maya's life to be in vain. If we can solve all their little puzzles, we might find something to stop them. Or, at the very least, discover what they want. If we have that sort of information, then we have power over them. Maybe we could even get them to do what *we* want for a change."

"All I heard was a lot of *ifs* and *maybes*." Bear shook his head. "The more we talk about this, the more I'm convinced we're digging ourselves in too deep. I'm not going to leave Luca or Antonio out to dry, but if that mural is as important as it seems, then destroying it might be the only way to stop them."

Mandy set her coffee cup down on the windowsill. When she turned back to Bear, her eyes held back tears. He also tracked the way her fists clenched at her side,

"I know this probably sounds stupid to you, but I feel like—like —" She swallowed and took a big gulp of air. "I feel like this was all meant for me, Bear. I was meant to find it. The girl in the painting—"

"It's gotta be a coincidence," Bear said, leaning forward to rest his arms on his knees. He refused to believe the alternative. "Or a way to manipulate you."

"You know, you're in the painting too." Mandy took a step forward, chin trembling. Her words came out wobbly. "Holding a dagger. That's gotta mean something."

"And what if it doesn't?" His voice shook, growing louder with every word. "At some point we have to stop being delusional and see what's right in front of us. Call it for what it is and then get the hell out of Dodge."

Now Mandy looked like she'd been slapped. "You think I'm delusional?"

Bear let out a heavy breath. "That's not what I meant."

"But it's what you said."

"It's what you wanted to hear, Mandy. I'm not the bad guy here."

"No, but you're still being a jerk." She strode across the room. "I'm going for a walk."

Bear jumped to his feet. "Not by yourself you're not."

She yanked open the door, already moving through it. "Isabella can come with me."

He took two steps toward her. "Mandy—"

Isabella appeared beside him, placing a hand on his arm. "She needs a minute to cool down. Maybe you do too. We're all stressed out. I'll keep an eye on her, okay?"

He cringed at the idea of letting his kid out of his sight, but Isabella had a point. The more he pushed Mandy, the more she'd pull away.

He couldn't help but think that's exactly what the Order wanted.

27

Mandy leaned against a brick building, letting the cool stone calm her rage. The flush warming her cheeks had nothing to do with the morning sun beaming down on her. She hated storming out of Isabella's apartment like that, but Bear had just made her so mad. The reasonable part of her brain argued that he had a valid point. But the emotional part could care less. He'd dismissed her in a way he'd never done before, and it stung.

Crossing her arms over her chest, Mandy watched as Isabella stopped on the corner of the street, her head on a swivel. It hadn't taken Mandy long to realize she had a tail, and even less time to lose it. Isabella had training. But Bear was better and he had taught Mandy everything she knew.

Temptation stirred in her to slip into the shadows and be alone for a while, but that would be a waste of time.

The morning crowd buzzed with energy, fueled by caffeine and the fresh ocean air after last night's storm. Mandy pushed off the side of the building and wove her way through the busy street. She stopped a few feet behind Isabella.

"Looking for me?"

Isabella whirled around, then looked Mandy over from top to bottom. Her wide eyes narrowed slightly as she gave Mandy a slight nod. "Thought I lost you there for a minute."

"You did." Mandy suppressed the urge to fling her words like daggers. Isabella had been on her side, after all. She shouldn't be punished for Bear's wrongdoings. "Did Bear send you to come get me?"

"No. Your dad wanted to come after you, but I convinced him you needed some time."

"So, we're supposed to, like, bond?"

So much for reining in that attitude.

Isabella's eyes crinkled at the corners as she smiled. "No, but I do need to keep an eye on you." She paused, tapping a finger to her chin. "You like museums?"

Mandy wanted to say no, just to give her anger an outlet, but she needed a distraction other than wandering aimlessly around the city of Venice.

"Yeah, why?"

Isabella motioned for her to follow and struck out across the street. Mandy hesitated, wondering whether Bear would approve of her following the woman to an undisclosed location. But she dismissed the thought the same way Bear had dismissed her.

As time dragged on, she swore they took the long way there. Keeping up with Isabella's long strides and staying aware of her surroundings occupied her mind enough that she could push down her annoyance and focus on the task at hand.

They had to cross back over the Grand Canal and walk a good distance south, but Mandy appreciated that Isabella had chosen not to rent a gondola, even if they were the faster option. It would be a while before Mandy wanted to get in a boat again.

The streets bustled with late-morning energy—vendors calling out their wares, gondoliers shouting greetings across the canals—as they reached an unassuming building labeled Gallerie dell'Accademia. Isabella stopped just outside the door and turned to Mandy. "I've got a deal for you."

Mandy put a hand on her hip. "I'm listening."

"We both go inside this museum and take a look around. We go our separate ways so it doesn't feel like I'm there to babysit you. We meet just inside the entrance in two hours, then we'll head back, and you and Bear can talk this out."

Mandy peered past Isabella at the groups of people walking through the entrance. It was crowded enough that she'd be safe on her own. There'd be plenty of security guards and cameras inside. The Order wouldn't dare try anything in there. And Mandy would get to spend a few hours by herself, even if that was mostly an illusion.

She barely held back a smile and shrugged as she said, "Works for me."

Mandy drifted toward the galleries, her mind half on the art, half scanning for anything that might echo the mural in Giulia's apartment.

People milled around her. The museum held plenty of room for everyone to have their own space but it was far from packed. Mandy liked that everyone kept their voices low and reverent, as though each word might disturb the brushstrokes. To see all these paintings and statues in one place was awe-inspiring. All this history, all this talent.

Mandy wandered wherever her feet took her. Eventually, she ended up in a room with pale blue walls. All the paintings here shared the same theme—Madonna and Child. Not really her thing, but one of the pieces caught her attention. Or, rather, the title did.

Madonna dello Zodiaco.

She didn't need to understand Italian to know that last word meant *zodiac*. Once again, it was as if she were being driven toward something meant for her. Bear's harsh words immediately followed, dismissing the thought that this was all meant to be.

She ignored the sick feeling of shame roiling inside her and stepped closer to peer up at the figures in the painting. A woman held a naked child. Small birds sat on top of a couple bunches of grapes hanging in the background. Her eyes took in every detail of how the artist painted Mary's robes, how they looked three-dimensional, appearing to drape over the edge. A big wooden frame, carved with leaves and flowers, surrounded the entire mural.

Golden symbols painted along the woman's right side caught her attention. That must've been where the name of the piece came from. She could pick out the signs for Aquarius, Pisces, Sagittarius, and Virgo. It was so different from the style of the paintings at Ca' della Maschera, and yet the connection to the zodiac was just as prominent.

Mandy wasn't sure how much time had passed as she stared at that painting, but before long, she noticed the atmosphere in the room shift. People had sometimes stopped a few feet away from her to look at the painting before moving on. Now, however, the room remained quiet except for the clack of a pair of heels against the floor. They didn't linger like the footsteps of those there to admire the art. They were confident and purposeful, and when they stopped beside her, Mandy knew the person wasn't there for the painting. It wasn't just the way their gaze skimmed past the artwork without lingering— it was the deliberate stillness in their stance, the subtle tension in their shoulders, the faint sense of attention fixed entirely on her.

It took all of Mandy's willpower not to react. She stood there staring at the painting for a few more seconds before slowly turning and looking up into the face of the woman beside her. Nothing could've prepared herself for what she saw.

A bright red dress hugged the woman's form. It looked classy and expensive- somehow modest even as it showed off the curves of her toned body. The stilettoes on her feet must've been at least five inches tall, but she seemed as steady on her feet as if she were wearing sneakers. Her nails were painted the same shade of red as her dress, and Mandy wondered if she wore lipstick to match. She'd never know, however, because the woman wore a mask that covered her entire face.

It looked a lot like the volto mask they'd seen on the island, only this one was—surprise, surprise—bright red. Gold dusted the cheeks and lips, and a thin piece of red mesh covered the eyes. It wrapped around the woman's head and tied in the back.

So, this was Libra, then. Blind justice. A member of La Velata Rossa.

Mandy turned back to the painting, fighting to suppress the tremors coursing through her body.

"Bit on the nose, don't you think?" Mandy hoped the woman didn't detect the slight waver in her voice.

The woman laughed. It was a soft, raspy sound. Genuine, too.

"Hello, Mandy. It's good to finally meet you."

"Wish I could say the same. Your friends haven't exactly been welcoming, you know."

"I'm sorry about that." She said, a little pout in her voice. She spoke in perfect English, yet her accent was Italian mixed with something else. British, maybe? She sounded posh, like she'd had an upscale English education. "It was important you be tested. We needed to assess your skills. Suffice it to say, we are quite impressed."

Mandy spoke through clenched teeth. "You could've killed my friend."

"Ah, the agent." Libra clasped her hands in front of her. "How very noble of her to throw herself on a knife for you. It seems you inspire loyalty in people wherever you go. That is an admirable trait. A useful one, too."

Mandy scoffed. "I bet you think so."

"I know so." The woman's voice grew firm, but not in anger. It was more like passion. No, *conviction*. "You are an incredibly intelligent young woman, Mandy. Forward-thinking and independent. Your potential is something to behold."

"Not everyone thinks so."

The words had slipped before she could stop herself. Mandy snapped her mouth shut. She hadn't meant to say that out loud, to show her hand. Even in a dress and stilettos, this woman was dangerous—lethal, even. Not the kind of danger you could see coming, but the sort that slid in under your guard and left you wondering how you'd agreed to something you swore you never would. She had the kind of poise that turned a crowded room into her personal stage, the kind of smile that could disarm suspicion while she steered the conversation exactly where she wanted it. Mandy didn't need to imagine the damage Libra could do in a fight—her posture said she could end one before it started. Worse, the sharp intelligence in her eyes promised she could dismantle someone's resolve piece by piece, make them think the choice was theirs all along. Power radiated from the woman's every pore, and it wasn't just physical. It was the kind that bent people without them realizing they'd been moved.

And it wasn't just the way she spoke and held herself. No one had entered the room since Libra had walked over to her. Mandy refused to turn around, to prove that she was nervous about having her back to the door. She bet if she looked over her shoulder, there'd be a museum guard blocking off this wing. Did Libra work at La Galleria dell'Accademia, or had she paid someone off so she could slip in here wearing her little mask?

"Your father is holding you back," Libra said. Not a hint of condemnation in her tone. She simply sounded matter-of-fact.

"He loves me." Regardless of the shame sitting in her stomach like a brick since their argument, she wouldn't let this person talk about him like that. "He wants to protect me."

"There is a fine line between protecting the ones we love and smothering them."

Mandy remained silent, hating that the woman's words had hit home.

Libra turned to her, waiting until Mandy met her eyes, hidden behind the mesh fabric. "You were always meant to decode the mural, Mandy. And you've done a brilliant job so far. Don't give up. We're rooting for you."

Mandy's jaw went slack. "Who's rooting for me?"

The woman didn't answer. She slipped a hand in her pocket and drew out something small and silver. When she held it out, Mandy took it instinctively.

"A gift," Libra said. "To remind you of what the future holds."

Mandy looked down at the object in her palm. She held a small ring, not unlike the one Signore Bianchi had given her before they left San Gimignano. Only this wasn't stamped with the face of Minerva. It bore the symbol of the Order—an iron serpent.

Mandy blinked at the object, wondering what it meant and why Libra had given it to her. When she looked up, however, the woman had disappeared.

People filed in as though the hall had been open the entire time. Mandy rushed to the door and peered through the crowd, trying to find the woman in the red dress. You'd think the mask would make people stop and stare. Give her a wide berth.

But no matter where she looked, Mandy couldn't find her.

28

BEAR HIT THE BUZZER FOR LUCA'S APARTMENT FOR THE THIRD time, but at this point, he'd given up hope of the man answering the door. Either he'd skipped town, or he was dead. One was better than the other, but neither helped Bear much.

With a sigh, Bear glanced down at his phone again, even though he knew there wouldn't be any updates from Isabella. Once he'd found out she'd taken Mandy to a museum and had promised to keep her busy for a few hours, he'd left Isabella's place to track down Luca. Giulia still had no leads, and Bear didn't know anyone else in Venice. His only option had been to head here.

To a dead end.

The sun peaked high in the sky. Yesterday's storm already a distant memory. Chatter from the next street over reached him, as did the smell of cooking meat. His stomach complained. He hadn't had anything other than that cup of coffee earlier this morning. He'd need to take the time to eat if he wanted to keep his brain sharp and his body ready for whatever the Order threw their way.

Bear scanned the street before he picked a direction and set off.

He didn't know where he was going, and he didn't care. He just had to work off some of the tension in his shoulders, the stress that had dug its way deep into his bones.

His stomach sank at the thought of fighting with Mandy. He still believed their best course of action was to torch anything and everything related to the Order, but he could've handled that conversation better. As soon as the words had slipped from his mouth, he'd seen how much damage they caused. She had to realize he hadn't meant it, but that didn't make it any less painful. When he saw her again, he'd apologize, and they'd figure out the best way forward. He could compromise if it meant fixing their relationship.

When Bear's stomach became louder than his thoughts, he stopped into a sandwich shop and ordered the biggest thing on the menu. He chose to sit outside at a round table, the little umbrella stuck through the middle working overtime to keep the sun off his shoulders.

Before he knew it, he'd finished half his sandwich. He'd barely registered what was on it. Each ingredient was there to fuel his body, and nothing else. Normally, he'd enjoy a meal like this under the Venetian sky, a gentle breeze ruffling his hair. But he kept thinking about the hurt in Mandy's eyes and the fear in Giulia's voice.

Something had to give, and he needed it to happen soon.

Like the thought itself had conjured him, a man stepped up to the table and grabbed the back of the chair opposite Bear. He slid it back and settled down into it, unbuttoning his suit jacket with one hand while he crossed one leg over the other. He folded his hands atop his knees and stared at Bear like they were two old friends catching up.

On a good day, Bear would've seen the guy coming a mile away.

Today was not a good day.

He didn't allow his body to react. He simply set the rest of his sandwich down, wiped his mouth with a napkin, and met the eyes of the man sitting across from him. The one who'd invited himself to the table without fear or preamble.

He wore a tailored suit. Expensive. The deep blue matched his sharp eyes and complimented his bronze skin and dark hair. When another gentle breeze rolled by, not a strand of hair blew out of place. The sun glinted off a gold ring encircling his pinky finger.

It took Bear the span of two heartbeats to place the face. René Bellevue. The art collector. It was debatable whether he was a thief himself or just hired thieves to get what he wanted. If Bear had to guess, he'd say a little of both. Bellevue was wanted by a lot of agencies. It wasn't surprising that he was in Venice, but the hairs on Bear's neck stood up because he was here, at this table, sitting across from Bear.

The little smirk on the other man's face said Bellevue knew exactly who Bear was and how much his presence at the table irked him.

Bellevue tipped his head in Bear's direction. "Monsieur Logan."

Bear leaned back in his chair. "René."

Bellevue's grin grew wider. "I hope I am not interrupting your meal. I saw you sitting here and decided I must not pass up the opportunity to say hello."

This was no coincidence, and they both knew it. How long had Bellevue been following him? Bear's rage rose like a tsunami, but he forced himself to appear calm. There would be time to chastise himself later.

"I must admit I'm surprised to see you here, out in the open." Bear let the words hang in the air for a moment. No one else at the cafe sat close enough to hear their conversation, but he couldn't stop from goading the other man. "Last I heard, you were running with your tail between your legs."

Bellevue offered him a playful frown, but his eyes were as cold as ice. "If that is what you've heard, I do believe you've been misinformed."

A lazy smile spread over Bear's face. "My sources are reliable."

"Ah, yes." He snapped his fingers, like he'd remembered something important. "Agent Fabrizio, yes? Though, perhaps I should just call her Isabella. Nearly as many agencies are as interested in finding her as they are me. I wonder who they will catch first?"

"Something tells me they'd be a lot more interested in putting you in cuffs."

Bellevue held up a finger and clicked his tongue. "I would not be so sure about that if I were you. Our mutual friend is much more devious than I think either of us has given her credit for."

"I don't think she would appreciate you calling her a friend."

"No?" Bellevue raised an eyebrow, his expression full of mirth. "Perhaps not. But are you so sure you can call her a friend? Do you trust her enough to, for example, keep an eye on your daughter while you're here, enjoying your lunch by yourself?"

This time, Bear couldn't control his reaction. His body stiffened, and while every nerve in his body screamed at him to call Mandy right now to make sure she was okay, he resisted. He'd already given Bellevue too much by rising to his bait.

"I'd choose your next words very carefully, Bellevue."

"Ah, no longer René, is it?" The man shook his head, yet his smile remained. "Tell me, how is Mandy? Did you find the gift I left for you?"

Just like that, Bear put the pieces together. The crown made of laurel leaves and the fleur-de-lis. Bellevue's calling card. He'd left it there for them. He'd almost gotten Mandy killed.

Bear clenched his teeth together so hard, his jaw popped. "You son of a bitch. You leave my kid out of this. You got something to settle, you come at me like a real man."

Bellevue tipped his head back and laughed, his eyes closed and throat exposed. If they were anywhere else other than this café, Bear would've pulled out his knife and given the man a permanent smile, from ear to ear.

"You Americans are all the same, are you not?" Bellevue wiped an invisible tear from his eye. The gold ring on his finger glinted in the sun again. "Please believe me when I say it was not personal. Simply business."

Bear changed the subject before he did something reckless. "What do you want with the Order?"

Bellevue studied his fingernails. "What else? Money, power, prestige."

"Falling on hard times already?"

"It is my personal belief that one can never have enough of those particular commodities."

Bear grew tired of this conversation. And he no longer cared if Bellevue knew it. "What do you want, René? This little tête-à-tête is not as stimulating as I thought it would be."

"It is funny you should say that." Bellevue stood and buttoned his suit jacket with precise movements that gave away his annoyance at Bear's comments. "Considering I have been two steps ahead of you this entire time. Tell me, what will you do without the dagger, hmm? Or have you not realized what a crucial part of the puzzle that is?"

Bear leaned forward. He'd calmed down enough to think straight. Now, he could see right through Bellevue's carefully crafted veneer. "You're desperate. You're missing a piece of the puzzle too, aren't you? Otherwise, you wouldn't waste your time sitting here poking at me. You need something."

Bellevue's eyes glinted as he stepped back and the sun bounced off his shoulders. "Perhaps that is a question better asked of Signora Fabrizio. Good day, Monsieur Logan."

Bear's mind spun as he contemplated the meaning of the man's words. Twice now, he'd hinted Isabella wasn't who she appeared to be. She hadn't once brought up Bellevue or the possibility of working with anyone else to solve the Order's puzzle, but it's not like he kept tabs on her when they weren't together.

Was she playing both sides? Playing him and Mandy?

Bear stood from his chair, not caring that heads turned as metal scraped against stone. He strode after the Frenchman, abandoning the rest of his sandwich. Bellevue was at the end of the street. He looked over his shoulder and saluted Bear before turning the corner and disappearing.

Bear stomped after him, hellbent on getting answers.

But when he made it to the end of the street, his target was no longer in view.

Bellevue had vanished.

29

BEAR STEPPED INTO FATHER BENEDETTO'S OFFICE AS THOUGH he were walking barefoot across glass. It was strange to think he and Mandy had been here the day before, and now the man was dead. Had they cut out his tongue before or after he'd been killed? Given the message written in his blood, Bear was certain he knew the answer to that question.

Sweeping his gaze across the room, Bear expected to see blood staining the carpet or the top of the man's desk, even though Giulia had told him he'd been killed in his home. Who had noticed he'd gone missing? More importantly, who had found him? Had the message been for that person, or did the killer intend for it to go public? He wouldn't be surprised if the note had been for him and Mandy.

Bear shut the door behind him, grateful that he hadn't had to answer any questions as to why he wanted to visit the priest's office. Giulia had pulled more strings to get him inside. The police had already combed through the room once, but her sources had said they hadn't spent long looking for clues. Either they didn't care to think too hard about who could've killed the man, or they already knew the answer and chose to look in the other direction.

Bear would've bet money on the second option.

He started furthest from the man's desk, pulling out each book on the shelf and riffling through the pages. He had no idea what to look for, but it was worth taking the time to search everything. Father Benedetto had known more about the Order of the Iron Serpent than anyone else, and it had very likely gotten him killed. Was it because of what he'd told Bear and Mandy about La Velata Rossa, or had he spoken to someone else?

Someone like René Bellevue.

Frustration still clung to him from having let his guard down, a low, bitter thrum he couldn't shake. But the moment he replayed how the Frenchman had needled him—how he'd taken the bait—it surged, hot and sharp, burning away the pretense of calm. It didn't matter that he'd managed to get under the art collector's skin, too. The damage was done, and it was his own lapse that had opened the door.

Bear moved from one book to the next, then through each shelf . A mindless task, giving him plenty of time to think about everything that weighed on him. His argument with Mandy firmly at the top of the list, along with Bellevue's comments about Isabella.

Something didn't line up.

Bellevue had tried to convince him Isabella wasn't who she seemed, that perhaps she was playing both sides. But she'd taken a knife to the gut for his daughter. Having stitched the wound himself, he saw how deep it had been. How close to fatal it could've been if the knife had gone just a little deeper.

With each new tome he pulled from a shelf, dust rained down around him. These books hadn't been touched in a while. This might have been a waste of his time but doing something with his hands always helped him calm down, even if it allowed his mind to wander.

After he'd lost track of Bellevue, Bear had called Mandy and made sure she was safe. She'd sounded distracted by everything at the museum, but he'd take that over bitter any day. He'd told her to be

THE MARKED DAUGHTER   183

extra vigilant, even with Isabella there. Mandy seemed to understand what he told her, even without him saying it directly. He promised to tell her more later.

They'd all be back under the same roof soon, and he'd get the answers he desperately needed.

In the meantime, he still had half of Father Benedetto's study to go through. When he finished with the bookshelves, he checked the armchair and couch for anything that looked out of the ordinary. Lumps or patches. Open seams or notes stuffed between cushions. He came up empty-handed.

The only untouched object left in the room was the desk. If Father Benedetto had hidden something, chances were it'd be in his desk, but Bear had needed to do his due diligence on the rest of the room first. He had no reason to believe the old man had left something behind, but something in his gut told him to keep looking.

Nothing appeared out of place on the desk, papers stacked, pens lined up meticulously. Bear opened every drawer, checking each item. He noticed nothing strange about any of the contents. Everything looked like it belonged, which was part of the problem. If Father Benedetto had wanted to hide something, would he have done it here or in his home? Bear would never be able to gain access to the crime scene until well after it had been scrubbed clean.

This place was his only hope for finding something that could help them.

Getting down on his knees, Bear ran a hand along the underside of the desk. It was solid. Solid and sturdy. Well-built. It would be easy enough to add some sort of secret compartment or hidden panel.

Bear paused, shaking his head and smirking. Mandy would love this. He couldn't help but feed off of her energy. He wished she were there with him. Looking for clues in an old wooden desk as if they had found themselves thrust into the plot of *National Treasure*.

Come to think of it, she'd never seen that movie. He promised himself he'd show it to her as soon as they put all this behind them.

Just as he started to stand up, dust off his hands, and call it quits, his fingers trailed over a notch in the wood- beneath the bottom drawer on the right side. Holding his breath, he pressed inward until he heard a click. A small tray dropped down, depositing a leather journal onto the floor.

Bingo.

Bear grabbed the journal and closed the panel, then strode over to the couch and sat down with the book in his lap. The leather had started to crack with age. This had to have meant something to Father Benedetto. Enough to hide it from prying eyes, at least.

Bear flipped open the first page, taking in the neat scrawl of the man's handwriting. It looked like calligraphy, each letter written with a practiced hand. The words were written in Italian, small but legible. A date lined the top. Father Benedetto had started this two years ago. Could there be others, ones much older than this one? Perhaps those had been hidden in the priest's house. Bear wondered if the police had found them. Or if the Scorpion had gotten to them first.

He flipped to the last page, checking the date. Ice filled Bear's veins. It had been written yesterday. It was one thing to find a dead man's journal. Another to know he'd written in it the day before he was murdered. Had he mentioned getting visitors?

Bear skimmed the page but saw no reference to them. He started again, this time reading more thoroughly. The writing on this page was sloppier than the first entry. Had he been scared or in a hurry? Or both? Had Father Benedetto known someone was coming after him? If so, why had he stayed in Venice?

Maybe he'd shared the same reason Bear had yet to leave.

He'd been too invested.

Bear had to read the final paragraph three times before the words sank in enough for him to understand the priest's meaning. La Velata Rossa was indeed an elite group within the Order of the Iron Serpent. What Luca had failed to mention—or perhaps didn't know—was that not everyone involved liked what the they stood for.

Ca' della Maschera had once been the home base for La Velata Rossa before other members of the Order slaughtered them one by one. The faction had gotten too strong, too ambitious. They'd risked everything the Order had spent so long trying to hide.

This had happened hundreds of years ago. According to Father Benedetto's journal, this violent history had been washed away with the tide. The House of the Mask had been buried right alongside the bodies of those who dared to rise above the Order of the Iron Serpent.

But some members must've learned of the elite faction and formed the group anew. Twelve people had led the charge, their masks always in place for fear that their identities would be revealed to the rest of the Order. That history would repeat itself. That they'd be marked for death.

La Velata Rossa had once again risen to the top of the Order, steering the group in a new direction. But not everyone agreed with their ambitions. A splinter group had formed within the Order, working to stop the Red Veil from gaining control of Venice.

And, eventually, the rest of Italy and beyond.

Bear closed the book and stared at nothing as he took in the information. The thought of working alongside the Order made his stomach turn.

Both the phrases *the enemy you know* and *the lesser of two evils* sprang to mind.

Neither put him at ease.

30

MANDY LEFT THE MUSEUM AS SOON AS SHE REALIZED THE Order could just as easily get to her there as they could anywhere else in the city. A woman wearing a mask had walked right up, had an entire conversation with her, and there had been no interruptions. No witnesses at all, really.

The thought sent a shiver down her spine.

She couldn't tell if it was from fear.

Mandy didn't know how long she had before Isabella realized she was gone. She tried to stay in the present moment as she strolled along the Grand Canal, the air was nothing like when they'd been swimming—no sharp tang of the water here. Instead, each breath was a blend of ocean salt, sizzling food from nearby kitchens, and the delicate perfume of fresh flowers.

Everything seemed more vibrant now, more interesting. Had they been wrong about the Order of the Iron Serpent and La Velata Rossa this entire time? Libra had said they thought she was intelligent and capable. That they were impressed with her ability to solve any puzzle they threw at her.

Mandy played with the ring in her pocket. The one with the

serpent on it. She hadn't put it on yet, and she wasn't sure she would. She had to remember that the Order was responsible for countless lives lost. Their power reached all the way around the world. She didn't think there was anything they weren't capable of.

Children laughed nearby, playing with a ball they bounced on the sidewalk. Had she ever been that carefree? If so, she couldn't remember. She'd never regret her time with Bear and all he'd taught her, but their life had been far from easy. She'd grown up around horror and bloodshed. She had blood on her own hands. That had been in defense of someone else, sure, but she'd ended a life all the same.

What would it be like to not be afraid anymore? To walk the streets of any city and know that she had nothing to fear? If she had impressed the Order, that meant they were willing to offer her a part in the role they played, pulling strings from the shadows.

Another shiver crawled down her spine from the thrill of that thought.

Mandy used one of the footbridges to cross over the Grand Canal. Once she reached the other side, she set off in the direction of Ca' della Maschera. She hadn't realized it until now, but that had been her destination all along. She wouldn't be able to use the tunnel in broad daylight, but the masked figures had come through from another entrance. Maybe she'd be able to find it on her own. That might be another way for her to prove herself.

She could practically hear Bear's lecture about where her thoughts were headed, but maybe they'd both been wrong about the Order. He'd called her right before she'd left the museum, and while he'd offered no explanation as to why, he'd told her to keep an eye on Isabella. Maybe they'd been wrong about her too.

Mandy had been too distracted by her conversation with Libra to be annoyed that Bear was once again holding back information. He must've been distracted too because he hadn't interrogated her about where she was or what she was doing. Isabella had likely filled him in on their whereabouts, but Mandy wondered if she realized she'd left the museum yet? Maybe she could make it to the hidden palazzo and back again before anyone noticed she'd dipped out right from under Isabella's nose.

Picking up the pace, Mandy wove her way through the crowd. She kept her chin held high, her gaze sharp. She classified every person she passed, sorting them into categories just like Bear had taught her. No one stood out as a threat. No faces repeated. She kept a wary eye on the direction from which she'd come, but as far as she could tell, she didn't have a tail.

It took some guesswork, but eventually, Mandy found the street that ran over the top of Ca' della Maschera. Somewhere below her, there were chambers of ancient artifacts and walls covered in forgotten paintings. She shook her head at the thought. Even as she itched to go back down there and study those frescoes in more detail, especially now that she'd found a connection to the zodiac. Perhaps there'd been something she'd missed. Something that would solve the riddle that had been clanging around inside her brain.

Mandy stopped and looked around. What would a secret entrance to those underground tunnels look like? It wouldn't be out in the open where anyone could just wander in, but would it be inside one of these buildings? There were apartments, shops, and restaurants all around her. Did one of them have a secret door in their basement? Would they even know it was there?

As Mandy studied the names of the storefronts, looking for a clue that could point her in the right direction, she noticed someone standing in the shadow of an archway. A man almost as tall as Bear, but not quite as wide. His muscles stood out beneath his pristine suit. The shadows hid his face enough that she couldn't make out any details, except that his jaw looked sharp and sturdy.

Every alarm bell in her head went off, screaming for her to run as far away as she could.

Instead, she placed one foot in front of the other and approached him. She stopped just on the other side of the shadow, the sun wrapping her in a warm embrace. She could breathe easier here, on this side of the darkness.

Up close, she could make out more details of the man's face. It struck her, then, that he didn't wear a mask- even though her gut screamed he must be from the Order. His skin held a deep tan, and his eyes crinkled at the corners. His face looked cleanly shaven, and his short hair had been styled into something modern and masculine. A few gray hairs at his temples indicated he must be about Bear's age, if not a little older. His rich, dark brown eyes stared back at her.

She saw none of Bear's warmth and comfort in his gaze.

"Hello, Mandy."

His voice came out soft and silky, with something close to an Italian accent. Greek, perhaps? It didn't surprise her that he knew her name—not after the day she'd had—but the open air felt more dangerous than the museum had. Out here, there were no cameras overhead, no security guards watching from the corners. Just people milling about, chatting in clusters or hurrying past, none of them paying her any mind. All it would take was the right opening, and he could vanish with her before anyone even realized she was gone.

Mandy crossed her arms, trying to hide her concern with a bored look. "Which one are you then?"

The man flashed his teeth in an approximation of a smile. "They call me the Scorpion."

She stiffened and dropped her arms. It took all her willpower not to back up a step. To not run away and put as much distance between them as humanly possible.

"You killed Father Benedetto." She hated the way her voice shook.

"I did." His remained calm and steady. "And Vittorio Rossi. I'm not sure if you've heard about that one yet."

Her mouth parted slightly. "Why?"

"Did you not get my message?"

"The Scorpion comes to sever false loyalties," she repeated. "That doesn't exactly answer my question."

The Scorpion glanced around, his gaze lazy as he watched couples and families walk by. After a moment, he met Mandy's eyes again. "Vittorio Rossi served his purpose and was no longer useful to the organization. I'm just the one they send in to prune the dead ends."

Mandy leaned forward, intent on getting as many answers out of this guy as she could. "And what purpose did he serve?"

"A misdirect."

She waited for him to say more, but he remained silent. Fine. She had plenty of questions she wanted answers to. "His men told us the Vatican was searching for something in the tunnels under San Gimignano, but that's not true, is it?"

The Scorpion shook his head, another smile that didn't reach his eyes lighting up his face.

"What about Father Benedetto?" Accusation dripped from Mandy's voice. "He was a priest."

The man shrugged, a slow and languid movement. "Priests are men, just like the rest of us. Human. Flawed. Fallible."

Mandy read between the lines. "He failed to keep his mouth shut."

"He spread the kind of lies we did not endorse."

"What lies are those?"

The Scorpion shook his head. "It no longer matters. I'd rather talk about you."

Mandy fought the urge to back up again, planting her feet even firmer against the stone beneath her shoes. "What about me?"

"There are members of the Order who wish to see you and Riley Logan buried six feet under. They fear you because of your capabilities. They fear him because of his hold over you. He has your ear. You listen to him."

She scoffed. "He is my father."

"Not biologically."

Mandy stiffened. Even when he irritated her, Bear would *always* be her father. "He's the only one that matters to me. The other one was just a sperm donor."

"Be that as it may, he's played a part in who you are. A larger part than you're aware of."

With a sigh, Mandy rolled her eyes in that exaggerated way that always got a growl from Bear. "I've got to say, Libra did a much better job than you're doing right now. She told me how impressive I am. Even gave me a present. All you've done is insult my father and spew cryptic bullshit. I'm over it."

Mandy made to leave, knowing the risk she took by turning her back on this man, but his next words stopped her dead in her tracks.

"Your biological father believed in our cause. Riley Logan may have been the one to mold you into the young woman you are today, but he's not the one who placed the clay on the wheel."

Mandy turned back to the man, squinting against the sun to get a better read on his face. "You knew him? My biological father?"

"I knew of him. He was one of us. If he had lived, he would have brought you here to learn the inner workings of the Order. He would have believed you to be the future of our organization."

Mandy's voice came out small as she said, "I'm just a kid."

"I was your age when I took a life for the first time. Children may lack the experience of adults, but they are no less capable of achieving whatever they put their mind to."

For the first time since she'd approached him, the Scorpion moved. He stepped out from under the shadow of the arch and into the sunlight. Mandy remained frozen.

"The man you call Bear is stuck. He protects the past. *Your* past. He's afraid of what the future brings, and how it might rip you away from him. But you were born to change the future, Mandy. Logan will only hold you back. We can set you free."

This would normally be the part where Mandy found something witty to say. A quip that disarmed her opponent. Made them feel off-kilter.

But her tongue lay heavy in her mouth. Hadn't she been thinking the same thing earlier that morning? Bear had dismissed the idea that all this had been meant for her, and here she was, being told she'd been right. She knew Bear loved her and only wanted to protect her, but at what point would he start letting her stand on her own two feet?

The Scorpion turned his back to her, walking away.

"Just something to think about," he called over his shoulder.

Even after he was gone, the shadow of his presence lingered, prickling the back of her neck.

31

BEAR WALKED THE STREETS OF VENICE TO PROCESS ALL THE new information he'd gotten over the last couple of hours. Navigating the crowds should've been enough of a distraction to let his mind work through everything in the background, but he kept coming back to the same questions.

What did Bellevue know about Isabella?

Was the Red Veil only a small contingent of the Order of the Iron Serpent?

And what of the members of the Order who opposed La Velata Rossa?

Would they be forced to work with the Order to stop the greater of the two evils?

A man bumped into Bear's shoulder as he passed by on the sidewalk. Bear's hands curled into fists, ready for a fight, but the man just apologized in Italian and kept walking. He'd been on the phone, distracted.

Bear stepped to the side, out of the flow of traffic. He unclenched his fists and took several deep breaths. He didn't dare close his eyes as he tried to ground himself, but he took a moment to focus on the warmth from the sun on his shoulders. To smell the ocean breeze on the air. To hear a laughing child as his mother played peek-a-boo with him. To feel the brick beneath his fingers as he leaned back against the building behind him.

People in suits or skirts emerged from restaurants. Parents held onto their children, tugging them away from the stray cats begging for food. Tourists consulted their books, then stopped to point up at the architecture.

It all looked so normal. So *ordinary*. Bear had grown accustomed to knowing more information about the dangers of the world than the general public, but these people had no idea of the secrets buried beneath the city. The weight of that knowledge pressed down, each second threatening to drag him through the stone beneath his feet and into the dark.

The need to find Mandy slammed into him, sharp and unshakable. To pull to protect her. To know beyond a doubt that she was safe. Pushing off the side of the building, Bear headed back in the direction he'd come from. La Gallerie dell'Academia wasn't far from where he'd ended up. Neither Isabella nor Mandy had told him they'd left yet. Maybe he'd get to check out the museum for himself as he searched for them. It might be enough to distract him for a few more minutes.

As Bear crossed the Ponte dell'Academia and made it to the other side of the river, the crowd in front of him shifted and a wild mess of copper hair caught his attention. The girl appeared to be about Mandy's height. Same build. Same walk. And that backpack—

Bear's steps faltered before he picked up his pace. Several people stood between him and her, and he closed the distance. Ahead, he saw Isabella standing outside the museum, clutching her phone and pacing. When she looked up, her eyes landed on the girl, and her shoulders sagged in relief. Then her gaze shifted to Bear, and she froze.

The girl noticed her reaction and turned. Familiar eyes met his, wide and panicked. Betrayal turned to anger, laced with fear. He hadn't wanted to admit it was Mandy, that she'd been reckless enough to leave the museum and Isabella's side.

Bear pointed to a spot away from the crowd, somewhere they could have a private conversation. Without a word, both Mandy and Isabella made their way down the street to the alcove Bear had indicated. It stood between a building and a small group of trees. The trees provided enough shade and privacy for them to have a sorely needed discussion.

"Dad—"

"Logan—"

Bear held up his hand. He looked away as he dropped it, pretending to take in their surroundings. They needed to hear what he had to say. But he needed a moment to get his anger in check. Isabella's gaze held his, unwavering, with the faintest downturn at the corners of her mouth. A silent concession that she understood and regretted what had just happened, even if she wouldn't take it back. "I trusted you to keep an eye on her. You, more than any of us, know how dangerous it is for her to be on her own right now."

"That's what I'm trying to tell you, Dad—"

Bear shook his head once. "Enough, Mandy. I'll deal with you in a minute. Right now, Isabella is the one who needs to do the talking."

Mandy snapped her mouth shut and stared down at her feet, where she scuffed the stone with the tip of her shoe. Bear's stomach twisted at having to talk to her like this, but one of these days, her reckless behavior would outweigh her ability to get out of any scrape by the skin of her teeth. And he had no interest in seeing that happen.

"We went inside the museum together," Isabella said, drawing Bear's attention back to her. "I thought she could use a little time on her own. We made a deal to meet inside the entrance after a couple of hours." She scowled down at Mandy. "A deal she clearly didn't follow through on."

"You never should have let her out of your sight to begin with." Bear took a step closer, using every bit of his height to make the woman feel small. "I trusted you with my daughter, Isabella. Why didn't you stay with her? What were you doing while she was off wandering on her own?"

"Nothing." Isabella's brows furrowed as she searched Bear's face. "I stayed in the museum. I only came out a few minutes ago to see if maybe she'd gone outside to get some fresh air."

Bear was tired of beating around the bush. She wouldn't admit her wrongdoings unless he confronted her directly. He'd mistakenly forgotten she'd spent so long pretending to be someone she wasn't.

"I ran into one of your friends earlier today. René Bellevue." Bear watched Isabella closely. Beside him, Mandy looked up with a gasp. "He shared some interesting information with me."

Isabella's eyes widened for a fraction of a second before returning to their normal size. She ran a hand through her hair, then wrapped her arms around her waist like she was trying to hold herself together. "It's not what it looks like."

"Go ahead," Bear ground out. "Tell me you're not working with him."

"I never wanted to lie to you." Isabella glanced at Mandy before returning her gaze to Bear. "Either of you. I'm not working with Bellevue. I'm using him."

Bear wanted to believe that, but Isabella had proven to be a master of lies. "Explain."

With a sigh, Isabella leaned back against the trunk of the nearest tree. She watched a family walk by, the parents laughing at the children as they danced in the street and sang a song in German. Isabella only spoke when they were out of earshot.

"I found out most of this information later, when my superiors told me about the Order and explained my real mission. Bellevue was also in San Gimignano looking for the puzzle box. We got to it first, and you disappeared before he could get it from you. But he managed to find a second one. Maya and I caught up to him soon after. Tried to convince him to work with us."

Bear snorted. "I'm sure that went over well."

The corner of Isabella's mouth turned up, but her eyes remained sad and wary. "We offered him protection and reduced sentencing if he handed over the puzzle box. He was about to agree, I swear it, but then Maya was shot. She died, right there in front of me. And Bellevue ran." She let out a sigh as she looked at the ground. "How could we protect him if we couldn't even protect ourselves? I barely got out of there alive."

Bear thought back to the gunshot wound she'd shown them. That part of the story lined up, but he'd learned that the best liars always used part of the truth. "Then what happened?"

"I followed Bellevue here." She spread her arms out, then let them drop to her side. "To Venice. This was before your phone call. I tried to steal the puzzle box from him. We fought. It broke. Everything inside turned to dust. There was no saving it."

A gentle breeze rustled the leaves overhead. Bear watched people come and go, trying to match up the pieces of her story to see if they fit together before he said, "Bellevue seemed desperate. He wouldn't have approached me if he wasn't. If you broke the box, then he's missing the riddle. And we're missing the dagger."

"I haven't spoken to him since I met up with you." Isabella's eyes pleaded with Bear. "After the box broke, he was furious. I barely got away."

"The riddle is specific to the mural," Mandy said, her voice quiet. "That means he must have access to it. Giulia never mentioned showing it to someone else."

Bear studied Isabella. "Had you seen it before that day we took you there?"

The woman shook her head. She no longer had her arms wrapped around her body. Instead, they were crossed over her chest, like armor. "No. I didn't know anything about the mural until you mentioned it. He must've found it on his own. Or someone reached out to him."

"Giulia?" Mandy asked. "Or someone else?"

Neither Bear nor Isabella responded, but the old woman was the least of their worries right now.

"You said the puzzle box broke open and the insides turned to dust," Bear said. When Isabella nodded, he continued. "Do you know what's inside the main compartment?"

Isabella chewed her lip before she answered. "I didn't get a good look at it, but if I had to take a guess, I'd say it was made of glass. Maybe porcelain or fine china."

"Told you busting open the puzzle box would've been a bad idea," Mandy muttered.

Bear ignored her. "What else do you know?"

"My superiors told me there was an artifact inside. Something that could bring down La Velata Rossa once and for all."

"What if—" Mandy stopped, looking up at Bear before she looked away again. "What if they're not the bad guys? What if they want to help us? Help...me?"

Bear read between the lines.

"Mandy," he said, forcing his voice to remain neutral. "Who have you been talking to?"

32

Mandy's body locked up. Bear used his Dad Voice, and it took everything inside of her not to make herself smaller. She wasn't afraid he'd yell at her. It would be way worse than that—he'd look at her like she'd disappointed him. Her chest heaved at the thought.

She clasped her hands in front of her to keep from fidgeting. She struggled to hold eye contact with him, so she stared at his left ear, hoping he wouldn't notice she couldn't meet his gaze. Going off on her own after talking with Libra had seemed like such a powerful move to make. She wanted everyone to see she wasn't afraid.

Now, the doubt crept in. Especially when Bear looked at her so expectantly, his eyebrows raised.

Squaring her shoulders, she tilted her chin up. "It didn't matter that I was in a public place. They found me anyway. Libra came right up to me in one of the gallery halls. There was a security guard keeping everyone else out. Maybe she works there. Or made a big donation to get that kind of access."

Bear shook his head. "Libra?"

"She wore a red mask with this bit of cloth over her eyes. Libra is the astrological sign for balance and justice. In the painting at Ca' della Maschera, there was a woman with a cloth over her eyes holding a pair of scales."

"Lady Justice," Isabella muttered. Then, louder, "So, a member of the Red Veil just walked right up to you in public wearing a mask?"

Mandy shrugged. She'd wondered the same thing. "Seems like it."

Bear pinched the bridge of his nose. "What did she say to you?"

The ring grew heavier like an anchor in Mandy's pocket. She still hadn't put it on. And for some reason, she didn't want to tell her dad about it. He'd probably take it away. She didn't like it as much as her other ring, but she'd felt special when the woman had given it to her. Like someone had seen the real her. Like she had a purpose.

"She said I was intelligent." Mandy debated how much she wanted to share. Libra hadn't exactly said the nicest things about Bear. "Said I had a lot of potential. She told me I was always meant to decode the mural."

Bear let out a world-weary sigh. "Of course she would say that."

Anger reared its ugly head inside of Mandy. Fire crawled along her skin. Her guts churned with acid. "Why is it so hard for you to believe that I'm meant for something special?"

"I've always known you were special, Mandy. That you'd do great things." Bear's gaze lingered on her a moment too long, his jaw tight, the corners of his mouth softening just enough to betray the thought he wasn't saying. "But this isn't it. They're just saying what you want to hear." He crossed his arms over his broad chest. "And after she'd proven she could get to you in public, you walked off on your own? You've been reckless before, Mandy, but that was—"

Bear looked down, his head shaking, But Mandy knew what he'd been about to say.

"Go on," she goaded him. "Finish it. Say that I'm stupid."

Bear dropped his arms and shifted his weight from one foot to the other. "It was a stupid mistake, but I didn't say *you* were stupid."

"Is there really a difference?" Mandy's fury was fueled by the tears she couldn't keep from her eyes.

"Yes." Bear's answer left no room for argument. "I don't think you're stupid. The opposite, actually, which is why I'm so frustrated that you keep doing this. It's too dangerous—"

"That's what I keep trying to tell you!" Mandy stomped her foot, acting every bit like a child throwing a temper tantrum but unable to stop herself. "They don't want to hurt me. When I left, I ran into another member of the Red Veil. He wasn't even wearing a mask. I think that was his way of offering an olive branch. He trusted me with what he looks like."

"Or he just knows he's untouchable," Isabella said.

Mandy shot her a look but held her tongue.

"Who was it?" Bear asked.

Mandy's mouth went dry. She'd expected this question , but she'd put off thinking about it. About whether she would tell Bear the truth or not. The thought of lying to him left a sour taste in her mouth, but she knew what kind of reaction he'd have if she shared the truth. If only he would *listen* to her.

"It was the Scorpion." The words rushed out of Mandy's mouth. "But he didn't want to hurt me. I swear. I think he was trying to protect me from the others."

Bear didn't even react. He didn't yell. He didn't draw any attention to them. In fact, he looked calm. But Mandy knew him well enough that she could see the fire in his eyes. She thought she'd find fury in those flames. But what shined through concerned her even more.

Fear.

Bear turned his back to her. "We're leaving."

"What? No!" Mandy lunged forward and grabbed his arm. He let her spin him back around. "Dad, please listen to me. He knew my biological father."

Bear froze under her touch. She dropped his arm like it had turned to ice. He spoke again, his voice barely a whisper.

"What?"

Mandy took a deep breath, steeling herself for this conversation. She hadn't had time to make sense of what she'd learned, and she wanted to know what Bear thought about it all. If only he could be reasonable.

"He admitted to killing Father Benedetto." Mandy needed to work her way up to the other conversation. "He also said he killed Rossi."

Bear looked to Isabella. "Rossi's dead?"

"We knew he went missing, but this is the first I've heard of it." She held her hands out to the side. "But I'm not exactly in the loop anymore."

"He said Rossi was a misdirect. All that stuff about the Vatican was a lie."

"Why would he tell you this?" Bear asked.

"To gain my trust." Mandy didn't know if that had been the Scorpion's intention, but nothing else made sense. She didn't think he'd been trying to scare her with this information. "He said there are some people within the Order who don't want to see me decode the mural. They're afraid of me. Of my potential. They think I could be a powerful addition to the group."

"The group," Bear said, drawing the words out. "La Velata Rossa. They want you to join the Red Veil? You're just a kid."

Even though she'd used the same argument with the Scorpion, it stung to hear Bear say it out loud. "I've done and seen more than most kids my age." Tears spilled over, her frustration bubbling up as she swiped at them with the back of her hand. "He said my biological father belonged to the group. That he would've brought me in to learn about the Order when I was ready."

"They're not good people, Mandy. They've done terrible things." Bear's voice trembled slightly. "You don't know what they really want from you."

Mandy straightened, hoping she sounded confident. "They want me to become who I was always meant to be."

Bear met her eyes. The fear that had erupted in them earlier had turned to hurt. "And I'm assuming that means leaving me behind?"

Mandy didn't know what to say to that, so she said nothing at all.

33

Bear stared at Mandy as she looked anywhere but at him. The silence stretched until it became a vice around his neck. Even the sunlight filtering through the leaves wasn't enough to warm him after the chill of her words settled over him. Venice's ambient noises faded into the background until he could no longer hear them. No more ocean waves lapping at the docks at the end of the street. Gone were the squabbling birds and chittering insects. People arguing and children shrieking with laughter reached him as though he were ten feet below the surface of the water.

The anger he fought to leash had nothing to do with her words.

It came directly for him.

Mandy had always been the type of kid who'd pushed back at being told what to do. She had a chip on her shoulder that convinced her she had to pave her own way forward, proving everyone else wrong in the process. He'd done his best to encourage her to stand on her own two feet. And even though they weren't flesh and blood, Bear was her father. He had a responsibility to protect her. Whether that be from the outside world or from herself.

The urge to drag her, kicking and screaming, out of this god forsaken city overwhelmed him. Standing here, doing nothing, the vise grew tighter, squeezing the last of the oxygen from his lungs.

Mandy had always been a smart kid, but as much as she'd seen and done in her sixteen years on this planet, she still had a lot to learn. Bear could remember being that age and feeling invincible. And after everything she'd survived, he couldn't blame her for thinking that.

But he'd seen enough death and destruction to last several life-times. He'd learned that no one was invincible. They were all just biding their time, trying to stay one step ahead of everyone else. To outrun fate.

Bear searched for the right words to convince Mandy, so she could see his side. He wasn't doing this to hold her back from achieving anything. On the contrary, he wanted to keep her safe for as long as possible, so she could have that opportunity.

But before he could open his mouth to continue, Isabella stiff-ened next to him. Bear looked over at her, noticing that her eyes had locked on something just over his left shoulder. He hadn't even started to turn before a heavily accented voice pierced their little bubble.

"Well," Bellevue drawled. "This is awkward. Perhaps I came at a bad time."

Bear turned on his heel, placing himself between Bellevue and Mandy. Isabella stepped up beside him so they stood shoulder to shoulder. The Frenchman smirked and held up his hands in response, his eyes alight at their show of solidarity.

"I come in peace, friends."

"We're not friends," Bear said, tone clipped.

Bellevue dropped his hands and tucked them into the pockets of his slacks. He'd changed since Bear last saw him, forgoing his suit jacket and rolling up the sleeves on his dress shirt. The strap of a brown leather satchel hung across his chest. He looked sharp but casual. He could pass as a businessman or someone on holiday. No one would ever think he could be a world-renowned art collector and thief.

The man's smirk didn't falter, his gaze shifting to Isabella. "Are we not?"

"We're not," she said, hands fisted at her sides.

"That hurts." But Bellevue's amusement never left his eyes, even as he turned his mouth down into a frown. "But I understand. I have not been much of a team player, but I am here to change all that."

Bear took a slow step forward. "I'm not in the mood for your games, René."

"Ah, we're back to René, are we?" His smirk returned. "I am delighted."

"What do you want?" Isabella asked, stepping beside Bear again.

He may have his doubts about her motives, but she seemed just as shocked and annoyed to see Bellevue as he was. Then again, he no longer trusted his instincts as he once had, not when it came to the former intelligence agent.

"Like I said, I'm here to be a team player."

Bellevue slipped a hand out of his pocket and flipped open the flap of his satchel. As soon as he reached inside it, Bear took two more steps forward.

"Don't even—"

Bellevue held up his other hand in surrender, even as the first stayed hidden within his bag. "You have nothing to worry about from me at this time, though I doubt you will believe me." He drew out the top of the item. The silver glinted in the sunlight. "Especially once you see what I have brought."

Once Bear's brain registered the shape, he closed the distance between him and Bellevue. A pair of hands tugged on his arm. Smaller than Isabella's. He looked down to see Mandy holding onto him, but she didn't return his gaze.

"It's the dagger from the island," she whispered.

Bear looked back to Bellevue, who held the knife just long enough for Bear to understand what he had, before he slipped it back into his bag and shut the flap. He returned both hands to his pockets before he spoke again.

"The girl is correct." The Frenchman glanced around them, growing more serious with each passing second. "None of us will benefit from drawing any unwanted attention, Mr. Logan. I suggest we play nicely until this is over."

"Are you even capable of that?" Bear growled.

"Of course." Bellevue broke out into a grin that didn't reach his eyes. They remained as sharp as the blade in his satchel. "As a token of my good faith, I will tell you that the dagger has a Latin phrase etched into its blade in the most beautiful script. It reads, *The Ouroboros consumes its own.*"

A beat passed before Mandy let out a gasp behind Bear. Three sets of eyes turned on her, and she flushed under their sudden scrutiny, even as she stared down Bellevue with a fierceness that made Bear's chest swell with pride.

"I know what it means." Mandy met Bear's gaze for the first time in several minutes. Hurt still swirled in the depths of her irises, but he could also see that familiar spark of determination, too. "I know what we have to do next."

Before Bear could ask her what she meant, his phone vibrated in his pocket. Drawing it out, he looked down at the name on the screen. "It's Giulia." He hit the answer button and lifted the device to his ear. Anticipation thrummed through his veins in time with his heartbeat. "Everything okay, Signora Vasari?"

He heard nothing more than a choked sob in response.

Bear's body went rigid. "Giulia? Are you all right?"

"No." Sobs garbled her words, but he could still make some of them out. "—have them—" Her cries grew louder. "—help, please—"

"Giulia, I need you to calm down." Bear forced a calm authority into his tone. "I can't understand what you're saying."

The woman took several deep, shuddering breaths. "They have them. The Order has Luca and Antonio."

"How do you know that?" Bear asked.

"They told me—" She broke off again to gulp in more air. "They told me they had both of them."

"Did they say where?"

Another sob escaped the woman. The phone crackled with static. "No, but they said you would know where to find them."

Bear closed his eyes. His instincts told him what would come next, but Giulia's words still stole the breath from his lungs.

"They said you have to finish what you started."

34

Bear stayed at the back of the group for the entire walk to Giulia's apartment. He refused to let the Frenchman out of his sights, but he had no interest in trying to make small talk with the man.

René stayed in front, several paces ahead of the others. His satchel bounced on his hip, and he kept both hands tucked inside his pockets. To the average person, he appeared to be out for a stroll on a sunny afternoon.

Every once in a while, Bear even caught the sound of him whistling to himself.

Isabella and Mandy walked side by side, though neither of them said a word. People moved around them, stepping out of their way or walking past without any idea what they had been up to over the last several days. They were better off not knowing. Safer.

Isabella looked over her shoulder every few minutes to check on Bear. He'd give her a curt nod or raise an eyebrow in question. She'd return the gestures and turn back around. Just checking in. Making sure he remained focused.

Mandy hadn't looked back once. Her shoulders were up near her ears, and she bounced her fingertips against her thigh as she walked. Bear didn't need to see her face to know her brain worked through every possibility. She'd said she knew what they had to do next, and no one had questioned her. After all, she'd been right about everything else so far.

But they'd needed somewhere safe to go while she worked her magic. Bear had suggested Isabella's apartment, but the woman had shot that down. One look in Bellevue's direction explained why. The Frenchman had only offered a lazy shrug in return.

Plenty of questions swirled around Bear's brain about the relationship between those two, but the tension rolling off Isabella indicated she had no love for the Frenchman. For the time being, at least, they'd all have to set their differences aside. Bellevue needed Bear and Mandy, and Bear took comfort in keeping the other two in sight, where he could account for every move.

He kept his gaze sharp as they approached Giulia's apartment. Bellevue hadn't needed directions—which didn't surprise Bear. But he'd save his questions until he had everyone in the same room.

They'd only just walked around the bottom of the steps when the front door to Giulia's apartment opened. The old woman stepped onto the landing and froze, looking from the Frenchman to Bear and back again. Her skin paled before she gestured for them to follow her inside.

Once they'd all filed in, Bear checked each room before returning to the living room. Everything looked the same as it had the last time they'd been there, with the exception of Giulia herself. Though there were no tears flowing from her eyes, they were red-rimmed and puffy. She couldn't quite meet Bear's gaze.

Bellevue clapped his hands together, looking like he'd just walked into a candy shop. "Well, isn't this delightful. It's wonderful to see you again Signora Vasari." He exaggerated his frown, even as the light in his eyes danced with mirth. "Though I wish it could be under better circumstances."

Giulia scowled at him before finally turning to Bear, choosing to stare at his left shoulder instead of meeting his eyes. "Thank you for coming." She hesitated, taking a slow, deep breath, then finally looked him in the eye. "I suppose I have some questions to answer."

Bear crossed his arms over his chest and leaned back against the wall, keeping everyone in sight. "You could say that. Since we're in a bit of a time crunch, I'll start with the basics." He jutted his chin in Bellevue's direction. "How long have you been working with him?"

"I met him the day before I met you and your daughter. I made the same request of him as I did of you—to find my Antonio." The scowl returned to her face as she looked at Bellevue. "I did not trust him to do what he'd promised, and so I returned to the basilica looking for someone else's help."

"Well, that's just rude." Bellevue stuck his nose in the air, then broke out into a grin.

Bear ignored the Frenchman. He had enough experience with people like him. Not responding to his dramatics would aggravate the guy. "How did the Order reach out to you to tell you about Luca and Antonio?"

"A phone call from a restricted number. I answered it, thinking perhaps it was Luca calling from a new number. But it was the voice of a strange man instead. He told me to pass along his message."

"Did he provide proof that they were still alive?" Bear asked.

Giulia opened her mouth to answer, but nothing came out. Then she buried her face in her hands and wept.

"Well, that answers that," Bellevue said, picking a piece of lint off the strap of his bag.

Isabella turned to Bear, raising her brows.

Bear sighed, "What choice do we have?"

The familiar tug of grabbing Mandy and running returned, pulling at his gut Responsibility for Guilia and Luca weighed on him. He'd made a promise to the old woman, and Luca had only gotten wrapped up in this mess because he'd helped them. Bear had been too late to save Father Benedetto, but maybe he could stop the other two men from suffering the same fate.

"I'm so glad we're all on the same page," Bellevue drawled. When Bear scowled at him, he merely smiled wider. The grin sharpened into something predatory when he turned his gaze on Mandy. "Now, you said you knew what the next step was? Do tell."

Mandy looked to Bear, trepidation and excitement at war on her face. Bear felt the same way. He'd been itching for a fight—mostly with the Frenchman—but they had to play this right. The Order wanted them to finish the puzzle, which meant they had something planned for them at the end of this wild goose chase. They had to ensure they were ready for whatever it was.

Bear nodded at his daughter. "Go ahead."

"I'll need the puzzle box," she said.

Bear swung his pack over his shoulder and unzipped the main pouch. He dug around until his hand found the wooden contraption, then drew it out and placed it in Mandy's open palm. He didn't miss the spark in Bellevue's eyes as the man fixed his gaze on the box.

Mandy knelt on the floor between Bear and Isabella, placing the puzzle box in front of her. She ran the tips of her fingers over the snake design on top, stopping once she reached its mouth. Then she retrieved something small from her pocket.

"*The Ouroboros consumes its own.*" She looked up at Bellevue. "That's what's on the dagger, right?"

Bellevue nodded. "What's that in your hand?"

"A ring." Mandy flushed, avoiding Bear's eyes. "Libra gave it to me in the museum. I thought it was just a snake ring, a way to offer me a spot within the Order. But I think it might actually be the last piece of the puzzle. Maybe I should have already found it, and she gave me a second chance by handing it over. Or maybe this was their insurance policy to prevent someone unworthy from getting this far."

Mandy gave Bellevue a pointed look as she finished her thought. For the first time, the Frenchman allowed his fury to spread from his eyes to his face. His lip lifted in a snarl as he spoke.

"So, I was never going to solve this on my own," he spat.

"Guess not," Mandy said, one eyebrow lifted.

Bear fought back a smirk. It wasn't easy to stare down a man like Bellevue. His kid had guts.

Mandy returned her focus to the puzzle box. Gripping the ring by the top, she inserted it into the snake's mouth. No one breathed, the room silent enough that Bear could hear the faint click. The ring disappeared and the top of the box shifted. Bear's angle allowed him to see that the pieces no longer aligned.

With shaking hands, Mandy pushed aside the lid of the box. It swung out, attached by a hidden mechanism. Everyone leaned in, peering down at the item they'd all been chasing for so long. Over the last week or so, Bear had run through hundreds of ideas as to what could be inside. Somehow, it had never occurred to him that it would be a tiny mask.

Mandy lifted the small item from where it'd been placed inside the box. After a moment, she spoke, her voice nothing more than a whisper. "It's light. Made of porcelain, I think. The eye pieces are glass."

Bear crouched down beside her to get a better look. It was red, like so many of the other masks they'd seen recently, but this one had been crafted small enough that it would only cover someone's eyes. If they'd smashed the box like he'd wanted to on so many occasions, it would've shattered into a million pieces.

Mandy caught his eyes, hers dancing with silent laughter. He had no doubt her thoughts mirrored his own. He resisted the urge not to peer up at Bellevue and rub it in his face that his kid had done what he couldn't.

"That's it?" the man said. "A mask? That's what all of this was about?"

"What were you expecting?" Isabella asked, as she pinned him with her glare. "A solid gold key to the city?"

"At the very least," Bellevue retorted.

Mandy spoke slowly, as she recited, "To wear a mask is to reveal one's true self." She shifted the item in her hands, letting the clear glass pieces of the eyes catch the light. "Do you see that?"

Bear nodded. The sheen on the glass had a rainbow tint to it, like it had some sort of coating on it.

"See what?" Giulia asked. "Do you know what it means?"

Mandy grinned up at the group, her smile stretching from ear to ear.

"It means the mural has one more secret to share with us."

35

MANDY PUSHED HERSELF TO HER FEET AND SPRINTED FOR THE back room, too excited to see the mural to care about anything else. She realized once she stood in front of the painting that she'd left the puzzle box behind, along with everyone else.

Mandy took a moment to stare at the mural and soak it all in before they joined her. Would this be the last time she laid eyes on it? Whatever the mask revealed could change everything she thought she knew about the painting and the messages she'd received so far.

The girl on the right side of the wall stared back at her, eyes bright and curious. The figure that looked like Bear painted just to her left, moving and spinning and holding the dagger aloft. She'd only seen the hilt of the knife when Bellevue had partially pulled it from his bag, but she'd recognized it as the one in the painting. Light shone off the silver handle in the painting just like it had when he'd exposed it to the bright Venetian sunlight.

So many of the other figures had looked mysterious and other-worldly when she'd first laid eyes on them. Now she could place them among the adventures she'd had, like the lion that had led them to that first church or the weasel-like creature that had taught her about Festa della Sensa. The bird mask remained just as imposing now that she knew it represented the plague doctor. It would be a long time before she forgot the creeping fog and broken buildings on the island of Poveglia.

Though not all of the symbols written across the face of the painting were entirely clear to her, knowing what some of them meant made her feel like she was tapped into the secrets of the universe. But where her spine tingled with excitement at solving the riddle, an inescapable weight had taken its place.

Mandy had yet to be convinced that the Order of the Iron Serpent or La Velata Rossa were as menacing as they'd first thought, but she'd never let her guard down. The Scorpion had killed Father Benedetto and Vittorio Rossi, and he'd shown no remorse. That didn't mean every member of the group knew about or had sanctioned those deaths, but would they have been able to oppose him if they had disagreed? Were a majority of the members like the Scorpion, cold and calculating, or like Libra, warm and full of praise for her potential?

The others filed into the room, spreading out around her. Isabella and Giulia stood to her left, while Bear put himself between her and Bellevue on her right. The old woman reached over and opened the blinds to the window closest to the mural. Sunlight poured in, highlighting the dust motes that hung in the air like falling ash.

"Well?" Bellevue asked, haughtier than ever now that he knew La Velata Rossa had given her the ring instead of him. "What do you see when you look through the mask?"

She wasn't sure why she did it, but Mandy looked to Bear. He'd just finished closing his bag after placing the puzzle box back inside when he met her gaze. She recognized his trademark warmth, hidden behind a new emotion she almost missed. Wariness. With a nod, he gave her all the encouragement she needed to take the next step forward.

With a deep, fortifying breath, Mandy brought the mask up to her face. She used both hands to hold it in place, feeling the smooth porcelain against her cheeks and forehead. The glass cooled her flushed skin, and she couldn't help the little shudder that coursed through her body.

The eye pieces were smaller than the lenses on a pair of glasses, and they had no magnifying effect. When she looked through them, she could see rainbow highlights dancing off portions of the painting, shimmering in the late afternoon sun as it filtered through the window. She gasped and lowered the mask, just to make sure she hadn't imagined it.

But no, the mural once again looked like it always had.

"What do you see?" Isabella asked, her voice low and reverent.

Aware that four people waited with bated breath for the answer to that question, Mandy once again raised the mask to her face and peered through the glass. Whatever coated them caused certain parts of the mural to pop out from the background, highlighting them in shimmering colors that took her breath away. She knew it was nothing more than science—light interacting with certain chemicals— but part of her thought it felt a little bit like magic, too.

Mandy's gaze skittered over the painting, trying to make sense of the shapes in the light. She took in every inch of the art in front of her. Then she took one step back. And another. Until she could see the whole mural and the picture superimposed on top of it.

"The mask is causing another design to pop out from the painting." Her words shook with excitement. "There's something written along the top and bottom." If she hadn't been so hyper-focused on trying to make sense of what she saw, she would've rolled her eyes. "Why does everything have to be in Latin?"

"You can't read it?" Bellevue asked. "Honestly, what are they teaching kids these days?"

"Languages that aren't dead." Bear shot back.

Mandy ignored them, trying to follow the swirl of colors between the two phrases. It wound its way along the bottom and up toward the girl on the right, but then it disappeared, broken up by her figure. It emerged from the side of her head and along the top of the mural, only to disappear again behind the figures that looked like Bear. Aside from that, it remained continuous as it wove its way around the others, curving and swooping in gentle meanders.

She could only make out the shape with any sort of certainty because she'd seen it so many times over the last few days

"It's a map of Venice. I can see the Grand Canal cutting through the center." She drew in a slow, steady breath. "But it's all one continuous loop. The line looks thicker than it would be on a traditional map."

She stepped forward now, never taking her eyes off the work of art in front of her. As she drew nearer, she saw thin triangular shapes overlap the larger line. Almost like scales.

"It's a snake." She followed the line until it flared out. "It's eating its own tail."

"The Ouroboros," Bellevue supplied.

"I think that's where we need to go," Mandy said. "It's right where—"

It hit her then. It made so much sense, and yet she'd never have thought of it on her own.

"What?" Bear asked, stepping up beside her. "Where does it point to?"

Mandy lowered the mask from her face to look up at him.

"Back to where we started, of course. The Santa Maria Della Salute Basilica."

36

Bear groaned at Mandy's answer. Going back to the Santa Maria della Salute Basilica was like realizing the key had been in his pocket all along after turning over every stone looking for it. "You're sure?" he asked her.

"Positive." She handed him the mask. "Look for yourself."

Bear took the delicate object in his hands, careful not to accidentally crush it between his fingers. He brought it up to his face and peered through the glass pieces. Colors jumped out at him, swirling along the painting in a jumble of lines. As he looked closer, he could see what Mandy meant by the snake eating its own tail. And, sure enough—

"Yeah, that's where the basilica is."

"What, they're being held in a church?" Isabella asked.

"Or underneath it," Bellevue supplied. He'd finally dropped his attitude. "But it sits right on the water."

"There are many hidden tunnels and chambers beneath the city of Venice," Giulia supplied. "Perhaps you start at Santa Maria, but it will lead you elsewhere."

Bellevue's voice turned wry. "You make it sound like you're not coming with us to rescue your precious husband and friend."

"I am an old woman," Giulia said, eyes turning to slits. "What would you have me do?"

Bellevue sighed, dramatics back in full effect. "I just love being the sacrificial lamb."

"Don't pretend like you're doing this out of the goodness of your own heart," Isabella snapped.

The Frenchman scoffed. "And you are?"

"Enough." Mandy's tone had them both shutting their mouths. "Dad, do you know what those words say?"

Bear hadn't taken his eyes off the map while the others bickered, but now he searched the rest of the painting for the Latin phrase Mandy had mentioned earlier. "Non est ad astra mollis e terris via."

The room quieted. Isabella spoke first. "There is no easy way from the earth to the stars."

Mandy sighed. "What does *that* mean?"

"It means," Bellevue said, "that if you want immortality, you have to work for it."

Mandy let out a groan. "Maybe it's just me, but I think we've been working hard enough."

Bear sensed another wave of bickering on the horizon. He returned his attention to the painting, looking at the spots where the figures broke up the shimmering light along the right side of the painting. He took a step closer. Whoever had painted the invisible map had done it last, so it would sit on top of everything else. But the girl's face—the one that looked so much like Mandy—obscured part of the line.

As much as he didn't want to, he looked to the figures that ran along the top. The ones that Mandy said looked like him. The man held the dagger aloft, pointed at the girl's chest. Did he mean to save her or stop her? He hated that he couldn't answer that question in any definitive way.

Bear lowered the mask from his face. It took everything inside him not to turn toward Giulia when he spoke. "This painting has been altered."

"What?" Isabella asked. "How do you know?"

Mandy stared at the mural, right where the shimmering lines cut off. "I knew something looked off."

"Why?" Bear turned to Giulia then. "Why did you do it?"

"I-I didn't." She took a step back toward the door. Isabella moved to block her. "I swear."

"Then who did?" The answer was so obvious, Bear almost laughed. "Your husband."

Giulia hesitated. Then she broke. "They threatened him. He had to do it. And once he was finished, they took him anyway."

Fury caused Bear's hands to curl into fists. He had to force himself to keep from crushing the mask to dust. "Why? So they could rope Mandy into all of this?"

Mandy looked from Bear to Giulia and back again. "What are you saying? That they used the mural to manipulate us?" She looked at the painting beside her, staring up into the face that mirrored her own. "It was never meant to be me?"

"I cannot pretend to understand why the Order does anything." Giulia's voice came out strained. "All I know is that they have Antonio and Luca."

"She's right," Bellevue said. "This changes nothing."

"Easy for you to say," Bear snapped, the vise closing in around his neck again. "It's not your kid."

"I can't believe I'm saying this," Isabella started, "but I agree with Bellevue. We came here to find out where they're keeping Antonio and Luca. We knew there was a possibility it was a trap from the beginning. And now we know they've been interested in Mandy and her connection to the Order from the beginning. Learning that Antonio altered the painting changes none of that."

"What connection?" Bellevue asked.

No one answered him.

"Dad." Her quiet word had him turning his head to meet her

gaze, finding her eyes glassy. "It doesn't matter. We can't just leave Antonio and Luca there. We have to go after them."

Bear's mouth pressed into a hard line, but he knew she was right.

"Fine. But we're making a pitstop along the way."

"Where?" she asked.

He turned to Isabella. "Any of your contacts in town have access to some weapons?"

Isabella gave him a feverish grin before responding.

"I'll make some calls."

37

In under an hour, Isabella had secured a handgun and a pair of knives for her and Bear. Mandy also had a few blades strapped to her, but she hadn't argued with Bear when he'd told her she didn't need to have a gun of her own. She'd had some practice, but nowhere near enough to be an expert marksman. Besides, if Giulia had been right about the tunnels beneath Venice, they'd likely be in close quarters while searching for Luca and Antonio. It'd be better for everyone if Mandy stuck with what she knew.

Bellevue hadn't appreciated the fact that Isabella had refused to secure any weapons for him. As far as Bear was concerned, the ceremonial dagger he'd pulled from the wall on Poveglia would be more than enough. Bear also considered that his complaints might all be for show. He hadn't let anyone search his bag, and it could have held several guns.

The group remained quiet as they left Giulia behind. The old woman hadn't shed another tear over her husband and friend, but she had all but shoved them out the door as soon as their plans were set. Bear wasn't happy about the part Giulia and Antonio had played in bringing them into this mess, but on some level, he understood their desperation.

Besides, that was all in the past. Now, they needed to end this.

The sun had set below the horizon an hour ago. The temperature dropped a few degrees cooler than it had been that afternoon, but the sky remained clear. Twinkling stars broke up the inky blackness above. The crescent moon crept ever higher, bright enough to illuminate their way forward even if they hadn't had the luxury of streetlights.

By the time the basilica came into view, Bear's tension had grown to an all-time high. His back had tightened with every step, the muscles in his shoulders bunched and straining. Every flicker of movement set his teeth on edge, and he had to force himself to keep from reaching for his weapon on multiple occasions. All of his instincts screamed at him to turn around.

But what choice did they have?

They stayed off the main street, choosing instead to walk down one of the narrower roads toward the church. Bear, focused on every movement and sound that caught his attention, missed what Mandy spotted once they'd reached the crossroads closest to the basilica.

"Dad, look."

She didn't sound alarmed, but his muscles tensed more anyway. He looked at her, gauging her expression for any flickers of fear. When he found none, he followed her line of sight to the building just ahead of them on the right. It looked similar to all the others in the city with one exception—a small mask had been carved into the stone above the door. A red cloth hung from the handle.

Mandy reached for it, touching the ends with her fingertips. "It looks just like the one Libra wore when I saw her in the museum."

"Guess we're in the right place then," Bellevue said, shoving past them and grabbing the doorhandle. "What is it you Americans like to say? Ah, yes. Let's get this show on the road."

Before Bear could protest, Bellevue pushed at the door and let it swing open. All four of them hesitated, leaning toward one another to peer inside. Darkness enveloped the room, but Bear could make out a black-and-gray marble floor. There were no light fixtures. No furniture. No decorations. Just a door at the other end of the room. It had been left open.

Bellevue reached into his satchel and pulled out a flashlight. He clicked it on, and the beam illuminated a stone staircase leading down.

Mandy straightened. "Well, that's not creepy at all."

"Feel free to stay here." Bellevue didn't even look at her as he strode forward. "I'm sure you'll be perfectly fine."

The three of them exchanged a look before following him. Isabella took the lead, staying close to the Frenchman, while Mandy stayed between her and Bear. In most circumstances, he'd rather Mandy be behind him so he could shield her with his body, but in this case, the thought of someone sneaking up on them from the rear concerned him more.

Besides, he didn't mind much that Bellevue would be taking the brunt of an attack if they walked into an ambush.

As each of them reached the opening at the top of the stairs, they clicked on their own lights. Bear waited until Mandy walked a few steps ahead of him before turning back and making sure they were alone. Satisfied no one had followed them, he descended the staircase at a measured pace, taking in every detail of his surroundings.

The steps beneath his feet were made of stone, as were the walls. They'd been smoothed over with a practiced hand. No matter how much he looked, he couldn't spot any other signs that they were in the right place. But the way the hair on his arms stood on end told him they were.

When they reached the first landing, the staircase pivoted before plunging deeper beneath the building. The stone underfoot was smoother here, worn down by centuries of boots and damp air. But as Bear ran his hand along the wall for balance, the texture changed. Rough, uneven, each edge still bearing the marks of hand tools. The grit scraped against his palm, leaving a faint sting, a sharp contrast to the time-polished surface above. He wondered how long ago someone had made this passage and how much longer it would last. Dripping water echoed in the tight space, but he couldn't find its source.

No one spoke as they continued descending for another two floors. Then, when Bear wondered if it would ever end, the ground evened out. Bellevue stopped and shone his light down the narrow stone passage. Moisture collected on these stones, heightening the chill in the air that had as much to do with how deep they were underground as it did with the anticipation settling over them.

Without a word, Bellevue strode forward. Isabella followed after him. Mandy looked up at Bear and waited for him to give her a nod of approval before she did the same. Bear stood there for a moment, straining his ears for any sounds that might be out of place. Boots against stone or whispers from the other side of the wall. But only their echoing footsteps and the constant *drip, drip, drip* of water reached his ears.

Ahead, the tunnel widened until it flared out into a chamber about the size of the one they'd first arrived in at Ca' della Maschera. Only this one lacked any ornamentation and was under at least two or three inches of water. The air sat heavy and undisturbed in the chamber, made worse by the moisture. The openings to three tunnels stood on the opposite side of the room.

Bellevue sighed, shining his flashlight down at his feet. "Do you know how expensive these shoes were?"

Mandy scoffed. "No one feels sorry for you."

Bellevue shot her a withering look, then lifted his light to peer at the tunnels ahead of them. "I don't suppose that little map of yours indicated which way we were supposed to go?"

When no one answered, Isabella said, "We could split up."

Her tone made it clear she liked the idea about as much as Bear did—which was to say, not at all.

Before he could say as much, a voice rang out from behind him.

"That won't be necessary."

Bear spun on the spot, sending water sloshing in every direction.

A man in a red robe stood in the archway they'd just walked through. He wore no mask, but he knew from Mandy's description that this had to be none other than the Scorpion.

Bear reached for his gun at the same time Isabella did. The Scorpion held up a single finger and clicked his tongue. They had no choice but to release their holds on their weapons.

In a matter of seconds, more than a dozen men filed in after him, fanning out and surrounding them. Had he been too distracted to hear them coming down the stairs, or had they been able to remain silent as they descended the stone steps? It didn't much matter either way.

"Come." The Scorpion's robe billowed out behind him as he strode forward through the water. "I will show you the way."

38

Bear's instincts had been screaming at him before entering the building, and as usual, they'd been correct.

He, Mandy, Bellevue, and Isabella stood in a large round chamber carved from stone. In the center stood a stone table much like the one they'd seen in Ca' della Maschera. The walls here had also been painted in a similar fashion to the other chamber, though he suspected these had been done more recently. On the plus side, this room had escaped the water and had an array of torches affixed to the wall that provided some dim lighting.

They had been relieved of their possessions, including their weapons, and were surrounded by at least two or three dozen masked figures. All of them wore matching red robes, with a wide variety of animals represented amongst their hidden faces. He recognized the bull and ram masks from their last run-in with La Velata Rossa and wondered if any of them were the same men or women. Was the person who'd stabbed Isabella here? Maybe she'd be able to enact her revenge.

If they lived long enough.

The Scorpion stepped up to the center table and flung his arms wide, a grin spreading over his face. Bear wondered why he didn't have to wear a mask. Was he that confident that he'd never be caught, or did he not care? Nothing in Father Benedetto's journal had pointed to a true leader of the Red Veil, but if Bear had to guess, he'd say their leader stood right in front of them.

"Welcome, everyone." His voice held a sense of reverence as he turned on the spot, surveying the crowd around him. "I hope you will forgive me for speaking in English, but I wish for our guests to under-stand every word I utter here tonight." He lowered his arms and clasped his hands together. "It is good to see so many of you in atten-dance. Our numbers are much higher than expected. Tonight, we prove that the Order of the Iron Serpent wears the Red Veil."

A cheer went up among the masked figures. Mandy jumped, and Bear stepped closer to her. The Scorpion hadn't bound any of their hands, but Bear still stopped himself from putting his arm around her, lest it draw unwanted attention.

"Many of you know our story did not start here, in this chamber." The Scorpion gestured to the walls around them. He sounded annoyed about this little fact. "The Order of the Iron Serpent has operated from the shadows for generations. The Red Veil has existed for almost as many years. Our group carved out the halls of the House of the Mask as a meeting space to share ideas and push the envelope. We have always been about progress, no matter how diffi-cult or dangerous."

Murmuring circulated through the group. People nodded their agreement. Bear searched for someone—anyone—who looked like they weren't enraptured by this man's words, but not a single person stood out from the crowd.

"It was within those halls that the Order descended upon the Red Veil and slaughtered each and every one of them. They buried this history beneath stone and water, but the truth cannot be hidden for long. No single entity can stop the advancement of our society." The Scorpion paused long enough to look around the crowd, stop-ping on the masked faces of several individuals. Did he know who they were under their disguises? "Generations passed, and the Red Veil reformed in secret. We took the lessons learned by our forefathers and applied them to the modern age. It has been a long road, my friends, but tonight we step from the shadows and into the light."

Another cheer went up. Several people raised their fists in solidarity. A few clapped each other on the back. Mandy didn't jump this time, but he could hear her shallow breaths when the echoes dissipated. Her breathing mirrored his own.

How the hell were they going to get out of this?

The Scorpion turned toward Bear and the others. His eyes reflected the flames around them, making them dance with the fervor of a fanatic. He paid particular attention to Mandy, and it took all of Bear's willpower not to step forward and block her from his view.

"Some of you already know what we have planned tonight," the Scorpion said. "The rest of you may be wondering who our guests are and why they are here."

Another round of murmurs coursed through the crowd. With masks covering their faces, Bear couldn't tell who looked confused and who already knew about tonight's events. At least half of them were looking around, perhaps trying to piece together the same information.

"First, we have the intelligence agent." The Scorpion gestured to Isabella. "She is responsible for keeping Lucia Moretti out of our reach for so long." The man tsked, like a child stood before him who had disappointed him. "Then we have the contender, René Bellevue. A collector of history, much like ourselves."

Bellevue blanched. "Contender?"

The Scorpion's mouth twisted to the side, nostrils flaring at the interruption. "As impressive as your skills have been, you would not have solved the remainder of the puzzle if it weren't for the others."

Bellevue scoffed, then flung his hand out in Isabella's direction. "Because she destroyed my puzzle box. I was one step ahead of them the whole time."

"Be that as it may," the Scorpion said, his voice as sharp as a whip, "you failed as many tests as you passed. Not all of them were as simple as reading a map and deciphering the clues left behind for you." He turned to Mandy, his face once again gaining the fervor from earlier. "Isn't that right, Mandy?"

Mandy remained silent.

The Scorpion continued as though she'd agreed with him. "Mandy Logan, daughter of Pieter Munier, former member of the Order of the Iron Serpent and the Red Veil."

This time, the murmurers transformed into astonished whispers. Mandy froze on the spot. Even Bear sucked in a breath at the information. He'd never been able to find Mandy's father. Never even known the man's name. Mandy had never asked, and if he were being honest, he hadn't tried very hard to track him down. What would he have been able to offer her that Bear couldn't?

"As many of you know, Pieter was killed years ago. Yet his bloodline lives on in his daughter." He turned to Mandy now, looking at her like she was a purebred show dog to be put on display. "For generations, your family has belonged to the Order. Your father dedicated his life to the Red Veil. Now, it's time for you to return home."

"But," Mandy started, her voice small, "I never even knew him."

The Scorpion's smile grew impossibly wide. "That only proves that this is all meant to be. You have solved every puzzle, deciphered every code. That is no accident, Mandy. You belong with the Order, with the Red Veil. We are your true family."

Bear's heart pounded in his chest. The adrenaline pumping through his veins made his head spin. Words wouldn't form on his tongue. He could barely breathe, let alone think of all the reasons Mandy didn't belong here, with these strangers. She belonged with him. He was her father, regardless of their DNA. He'd been there for her from the moment he met her, and he'd be there for her until his dying breath.

"What do you want from me?" Mandy asked, her voice louder now. "What are you even trying to accomplish?"

The Scorpion bobbed his head in acknowledgement of her question. "The Order of the Iron Serpent has spent centuries pulling strings from the shadows. They have laid the groundwork for all that we have now, but times have changed. Our family has focused too long on staying hidden. We deserve to step into the light, to have the common people bow to us like the kings and queens we are."

Mandy's jaw dropped. She looked like she wanted to say something else, but the Scorpion turned his back on her. He held out his hand to one of the robed figures. The person stepped forward and placed a mask in his open palm. When the Scorpion turned back around, he placed it in the center of the stone table.

A simple red mask that would cover the entire face. Its gold-painted lips were bright in the firelight, as was the gold splashed around the eyes. It dripped down the cheeks like water droplets. It stood out from every other mask in the room.

"Aquarius," the Scorpion said. His voice barely more than a whisper, like he spoke just to her. Like no one else was in the room with them. "Innovative. Progressive. Future-oriented."

Mandy stared at the mask, her eyes huge as she took in the item. When she finally dragged her gaze away, her brows were furrowed.

"But I'm an Aries."

No one spoke or made a noise. The Scorpion stared at her. She stared back.

Bear tipped his head back and laughed.

He'd tried to hold it in, but the tension, the anticipation—it had become too much.

The Scorpion's gaze landed on him. The man's eyes were hard. The feverish look had been replaced with ice. He spun on the spot and motioned to a small group of people. They strode forward, to surround Bear and the others. One grabbed Bellevue while the other grabbed Isabella. Two men wrapped their hands around Bear's upper arms. All the humor drained from his face in an instant.

"Hey, what are you doing?" Mandy demanded.

"It's time."

The Scorpion gestured to someone else. They strode forward

with Bellevue's satchel. The masked figure retrieved the dagger from the bag and placed it in the Scorpion's hand. He grasped the blade and then turned to Mandy, offering her the hilt.

Mandy paled as she stared down at it. "What do you want me to do with that?"

"Non est ad astra mollis e terris via," the Scorpion recited. "There is no easy way from the earth to the stars. You must sever the last of your earthly ties. Riley Logan has only held you back from achieving your true potential. If you rid yourself of him, you will find you no longer have limits."

Mandy trembled. She looked over her shoulder at Bear, confusion and fear at war in her eyes. His heart broke as he read her expression. She'd never hurt him, he knew she wouldn't, but is this what she wanted?

To belong to a new family?

Mandy turned back to the Scorpion.

She struck out with her hand.

And knocked the knife to the ground.

She leaned toward the man standing in front of her, speaking loud enough for everyone to hear.

"Eat shit."

Bear grinned from ear to ear.

He'd never reprimand her for cursing again.

39

MANDY'S HEART HAMMERED AGAINST HER RIB CAGE. SHE forced her breathing to remain slow and steady. She never looked away from the Scorpion's gaze, not even when he looked down at where the dagger had landed between his feet. Her whole body trembled, but maybe the others would think it was from rage instead of fear.

The Scorpion sighed. His gaze met hers again. Disappointment in his eyes. He shook his head.

She laughed. His opinion didn't matter, not one bit.

Sure, she'd liked what he'd said about her, how strong and tough she was. Libra's words had been kinder, more encouraging, but she'd said the same thing that he had. The woman hid among the crowd. Mandy would bet money on that. But none of it mattered.

Did they really think she'd kill Bear?

He might not be her biological father, but he'd always be *her dad*. No matter how much they fought, no matter how many times they didn't see eye to eye, nothing would ever change the fact that he raised her. Bear had helped her become the person she was today. *He* was the reason the Red Veil was so enamored with everything she'd accomplished so far.

How could they ever think she would turn her back on him?

"I'm disappointed." The Scorpion's words were quiet. Lethal. "But I can't say I'm surprised."

Mandy crossed her arms over her chest. She hoped she looked tough. She hoped no one knew she did it because she couldn't stop her hands from shaking.

"I'd say I'm sorry to disappoint," Mandy replied, "but that would imply I care about what you think of me."

The Scorpion nodded like he'd expected her to say as much. He kept his eyes locked on hers, even as he addressed the crowd. "As many of you know, teenagers like to keep us on our toes." The crowd tittered. "But the Red Veil has made even the most stubborn person come to heel. Mandy will be no different."

"No?" She raised a single eyebrow in challenge. "What makes you think that?"

When the Scorpion smiled, it was all teeth. "Because I came prepared with the proper motivation."

He swung his foot and kicked the dagger. It skittered across the stone floor and stopped halfway between her and where Bellevue and Isabella were being held. They both stared down at the knife, concern etched all over their faces.

"Release the contender. Keep the other two out of the way."

The member holding Isabella dragged her to the other side of the circle at the same time the two men securing Bear did the same. They both put up a fight, but several others stepped forward from the crowd to ensure they didn't get away. It took four men to keep Bear back. Mandy watched as he struggled against his captors, swallowing down the bile rising in her throat.

"Go ahead," the Scorpion said. "Let him go."

Mandy turned back to the crowd and watched as the man holding Bellevue released him. The Frenchman scoffed and ran a hand down his now wrinkled shirt. When he spoke, his voice contained all the haughtiness Mandy had grown used to. In a way, it steadied her to hear it turned on someone else for a change.

"You expect me to fight a child?" Bellevue asked.

The Scorpion spread his arms wide as he took several steps backwards. "I'll make it easy on you. It's a fight to the death. The person left standing will be welcomed into the Order with open arms, no questions asked." He came to a stop as he reached the ring of masked figures surrounding them. "The only weapon allowed is that dagger. Getting to it first could mean the difference between living and dying today."

Mandy locked eyes with Bellevue. She didn't want to fight him, but she saw the second he decided to go for it. His whole body coiled tight like a spring as he prepared to lunge for the dagger. She'd never seen him fight, but there was no doubt in her mind that he could kill just as easily with or without a weapon. He was tall and lean, which meant he had good reach. She expected him to be fast, too.

But she was faster.

She dove forward. Leaving no room to second-guess herself. All those years of training had given her instincts most people didn't have, and she wasn't about to ignore them now.

As soon as her hand wrapped around the hilt of the blade, she rolled out of the way and popped back up to her feet. With Bellevue's background, he'd likely have a contingency plan if she got to the weapon first.

Sure enough, he'd already pivoted, ready to tackle her to the ground.

She rolled out of the way again, momentum carrying her into a crouch beside Bear. His captors strained to hold him, muscles taut, eyes wild. She kept her gaze fixed forward—because if she looked at him, she might lose her nerve.

Bellevue closed the distance between them. She clutched the hilt in her hand, her breathing coming easier because she could wield a knife in her sleep. If she could stay ahead of the Frenchman, she might be able to gain the upper hand. If he managed to get ahold of her, it'd all be over. He'd be too strong for her to throw off.

She saw a certainty in his eyes that he wouldn't stop until he'd won.

Mandy sprinted around the table in the center of the circle, hoping to put it between them and give herself a second to catch her breath. But Bellevue didn't let up. Whenever he lunged, it forced her to pivot away from him. Her feet hardly had the chance to touch the ground as she danced out of his reach time and time again.

After a minute or two of this complicated routine, as Bellevue started to lose momentum, Mandy realized she had another advantage. Bellevue had clearly kept in shape, but he also had quite a few years on Mandy. Even as he slowed, she didn't let her guard down.

As his steps seemed to falter, he lunged forward and made a grab for the knife.

Mandy drew her hand up and away, even as she skittered backwards.

Bellevue shouted as a spray of blood erupted from his palm. He stopped dead in his tracks as he laid his uninjured hand over the wound. A cascade of French words streamed from his mouth.

"You don't want to kill me," Bellevue said, stalking toward her.

She backed up, keeping the distance between them. "No, I don't."

"And that's why you're going to lose."

Mandy didn't bother wasting her breath on a retort. She feinted left as though she wanted to put the table between them again. When he lunged to cut her off, she sprang to the right and dragged the edge of the dagger across his left arm. He howled in pain as another river of blood poured from his skin.

The crowd around them murmured, but Mandy didn't care. She didn't think anyone would interfere with the fight, but she still kept as much distance between her and the masked figures surrounding them as possible. Bellevue might be injured, but he'd take advantage of any simple mistake she made.

Like tripping over an uneven stone.

She stumbled and, with a growl, Bellevue launched himself at her again. His hand wrapped around the wrist that held the dagger. But she didn't try to yank free of his grasp.

She simply dropped the blade.

It landed in the open palm of her other hand. With practiced efficiency, she jerked her captured arm up to expose his and dragged the blade across the inside of his wrist.

On instinct, Bellevue let go with another bellow of pain.

Instead of dancing away again, Mandy pivoted on the ball of her heel and ducked low, dragging the blade across the back of his knee. It sliced through skin and ligaments like softened butter. Her stomach churned, but a grim satisfaction coiled tight in her chest at the precision.

The Frenchman went down on one knee. He sprang back up a moment later. His arms shot out to keep him balanced.

That's when Mandy struck again.

She passed the knife back to her dominate hand and sliced into the back of Bellevue's other knee. He fell to his knees again. When he hit the stone floor, he tipped forward. His hands shot out, and he caught himself inches from landing on his face.

Crimson blood pooled beneath him.

Mandy watched as he flipped over to face her, his breaths coming in heaving gasps. Perspiration dotted his forehead, his shirt and pants now stained with blood. His gaze locked on her—sharp, unblinking, and dangerous—like a cornered predator deciding whether to strike.

Was that fear?

Mandy stood there, staring at him, with her feet planted wide. She didn't think this was another trick, but she wouldn't take the chance. The cuts to the backs of his knees were deep enough that he'd have trouble standing, never mind the amount of blood he lost with each passing second.

As they stared at each other, the rest of the room came back into focus. The crowd muttered amongst itself. The Scorpion clapped loud enough to quiet the rest of the people in the room. To her right, the mask stared back at her from the center of the stone table.

"Well done." The Scorpion kept his gaze trained on her face even as he approached Bellevue's prone form. "What a performance."

Mandy met his gaze. "I'm not going to kill him."

"Why not?" The Scorpion frowned at her. "He would kill you."

"Exactly." She stood taller. Jutted her chin out. "I don't want to be like him."

"The man you call your father has killed people." He paused for a moment. "You've killed people."

"Not like this," she said, her knuckles turning white as she clenched her fists. "Not for your entertainment."

But what the mask represented is what held her attention. The gold caught the light of the flames licking along the stone walls, each flicker breathing life into its intricate details. In another place, another time, she might have called it beautiful. Art to be admired. Here, the beauty felt wrong, like finding elegance in the curve of a predator's teeth.

The Red Veil offered her an alternative.

But it would cost too much.

Mandy reached out for the mask with her free hand. She touched the cool porcelain, bringing it closer. It really was a piece of art. She wondered how old it was.

"You can keep my destiny."

She raised the mask and threw it against the stone, watching it shatter into a million pieces. She looked the Scorpion in the eye, holding his gaze for a moment, before she spoke again.

"I don't want it."

With a sigh, the Scorpion drew one hand out from beneath the folds in his robe. Silver glinted in the firelight. Her body tensed, readying itself for another battle.

She couldn't have prepared herself for what came next.

He leaned down and dragged the blade of his own dagger across Bellevue's throat.

The Frenchman didn't even have time to react. Blood flowed from his throat. He scrabbled at it with his hands, like he could hold back the flood of crimson. Then he simply stopped moving.

"You know, Mandy," the Scorpion began. He wiped his blade off on the fabric of Bellevue's expensive shirt. One last sign of disrespect to the Frenchman. "You're not who I thought you were."

A familiar voice rang out from the other side of the chamber.

"Neither are you."

40

Bear froze as soon as he heard the voice. In the second or two it took him to place it, the room erupted with murmurs and gasps. Unfortunately for Bear, the men holding him back didn't slacken their hold. If anything, they wrenched his arms back more.

Pain coursed down his shoulders. His arms were bent at the elbows, and each time he struggled, they would pull them higher. He could feel his skin stretching around the bullet wound he'd gotten in San Gimignano.

A third man had his meaty forearm wrapped around Bear's neck. He squeezed hard enough to constrict the blood flow to Bear's brain, but not so much that he was in danger of passing out. The pain kept him sharp, even if he remained immovable. It would only take a single mistake for Bear to get the upper hand, and he wouldn't waste the opportunity if it presented itself.

A figure from across the room stepped away from the crowd. She wore a red robe like everyone else, but her mask stood out with its simplicity. She lifted it from her face and held it in one hand, staring down at it like she was disgusted to even have it touching her skin.

"Signora Vasari," the Scorpion said. His voice had lightened, but his sharp eyes never left her face. "What a surprise."

Bear watched the woman closely. She looked so different from the person he'd seen a few hours ago. The puffy, red skin around her eyes had faded, and she stood taller than he'd seen her in the past. She carried a gravitas about her that transformed her entire persona.

"I don't know why you're surprised." Giulia tore her gaze from the mask in her hand to look at the Scorpion. "This has been a long time coming."

"Ah, is this your little revenge plot for your husband? Dear, he died weeks ago. It's time to move on."

Bear forced his body not to react, but his mind reeled with the influx of information.

Mandy, who'd hadn't moved from where she stood amongst the shards of the mask she'd broken at her feet, stared at Giulia with a slackened jaw before saying, "Antonio is dead?"

The Scorpion addressed her but never tore his eyes from the old woman standing in front of him. "Oh, she didn't tell you? Has she still been playing the role of frantic wife looking for her missing husband?"

Giulia turned her attention to Mandy. Bear could have sworn he saw regret in her eyes, but her face remained stony. "Most everything I told you was true. I just didn't include that Antonio and I both belong to the Order of the Iron Serpent. He defied the Red Veil and was punished for it. He was a beautiful artist, my husband, and they made him alter the mural to draw you in. Then they slaughtered him." Her gaze flickered to the lifeless form of Bellevue in the center of the room. "It is something they're making a habit of it seems."

"You lied to us." Mandy's mouth still hung open, her brows scrunched. "You sent us here knowing we were walking into a trap. You knew Antonio was already dead." She shook her head. "What about Luca? Is he still alive?"

The Scorpion chuckled. "No, I'm afraid he also had to pay for his crimes against the Veil, just as Father Benedetto did. Perhaps his body will one day wash up on the shore." He pressed his lips together, but the corners of his mouth twitched. "Or parts of him, at least."

"You're a monster," Mandy spat.

The Scorpion shrugged. "What is more monstrous, showing your true face as I always have, or hiding behind a mask?" He gestured to Giulia. "Which one feels like more of a betrayal?"

Mandy remained quiet. Bear fought the urge to struggle against his captors to go to her. His hands started to tingle from his cutoff circulation. The muscles in his shoulders screamed at him. If he didn't change positions soon, his ability to defend himself and his daughter could cost them their lives.

"I will offer you thanks, however." The Scorpion tipped his head in Giulia's direction. "For the part you played in bringing them here."

Giulia stood taller. "Someone needed to stop you."

"And you think they can?" the Scorpion asked.

"Not just them," Giulia said. "But all those who have put their heads down for too long and lived in fear of the future you want to build."

The hands holding Bear's arms disappeared, and he would've sagged in relief if the man with his arm around his neck weren't still holding him. Beside him, the two men stepped forward, along with almost half the masked figures in attendance. Each of them removed their masks, tossing them against the wall or floor and watching them shatter.

For the first time, the man who called himself the Scorpion appeared unsure of what to do. The whole room waited with bated breath as he contemplated his next move. Meanwhile, the blood rushed back into Bear's hands even as the muscles in his shoulders continued to scream.

The Scorpion adjusted his grip on the dagger. "So, this is how it's going to be?"

Giulia held her chin high. "We will not allow you to destroy everything we've worked so hard to build."

"We'll see about that," the Scorpion snapped.

Then he charged.

Chaos erupted within the chamber. The men who'd held Bear's arms attacked the member who'd kept his grip around Bear's neck. As the man's arm fell away, Bear stumbled forward. He rolled his shoulders and wiggled his fingers, urging the blood to return to his hands even faster, and scanned the room to get a better idea of what they were up against.

His gaze first landed on Mandy, who kept the length of the stone table between her and the Scorpion even as she turned to search the room. Their eyes met, and he gave her what he hoped was a reassuring nod. He'd nearly been sick while watching Mandy fight for her life, except for the pride that swelled in his chest as he'd watched her outmaneuver a man much bigger and more experienced than she was.

Bear broke eye contact long enough to look for Isabella, who'd also been released from the grip of her captor. She'd picked up a knife from somewhere and was holding her own against two combatants. He wasn't worried about whether she'd make it out alive. Isabella had proven herself to be as much of a survivor as any of them.

Bear turned his focus back to Mandy in time to see a body crumple to the ground just beyond where she was standing. Bear shifted his gaze and saw the Scorpion standing over Giulia. She'd collapsed a foot or so from Bellevue, the same grisly wound taking her life that had taken his. Bear tried to find some remorse for the way the woman's life had ended, but she, more than any of the others, had brought him and Mandy into this mess.

Giulia might not have the same amount of blood on her hands as the Scorpion, but that didn't make her any less guilty.

In a blink, the man in question spun on his heel and searched the room. When he spotted Mandy, his lips curled into a cruel smile. Mandy caught sight of him and backed up a step—right into the waiting arms of a masked member of the Veil.

Without a weapon, Bear charged forward. He closed the space

between him and his daughter in three steps. The tingling in his hands had diminished, replaced with the pinpricks of pain as blood returned to his vessels. It hurt more when he reared back and punched the man in the face, but Bear would endure ten times the pain to ensure Mandy's safety.

The man's mask shattered, cutting ribbons into his flesh and embedding shards into his cheeks. He howled in pain and brought his hands up to cover his wounds. Rookie mistake. Bear lifted his foot and kicked him in the gut with all his strength. The man flew back into the stone table. Even above the surrounding din, Bear heard the crack and crunch of bones.

His knife went skittering across the floor. Mandy dove for it. In one fluid motion, she picked it up and tossed it to Bear. He caught it by the hilt and held it at the ready. The Scorpion watched all of this with a curious, impassive look on his face. Bear shoved Mandy behind him.

"Watch my back," Bear shouted. "Don't take any risks. Defense only. This is no time to be a hero."

"You gonna take your own advice?" she shouted back.

Bear cracked a smile. Fair point.

As masked figures battled their unmasked peers, blood flowed freely from wounds and shouts echoed around the chamber. From the corner of his eye, Bear saw that Isabella had moved closer to the center of the room to join them. Just because the unmasked members seemed to be on their side, it didn't mean the three of them would walk out of here when all was said and done.

The Scorpion approached, stealing Bear's attention once again. He moved with the grace of an experienced fighter. Bear's back might not have been against the literal wall, but he could see the disadvantage here. The last few days had taken their toll on his body and mind, and as much as he wanted to keep Mandy in his sights, he had to trust that she knew how to defend herself enough to stay alive. He just needed to focus long enough to defeat the man stalking in his direction.

"As disappointed as I am that Mandy did not sever her connection with you," the Scorpion said, "I am glad to be the one to end your life, Riley Logan. I promise to make it quick."

Bear let a wild grin cross his face.

"Now, where would the fun be in that?"

41

Adrenaline pumped through Bear's veins as the Scorpion stepped over Bellevue's dead body and crossed the space between them. Bear's hands had stopped tingling, and the dagger Mandy had tossed him sat firmly in his grip. He kept searching for the gun they'd taken from him, but he was thankful that none of the others had brought firearms or thought to take his and Isabella's.

Secret societies sure did love their ceremonial daggers. He could've laughed at the thought.

The Scorpion shrugged out of his robe, revealing a plain collared shirt and pair of slacks underneath. They were both tight enough that Bear couldn't grab the excess fabric like he would have if the man had kept on his cloak.

Trying to forget that Mandy fought at his back, Bear assessed his adversary. Small enough to be quick on his feet but large enough that there'd be power behind his blows. If Bear wanted to come out on top, he'd have to finish this quick.

The other man made the first move, lunging forward and swiping at Bear's chest. The resulting whoosh of air brushed across his face, but he dodged out of the way before the tip of the blade could graze his skin. The Scorpion laughed, delighting in their little dance.

"I thought all good parents would be willing to lay their lives on the line for their children," he taunted. "Don't you want the best for your daughter?"

He didn't bother answering. The Scorpion slashed at him again, but Bear knocked his arm away and took a shot of his own. A shallow cut appeared along the man's left shoulder, and within seconds, his shirt began to match the color of his robe.

"You should've left your robes on," Bear said. "Now all these people will see that you can bleed."

The man snarled. "Let them know that I am no different than them, and they will follow me to the ends of the earth."

Someone stumbled close to where they fought, distracting Bear for a split second. He glanced at an unmasked fighter who'd been knocked off balance by her assailant. She righted herself and jumped back into the fray.

It gave the Scorpion the opening he needed.

He stepped close and reached for Bear's wrist. The Scorpion's fingers clamped down in an iron grip, stopping Bear from using his weapon. The man then brought up his own dagger and drove it toward Bear's chest. Bear had just enough time to bring up his other arm and block the action, but the blade sliced across his skin. Within seconds, blood dripped onto the floor, even as he used his remaining strength to keep the other man from driving the knife in deeper.

The Scorpion's eyes had become wild. Bear was sure his looked the same. His arm stung, but he pushed the pain from his mind. It would pass. If he defeated the Scorpion, he had to be ready in case someone else stepped up to finish the job.

With a deep breath, Bear shoved the man to the side, letting a roar erupt from his mouth. The Scorpion stumbled into the stone table but caught himself before he fell over. Before he could fully regain his balance, Bear launched himself at the other man, sweeping his knife around and plunging it in his side once, twice, three times.

The Scorpion's eyes widened, the gleam in them unhinged—like he was savoring a private joke no one else wanted to hear. Before Bear could drive the knife in again, the other man brought his arm down and took the brunt of the blade with his forearm. It drove in deep, glancing off bone, and the Scorpion twisted the weapon out of Bear's hand. It stayed stuck in his arm. Bear hesitated at the sight of it.

That's all the Scorpion needed.

With a howl of pain-filled rage, he brought his other hand up and then down, burying his own dagger in Bear's shoulder- up to the hilt. Bear cried out in pain and staggered to the side. The Scorpion never let go of the handle, twisting it until Bear thought he'd black out from the pain.

And then something cool and smooth pressed into the hand that hung limp by his side. He wrapped his fingers around it, making sure he wouldn't drop it because of his blood-slick palm. Mandy's voice yelled at him to move, to do something. She sounded so far away, but she'd given Bear all the encouragement he needed.

The Scorpion leaned forward to make one final quip. Bear drove the dagger up between them and through the bottom of his jaw. Then, without hesitation, he pulled the knife free. Blood poured from the man's neck. He let go of the dagger sticking out of Bear's shoulder and scrabbled at his throat. Bear brought his knife up and down again one final time.

He drove it straight through the man's eye.

A sickening squelch told Bear he hit his mark.

The Scorpion stumbled backward. His face now slack.

Then he crumpled to the ground.

"Dad!" Mandy was at Bear's side before the body even hit the stone floor. "You're hurt!"

Bear grunted. "I'll be fine."

"We have to go." She tugged on his good arm. "Before there's no way out."

Bear blinked down at her, struggling to comprehend her words.

He then noticed a haze in the air that had nothing to do with his blood loss. The acrid stench of smoke finally registered in his brain.

Isabella appeared on his other side. "I got our stuff. Managed to set a fire. Open flames can be such a hazard, you know?" Her grin turned into a wince as she looked at the knife sticking out from Bear's shoulder. "What the hell happened to you?"

"Oh this?" He watched as she handed Mandy both their backpacks and slung hers over her shoulder. People still fought all around them, but some had started to slow as they noticed the chamber filling with smoke. "It's nothing. Can barely feel it."

"I'm sure." Isabella pressed her lips together but the corners of her eyes crinkled. "I hope you can make it up all those stairs because I don't know of another way out of here."

"He better," Mandy said, slinging his good arm over her shoulder. "Because I sure as hell ain't gonna carry him."

42

MANDY LIFTED HER COFFEE CUP TO HER MOUTH AND INHALED the sharp aroma wafting toward her. She and Bear sat outside a small café on a side street not far from their new hotel. The sun hung low, stretching the shadows across the cobblestones, and the city had settled into that easy, unhurried rhythm between day and night. The coffee shop bustled with life, but for some reason, it didn't bother her.

The bliss of this moment wouldn't last forever, and she wanted to soak in every possible second of it.

She took a sip of her coffee, reveling in the way it warmed her from the inside out. She sighed and set the cup back down on the table. "Is there anything better than Italian coffee?"

"I'm sure there is." Bear looked as relaxed as she felt. "But I can't think of a single one right now."

Someone bumped the back of her chair and then apologized in Italian. She smiled up at them with a shake of her head. She had yet to master the language, but she'd started picking up on individual words here and there. Maybe she'd take classes someday.

Bear tipped his head at someone behind her. "Isabella's here."

Mandy scooted to the side, closer to Bear. They hadn't seen

Isabella in three days, and Mandy wasn't sure what to expect from the other woman. They weren't friends, not after all the lies between them, but they weren't enemies either. Associates, maybe? That seemed right for Bear and Isabella's relationship, but Mandy didn't know where she fell on the scale. Young enough to still be a kid, experienced enough to know what sort of horrors hid in the dark.

Isabella walked up to the table and slid the remaining chair back. "Buongiorno."

"Hey," Mandy said, looking down at her coffee.

Bear nodded his head in greeting, lifting his own coffee cup to his mouth now.

The server arrived and took Isabella's order. When the woman left, Isabella's gaze fell on Bear's shoulder. He winced as he lowered his arm and placed his mug back on the table.

"Doing okay?" she asked.

Bear shrugged with the opposite shoulder. "More or less. Stitches are holding up. Thanks again for that."

Isabella grinned. "Seemed only fair to repay the favor."

Bear chuckled. "How's the side doing?"

"A little inflamed. I'll blame that on the dirty canal water and our other extracurricular activities." She shrugged. "But otherwise, it's good."

"Good."

A beat of silence passed between them. The server returned with Isabella's coffee and left. They took turns staring at the table, the other customers, the sky. Anywhere but at each other.

"Well," Isabella said after taking a sip of her beverage. "Thanks for meeting me. I wasn't sure you would."

Mandy hadn't been sure they would either. After the fight in the underground chamber, the three of them had holed up together for the rest of the night. Isabella had stitched up Bear's wounds, and Mandy took an hour-long shower before falling into a fitful sleep on the cot set up in the living room. They'd parted ways the next morning, planning to lay low over the next few days to see what the fallout with the Order would be like.

So far, nothing had been out of the ordinary.

"Figured it wouldn't hurt to say goodbye before we left the city," Bear replied.

Isabella bobbed her head. She wrapped her hands around her mug but didn't bring it to her lips. "When are you heading out?"

"Probably tomorrow. Maybe the next day. We're still trying to decide where we want to go next."

Mandy held up her hand and ticked the items off on her fingers. "Somewhere dry. Somewhere quiet. Somewhere with good coffee."

"Ah." Isabella grinned at her. "Then you'll be staying in Italy?"

"Doubt it," Bear said. "I think we've had our fill for the time being."

"I understand." Isabella tucked a piece of hair behind her ear. She played with the handle of her mug, not meeting their eyes. "I'm staying."

"In Italy?" Mandy asked. "Is that safe for you? Have you talked to the agencies yet?"

"Yes, in Italy," Isabella replied. "But no, I have not talked to them. I've had to think long and hard about what I want to do next, and I don't think it involves being an intelligence officer."

"Oh?" Mandy couldn't picture her doing anything else. "Then what?"

"Well." When she looked up, she made a point to meet Bear's eyes. "I've been recruited. To the Order."

Mandy exchanged a look with Bear. The muscles in her shoulders grew tight and a chill ran down her spine, despite the warm sun on her back.

Isabella put her hands up. "I know what you're thinking—"

"Is it something along the lines of *are you crazy?*" Mandy asked.

"I don't blame you for thinking that." Isabella put her hands flat on the table and took a deep breath. "It might even be true. I'm still waiting for the other shoe to drop. Maybe this is all a giant mistake."

"Then why'd you do it?" Bear asked.

"If you can't beat them, join them, right?" Isabella smiled, then stared down into her coffee mug. "A few of the remaining members approached me after the fight. Many did not make it out of that chamber alive. Most of them were La Velata Rossa. Others belonged to the Order and were there because they'd followed Giulia into the lion's den. Many have felt dissatisfaction towards the Order's ambitions for some time. They'd like to go in a new direction."

"They want to be, like, the good guys now?" Mandy asked, unable to keep the skepticism out of her voice.

"This branch of the Order does not represent the whole. There is so much more we still don't know about their power and reach. Some use it for the good of the people, and others use it for their own gain. It was never my intention to join the Order, but I can't see a better way forward. Both the AISI and AISE will want answers I can't give them. With the Order's resources, maybe I can make a difference like I've always wanted to."

"Those are some high ambitions," Bear said. "Are you sure they're on the same page?"

"There has been a massive restructuring. I can't guarantee that what I've been told is the whole truth, but I would rather bear witness to their actions myself. If I find out they're lying about trying to make up for the sins committed by La Velata Rossa, then I have enough evidence to bring them down on my own."

The table grew silent at her words. They each sipped at their coffee. Mandy wondered what the future would bring. Somewhere down the line, years from now, would she run into Isabella again? And if so, would they be friends or foes?

Bear asked the other question on Mandy's mind. "What about us?"

Isabella smiled. "The Order has agreed to leave you alone. As long as you stay out of their business, they'll stay out of yours."

"Just like that?" Bear asked, his mouth tipped up in a wry grin.

"More or less."

"What about Lucia?" Mandy asked. "She started all of this when she found the puzzle box. She's been in hiding because of the Order."

"I know how to get in contact with Lucia," Isabella reassured her. "I'll make sure she knows she's safe. It won't be easy to return to a normal life, but she's a survivor. If anyone can do it, she can."

A pang of disappointment tugged at her—she'd never meet the real Lucia Moretti. But if that was the price of knowing the girl could build a new life, it was one she'd gladly pay.

Bear lifted his coffee mug and tipped it back, draining the last of the liquid. Mandy did the same.

"You two will be okay?" Isabella asked, getting the hint that their time was coming to an end.

"Yeah." Mandy beamed up at Bear. "We're always okay."

He nudged her with his elbow. "Damn right."

"Good." Isabella reached into her pocket and drew out a piece of folded paper. She slid it across the table until it sat between the two of them. "This is for you. One last parting gift."

The breeze jostled the note. Mandy placed her hand on top of it to keep it from flying away. "What is it?"

"An address. The location of the original painting that the mural in Giulia's apartment was based on." Isabella locked eyes with Mandy. "Many years ago, the Red Veil commissioned the one that Antonio altered. The plan had always been to hide it and then reveal it when the time was right. But it was based off another painting. The Order paid for the original. It was never meant to be a twisted treasure hunt. Just a work of art created to tell a story."

"Have you seen it?" Mandy whispered.

"I have." Isabella drained the last of her coffee too, then set her cup to the side and stood. "It might not answer your lingering questions, but I think it could offer closure. For whatever that's worth."

Mandy stared down at the slip of paper trapped beneath her hand long after Isabella walked away.

Closure.

Was it possible?

She'd like to think so.

43

Bear held the door open for Mandy, letting her exit the jewelry store first. Her eyes were wide and glassy, mouth slightly open. He couldn't stop the laugh that worked its way up his throat. Her eyes had been wide as saucers for the last twenty minutes, and it only got funnier the longer it went on.

She walked a few paces, then stopped and leaned back against the brick building. He came up beside her and mirrored her posture. The crowd continued to pass by, unaware of the conversation they'd just had with the appraiser inside the store.

"Wow," Mandy muttered. "I mean—wow."

"Yeah, that about sums it up."

She looked up at him. "Are you not shocked?"

He shrugged. "Not really. It was a pretty big gemstone."

"I know, but *still*." She dug the sticky note that the man had handed them out of her pocket and looked down at it again. "Did you see how many zeroes are in this number?"

He bobbed his head up and down. "It's a lot of zeroes."

"You don't seem as impressed as I am."

Bear threw an arm around her and squeezed her to his side.

They'd gathered all the jewels from the puzzle box and the cipher wheel and brought them into the jewelry store to get them appraised, saying that they were in Venice to deal with his mother's estate. The man hadn't asked any follow-up questions. He just studied each ruby under the light and wrote down an approximation of its value. Then he tallied it all up and handed over the final number. Easy as that.

Bear had grown accustomed to having money. He'd earned plenty over the years. Neither he nor Mandy would ever want for anything. But still. It gave him peace of mind to have a little extra cushion.

"Maybe this will help pay for grad school," she murmured.

It was the first time she'd ever mentioned it to him.

"Any idea what you want to do?"

"No." Mandy slipped the paper back in her pocket and pushed off the brick wall. "But I know I'll figure it out. It doesn't seem so scary anymore, you know? I think I might be able to do anything I put my mind to."

Pride swelled in Bear's chest, numbing the dull ache of his shoulder. The sun warmed his skin, and he breathed deeply for the first time in forever.

"You *think* so?" he asked her. "Well, I *know* so. Besides, you've got time to figure it out. No rush."

He had no desire to push her out of the nest.

She smirked, knowing exactly where his thoughts had gone. "You still want to make our final pit stop before we leave?"

"Only if you do."

She nodded. "Let's do it."

Bear stepped away from the wall and into the flow of traffic with Mandy at his side. The address of the gallery Isabella had given them was just around the corner. The location had been part of the reason he'd picked this particular jeweler. He'd told Mandy they could go after they got the rubies appraised. It wouldn't be out of their way, and if she changed her mind, they could head straight for the train station.

In minutes, they stepped into the gallery's air-conditioned hall. A woman in a smart skirt and blouse greeted them. Told them to let her know if they had any questions. Bear thanked her and kept walking. He'd already spotted what they'd come to view.

It hung on a wall all by itself, surrounded by a wooden frame similar to the one Mandy had found in one of the rooms in Ca' della Maschera. If he had to take a guess, he'd say it was a little bit smaller. The paint was better preserved, too.

But most of the iconography matched the mural they'd studied.

As they stopped in front of the painting, Bear let his gaze roam over the details. There were the symbols that he knew spelled out the phrase, "To wear a mask is to reveal one's true self" in Latin. He understood the sentiment when he'd first read it back in Isabella's apartment, but now it hit him on a deeper level. People always showed their true colors under the guise of anonymity.

He could see Mandy staring up at the symbols and had a gut feeling she was thinking the same thing.

Masked figures still crowded the edges. It might just be the gallery lighting, but he swore they looked less sinister now. Less mysterious. Even the plague doctor appeared less ornery.

Or maybe he was the one that had changed.

Bear couldn't put off looking at the far side of the painting any longer. He let his gaze drift from figure to figure until it landed on the girl who stole the viewer's attention with her unwavering gaze. Her hair was now lighter than Mandy's, and this one had a splash of freckles across her nose. Even the shape of her eyes had changed. There would be no mistaking the two, but Bear could still see the same tenacity in the set of her jaw.

Even if the girl had never been meant to be Mandy, they shared the same strength. The same sense of adventure.

When Mandy had mentioned seeing Bear in the painting, he'd wanted to deny it. Back at Giulia's apartment, however, there was no arguing with the truth. His face had stared back at him from the top of the mural. His hand held aloft the dagger aimed at the girl's chest.

Seeing that dagger in Mandy's hands in the underground chamber had set his soul on edge. For the span of a single heartbeat, he'd allowed himself to consider the worst-case scenario. What if the Red Veil had gotten to Mandy and convinced her that Bear was nothing but a hinderance? What if she'd decided there was no other option but to sever her ties with him forever?

Bear never would've lifted that knife against his daughter, only in defense of her. The mural in Giulia's apartment told a story of the first scenario, but this one told the story of the second.

The figure painted along the top of the mural looked nothing like Bear, but the man's similarities to the girl were undeniable. They were father and daughter. And instead of raising the knife to plunge it through his child's chest, he raised it to shield her from the cruelties around her.

Because that's what fathers did for their daughters.

They taught them.

Protected them.

Then watched them take flight.

Mandy pressed into Bear's side. He peered down at her, not caring if she could see the tears in his eyes. Hers weren't dry either. They'd been through so much together. The world had tried to drive them apart time and time again. And still they stood there, shoulder to shoulder.

"I wonder if there's a message written in this one too," Bear said, his voice soft. "You want to use the mask and check it out?"

Mandy shifted her backpack until she could reach inside and pull out the mask they'd found inside the puzzle box. For a moment, she just held it in front of her and stared down at it like it might whisper the secrets of the universe in her ear.

When she stepped forward, he thought she'd raise it to her face and peer through the glass eyes.

Instead, she walked over to the nearest garbage can and dropped it inside.

Even from where he stood, Bear could hear the porcelain shatter.

A few heads turned in their direction, but after a few seconds, everyone went back to their own business. Mandy returned to his side, her jaw set in fierce determination. Just like the girl in the painting.

"They wanted me to follow their story," she said, squaring her shoulders. "But I'm going to write my own."

Bear hooked an arm around her and led her out of the gallery, a mixture of pride and trepidation swirling inside him. As each day passed, Mandy got closer and closer to striking out on her own. He always knew the time would come, yet he was no more prepared for it than the day he first set eyes on her.

Still, he had no doubt she'd do just fine out there in the great, wide world.

Their time wasn't up yet, and determination rooted itself deep inside of him to hold onto every remaining second.

The fact that it was limited didn't diminish it in the slightest.

It made it all the more precious.

The story continues in *Beneath the Frozen Sky*. Pre-order your copy on Amazon today!
https://a.co/d/9269bJo

THE BEAR & MANDY LOGAN SERIES

ALSO BY L.T. RYAN

Find All of L.T. Ryan's Books on Amazon Today!

Beyond Betrayal (Clarissa Abbot)

Noble Judgment

Never Cry Mercy

Deadline

End Game

Noble Ultimatum

Noble Legend

Noble Revenge

Never Look Back

Bear Logan Series

Ripple Effect

Blowback

Take Down

Deep State

Bear & Mandy Logan Series

Close to Home

Under the Surface

The Last Stop

Over the Edge

Between the Lies

Caught in the Web

The Marked Daughter

Beneath the Frozen Sky

Rachel Hatch Series

Drift

Downburst

Fever Burn

Smoke Signal

Firewalk

Whitewater

Aftershock

Whirlwind

Tsunami

Fastrope

Sidewinder

Redaction

Mirage

Faultline (Coming Soon)

Mitch Tanner Series

The Depth of Darkness

Into The Darkness

Deliver Us From Darkness

Cassie Quinn Series

Path of Bones

Whisper of Bones

Symphony of Bones

Etched in Shadow

Concealed in Shadow

Betrayed in Shadow

Born from Ashes

Return to Ashes

Risen from Ashes

Into the Light (Coming Soon)

Blake Brier Series

Unmasked

Unleashed

Uncharted

Drawpoint

Contrail

Detachment

Clear

Quarry

Dalton Savage Series

Savage Grounds

Scorched Earth

Cold Sky

The Frost Killer

Crimson Moon

Dust Devil

Savage Season

Maddie Castle Series

The Handler

Tracking Justice

Hunting Grounds

Vanished Trails

Smoldering Lies

Field of Bones

Beneath the Grove

Disappearing Act (Coming Soon)

Affliction Z Series

Affliction Z: Patient Zero

Affliction Z: Abandoned Hope

Affliction Z: Descended in Blood

Affliction Z : Fractured Part 1

Affliction Z: Fractured Part 2 (Coming Soon)

Alex Hayes Series

Trial By Fire (Prequel)

Fractured Verdict

11th Hour Witness

Buried Testimony

The Bishop's Recusal (Coming Soon)

Stella LaRosa Series

Black Rose

Red Ink

Black Gold

White Lies

Silver Bullet (Coming Soon)

Avril Dahl Series

Cold Reckoning

Cold Legacy

Cold Mercy (Coming Soon)

Savannah Shadows Series

Echoes of Guilt

The Silence Before

Dead Air (Coming Soon)

Receive a free copy of *The Recruit*. Visit:

https://ltryan.com/jack-noble-newsletter-signup-1

ABOUT THE AUTHOR

L.T. RYAN is a *Wall Street Journal, USA Today*, and Amazon best-selling author of several mysteries and thrillers, including the *Wall Street Journal* bestselling Jack Noble and Rachel Hatch series. With over eight million books sold, when he's not penning his next adventure, L.T. enjoys traveling, hiking, riding his Peloton,, and spending time with his wife, daughter and four dogs at their home in central Virginia.

* Sign up for his newsletter to hear the latest goings on and receive some free content ➜ https://ltryan.com/jack-noble-newsletter-signup-1
* Join LT's private readers' group ➜ https://www.facebook.com/groups/1727449564174357
* Follow on Instagram ➜ @ltryanauthor
* Visit the website ➜ https://ltryan.com
* Send an email ➜ contact@ltryan.com
* Find on Goodreads ➜ http://www.goodreads.com/author/show/6151659.L_T_Ryan

K.M. ROUGHT is a writer and editor hailing from Upstate New York. Though she graduated with a degree in Art History, she fell into a career of freelancing, fulfilling her childhood dream of being a published author.

Now residing in Ohio, K.M. spends her days writing, playing video games, and telling her cat that no, it's not time to eat yet. Her obsessions include foraging for mushrooms, daydreaming about her next tattoo, and adding to her to-be-read pile.

You can find her on Instagram @karenrought

Made in United States
North Haven, CT
23 August 2025

71938830R00157